Was it possible that Declan might still be here?

Oh God. I brushed my hair back from my face, gave thanks that I'd worn the figure-hugging T-shirt, licked my lips. The attraction I'd felt for him when I first met him, when I first started working at the bar, had dissipated in the face of his many high-drama romances and our developing friendship.

But then I slept with him, and all those years of friendship went out the window. I thought of him now only as an ex-lover, as a fantasy who'd fueled hundreds of orgasms in the time since I'd last seen him. Oh God. I pressed my nose to the blackened window, and there, drawing a Guinness from the ancient brass tap, was my fantasy.

I could just walk away, leaving him none the wiser. I could go home, work on creating my future.

Or I could go through that door. Say hello. Have a beer. Revisit my past.

the
man
i should
have
married

Pamela Redmond Satran

New York   London   Toronto   Sydney

This book is a work of fiction. Names, characters, places and incidents are products of the author's imagination or are used fictitiously. Any resemblance to actual events or locales or persons, living or dead, is entirely coincidental.

DOWNTOWN PRESS, published by Pocket Books
1230 Avenue of the Americas
New York, NY 10020

Copyright © 2003 by Pamela Redmond Satran

Originally published in trade paperback in 2003
by Downtown Press

All rights reserved, including the right to reproduce
this book or portions thereof in any form whatsoever.
For information address Pocket Books, 1230 Avenue
of the Americas, New York, NY 10020

ISBN: 0-7434-9701-5

First Downtown Press mass market paperback edition May 2005

10 9 8 7 6 5 4 3 2 1

DOWNTOWN PRESS and colophon are
trademarks of Simon & Schuster, Inc.

Cover design by Regina Starace
Front cover photo credits: fish © Bill Steele/Stone;
hook and ring © Photodisc

Manufactured in the United States of America

For information regarding special discounts for bulk purchases,
please contact Simon & Schuster Special Sales at 1-800-456-6798
or business@simonandschuster.com.

For Dick Satran,
the man I should have married . . . and did.

ACKNOWLEDGMENTS

Thank you to Amy Pierpont, my visionary editor; to Michael Carlisle, my ever-positive agent; and to Laura Mathews, literary midwife extraordinaire. At Carlisle & Co., warm thanks to Kathy Green and Whitney Lee, as well as to Louise Burke and Deirdre Dore at Downtown Press/Pocket Books. In Britain, my appreciation goes to Clare Conville, Louise Moore, and Harriet Evans. Two of my teachers, Elizabeth George and Ann Packer, contributed immensely to the shaping of this book. My friend Rita DiMatteo tirelessly read, cheered, and critiqued my many drafts, and I am grateful to her along with the many other friends and colleagues who gave me invaluable insights and support: Alice Elliott Dark, Alexa Garbarino, Kim Bonnell, Josh Lerman, Linda Rosenkrantz, Christopher Finch, Liz Werby, Harvey Araton, Nancy Rivera, Marty and Kathy Beiser, Rachael Grossman, Jane Sandor, Chris Cosgrove, and the Fictional Sluts of Northern California: Andy Schell, Joel Gardner,

Ginny Horton, Cameron Tuttle, Bill Taeusch, and Dave Betz. And of course, the ultimate love and thanks to my family: Richard Redmond, Rory, Joe, and Owen Satran, and especially Dick Satran, who knows that he's the only man, apart from the fictional ones, in my dreams.

CHAPTER *one*

"**M**ommy, Mommy!" my five-year-old daughter Amanda yelled, slamming her way out of her father's car. "Maya called Daddy a jerk-off!"

She hurtled up the front walk toward where I was crouched under the hedges, trying to clear the dead leaves away from the hyacinths and tulips, and leaped on top of me, knocking me backward onto the wet lawn. I shut my eyes and pulled her close, burying my face in her mango-and-sweat-scented hair.

"That's not a nice word, sweetie," I said, feeling her heat above me, while below the damp from the grass was already seeping through my clothes.

"I know," said Amanda, pulling back and looking at me gravely. "That's what Daddy told Maya. And then she said, *okay*, she was sorry, he wasn't a jerk-off, he was a dickhead."

I bit back a laugh.

"Why did she call him that?" I said, working to keep my face as serious as hers. "Did they have a fight?"

Amanda only shrugged. "Can I go play Barbies?"

"Sure."

She scrambled off me and ran up the stairs into the house. I had barely made it to my feet, and was still trying to get a look at what was going on inside the car, when the passenger door shot open. Now it was Maya tearing up the walk.

"Mom," she said, as she whizzed past me, "tell Frank to leave me alone."

Frank was already out of the car, also hurrying my way. This was a real shocker: Usually he was peeling out within nanoseconds, heading back to New York, not even cutting his engine in his eagerness to flee. It had been weeks since I'd gotten so much as a glimpse of him, and now I tried to keep from gawking, so transformed was he with his newly lean body and his bleached blond spiky hair, his suede jacket and—my God, could it really be?—teeny tiny hoop earring dangling what looked like an ankh.

"What's going on?" I asked him.

I could feel Maya breathing behind me, sucking her rage in and out through her teeth.

"Nothing," said Frank, trying to look around me to where she hid. "She's just being fifteen."

"If you don't fucking tell her," Maya said, "I will."

"See how she talks now?" Frank said. "This is okay with you?"

Dickhead, I thought. "Tell me what?"

Frank took a deep breath. "I'm leaving the firm, Kennedy. I'm becoming a yoga instructor."

Frank, who couldn't make it through a cocktail-party conversation without mentioning he'd gone to Harvard Law. Frank, who used his legal stationery to write to the local newspaper to complain about faulty garbage collection. Chucking it all for the downward dog.

Now I really did burst out laughing.

He drew himself up to his full height, which wasn't all that tall. "I object to your ridicule."

"You're not a lawyer anymore, Frank," I said, still chuckling. "Remember?"

"This is about healing," Frank said. "This is about giving back to society."

"This is about you covering your ass," Maya said.

Frank opened his mouth, then shut it again. "I don't have to put up with this," he said, lifting his hands in surrender. "I'm out of here."

He half-turned and had started to move back down the path when Maya spoke again.

"The thing he didn't want me to tell you, Mom, is that we met her. We met Sunny."

Frank froze. Maya held her breath, waiting for my reaction. And I stood rooted in my spot, trying to take it in. I knew about Sunny, of course, the high school surfer girlfriend Frank had run into last fall at the Oyster Bar. Had gotten reacquainted with, had slept with, had left me for. I knew all about her, but my daughters were not supposed to. Not yet.

"What do you mean, you met her?"

"She came to the apartment, Mom. Duh! She came for dinner Saturday night and she was still there when we woke up this morning."

Frank broke in. "Maya, I warned you not to go running to your mother with all this misinformation." He took a step back toward me. "Kennedy, this is not what it seems."

"She was wearing a diamond ring, Mom," Maya said from behind me. "Way bigger than yours."

Without thinking, I reached out and pushed Frank. Hard. Leaving a muddy handprint on his pristine suede. I should turn him in to the maharishi for wearing dead cow.

"You promised me, Frank." I advanced on him. "You agreed we were going to give them time to adjust to the separation before we introduced other people into their lives."

"It's been four months, Kennedy," he said, backing away.

"Four months is nothing. They're nowhere near ready."

He stopped. "I think you're the one who's not ready."

He said this so quietly that it didn't even sound at first like it had come from him. It was more like a voice in the air, one of those voices that crazy people heard. Behind me, the screen door slammed; Maya had retreated into the house, leaving the two of us alone. I blinked.

"What do you think I'm not ready for?" I asked him.

"To leave the past behind. To start a new life."

That uncharacteristically straightforward no-bullshit statement coming from Frank hit me like a hardball between the eyes. Reeling, my gaze swerved and I looked blindly beyond him, desperate for something, anything else to focus on. What I found was Mrs. Husk's cherry tree across the street, which seemed overnight to have come into bloom. For months I'd seen only a tangle of black branches, and now suddenly there was this cloud of pink. Gaping at that pinkness, I realized that Frank was right. I had not, until that moment, accepted that he was gone and that my life was once again my own. And right then, ready or not, I knew that my future had already arrived, and that I was sailing into it by myself.

Unfortunately—or maybe not—I didn't have much time to think about what I was going to do now that I had again become master of my own domain. As soon as Frank left, Amanda pulled me into playing Ken to her Barbie. And then there was the evening's pizza to order—one of the main advantages of single motherhood: not having to give a fuck what *he* wants for dinner. And then once I had Amanda bathed and settled down in front of her Sunday night TV shows, I had to go see what Maya had been doing all evening barricaded in her room.

Halfway up the stairs to the third floor, I could hear the *clack clack clack* of her computer keys. Her door was open and she was sitting in the dark near the window, illuminated only by the blue glow from the screen. She'd outgrown the green-painted antique chair at her desk—she was taller than me now—and her long, muscled legs sprawled into the shadows. When she saw me, she stopped typing and covered the screen with her hands.

"Homework?" I asked, trying for a casual tone, attempting a smile.

"No."

"E-mail?"

"No, Mom. Don't you have, like, something else to do?"

"Not really." I crossed the room and perched on the edge of the wicker chair near her desk, one of my flea market finds Frank would not allow downstairs, in "his" part of the house.

"Well, I do, Mom, okay?"

"No," I said, hearing the nervousness in my own voice. It wasn't often these days that I confronted her about anything, not wanting to piss her off any more than adolescence and her crumbling family already had. "Not okay. I want to talk with you about what happened today."

She let her mouth drop open and batted her eyes,

which I guessed was as much encouragement as I could hope for.

I took a deep breath, trying to summon what little advice I could remember from those books on how to talk to your teenager. "I know what's happened between me and Frank is hard for you," I said. "But Frank loves you, Maya. You've got to know that."

"Well, I don't love him."

"Oh honey," I said, "Frank may have done some things that weren't very nice, but he is your dad."

"He's not my dad."

I sighed deeply. I'd started going out with Frank when Maya was five, the age Amanda was now, moved in with him when she was six, married him when she was eight. Her biological father hadn't lived with us or supported her since before she could remember, and she'd seen him only a handful of times after that.

"He's the only dad you have."

"No, he's not." And that's when she dropped her hands from the computer screen and I saw what was there:

> Marco Rivera
> Bronx, N.Y.
> 718-555-6987
>
> Marco J. Rivera
> Bronx, N.Y.
> 718-971-2910

Marco Rivera
Manhattan, N.Y.
212-987-2335

"Maya," I said, my breath catching in my throat. "What are you doing?"

"I'm trying to find him, okay?" she said, her hands fluttering back to the screen, too late. Through her fingers, I could still read the name: Marco Rivera. Her real father.

"Oh, Maya," I said. "You don't really want to do that."

"Yes, I do."

"Maya. There are things I haven't told you."

She narrowed her eyes at me—the amber eyes with the Asian tilt that were so like his. As was her thick hair, darker even than mine and as straight as mine was curly. And then there was that aggressive streak that made her seem to almost relish confrontation. "What?" she said, sticking out her chin, just like he used to do.

I took a deep breath. "Drugs."

She laughed, startling me. "I know about the drugs."

"How do you know?"

"What do you think, Grandma's jabs just whizzed by me all these years?"

"It wasn't only grass, Maya."

"I know, I know: coke, crack." She waved her hand impatiently. "What else?"

I thought about it. What hadn't he done?

"He stole to get money for drugs," I said. "He was arrested."

"He was young. George W. Bush was arrested when he was young. What else?"

What else? She needed more?

"I'm just afraid for you, Maya," I wailed. "It's been so long." When I thought of Marco at all, I imagined him in an alley somewhere, on a bench, drunk, strung out, toothless, as good as dead. I tried a different tack: "If he was capable of being a father to you, I think we would have heard from him long ago."

The chin came out again. "You don't think he wants me."

Just knowing this thought had passed through her mind made tears spring to my eyes. "No, no, that's not what I'm saying."

In fact, we'd both really wanted Maya, me as much as him. Whenever I told anyone I'd gotten pregnant at nineteen, they always assumed it was a mistake. My own mother offered me $100,000 at the time to have an abortion, which made me so angry that I cut off all contact with her. Even after my mother and I made up, when I finally broke up with Marco, I swore I would never take money from her for any reason, never let her control me that way, a resolution I still kept.

Marco not only wanted Maya, he aspired to being an ideal father, which was what started his trouble

with drugs. He'd played major league ball for about
two minutes and when we got together, he worked
construction, as a bicycle messenger, whatever job he
could get that—combined with my waitressing tips—
would pay our East Village rent. But having a baby,
that introduced a whole different way of life, an entirely new side of Marco. He knew I was from a rich
family—the reality, more precisely, was that my
mother had married a series of progressively richer
men—and he wanted to "take care" (his words) of us
in "high style" (his words, too). It didn't matter that I
told him that I'd never cared about having a lot of
money, either making my own or living off my
mother's. When I protested that I wanted to keep
working, that I was happy to contribute to our household expenses, he only laughed. His outmoded brand
of Latin pride would never allow his wife, the mother
of his baby, to work.

And so he started dealing drugs. He told me he was
working as a trader on Wall Street and I believed him.
I was naive, and I wanted to believe him. It was the
golden age when people rose from the mud to make
millions in mergers and acquisitions, as well as the era
of crack cocaine. Marco kept the yuppie charade
going—he'd even get up in the morning, put on a
beautiful suit, and leave the apartment—until he
started using drugs himself. Then it was downhill fast.

"Marco really loved you," I said, thinking carefully
now about how to explain all this to Maya. "You were

the most important thing in the world to him. But he just couldn't hold it together, sweetheart. He wasn't capable of being a good father to you, and I think that broke his heart."

Her face softened as she considered this. Then suddenly her eyes widened and brightened as if she'd seen something wonderful. "You know what I remember?" she said. "I remember him coming to Frank's apartment on my birthday, and bringing me that pink dress with all the ruffles, and I remember he and Frank got in a fight."

That had happened. Marco had been high, as usual, and Frank had challenged him, and they'd gotten into a shoving match that Frank won only because Marco, who had been muscled and powerful when I first met him, was by that point so dissipated he could barely stand up. The next year on her birthday, Maya had put on the ruffled dress, by then so tight it bit into her waist and strained across her shoulders, and waited in Frank's vestibule, certain Marco would appear. She waited for four hours. Then she took off the dress, marched out into the hallway in her underwear, stuffed the wad of pink ruffles down the chute to the incinerator, and never asked to see Marco again.

But that wasn't what she remembered now. She remembered getting the dress; she remembered feeling her father's love. And I could understand, despite all my misgivings, why she wanted to feel that again.

"I'll help you," I said, hearing the tremble in my

own voice even as I tried to convince myself I was on Maya's side. "I'll help you look for him, and if you find him, I'll help you connect with him."

"You really want to do that?" Maya said.

"No," I admitted. But I'd already decided I would do it anyway. Marco had scared me for a long time, but it scared me even more to think of my teenage daughter going to see him without my backing her up. And, I thought, I'd been too afraid of too much for too long. I'd gone from being a teenager so self-confident I had a baby and supported her on my own to a thirty-four-year-old woman who was scared to drive on the highway, who was afraid to walk alone through New York streets where I'd lived for years. How had that happened? I didn't know. I just knew I wanted to be different.

CHAPTER *two*

Once I had accepted that Frank was really gone from my life, I wanted his stuff out, too. The Brooks Brothers suits and the hole-ridden jockey shorts. The ponderous history tomes and the pretentious jazz records. It all went into bags and boxes, down to the basement or off to Goodwill. The only thing I didn't pack up or give away were the antique Fendi and Brooks Brothers ties I'd collected for Frank over the years, and that I'd always liked way more than he had. These I loaded into the back of the Volvo and carted over to my friend Jeannie's shop.

It was my favorite time of year in Homewood, when the weather first turned warm and all the tiny green leaves popped out on the huge trees that arched over the town's boulevards. The sidewalks seemed suddenly thronged with young mothers, pushing carriages holding the winter's crop of babies, little legs flailing free for the first time. The new Starbucks, just down the street from Jeannie's, had put tables out on the sidewalk and it seemed as if the half of Homewood that wasn't pushing baby carriages was sunning itself there, reveling in a caffeine-fueled frenzy of believing itself finally and officially hip.

Jeannie's door was propped open to let in the warm air, and I burst into the shop, buoyant from some combination of the weather and the new forward thrust of my life. Since Frank's December 26th departure, I had spent far less time with Jeannie and in the shop than usual, burrowing in at home and wanting to avoid Jeannie's lectures about how beneficial a stable two-parent home was for women and children. I loved Jeannie. She had been my best friend since we were fourteen, and would be my best friend, I hoped, forever. But now I needed her to help me grab hold of my new life, whatever that might be, rather than clutch at the one I was leaving behind.

"Do you think you can sell these?" I asked, dumping Frank's ties on the scrubbed pine table that served as the shop's counter.

Jeannie slowly turned to face me, looking, in the shadows of the shop, like the teenager she'd been when we met as roommates at Miss Forster's School for Girls in the hills of Virginia. Her hips were narrow in her skinny lime-green silk capri pants and her tawny brown hair was piled high atop her head in some retro do, huge antique Mexican silver hoops swinging from her lobes.

"What's the matter?" she said. "Doesn't Frank want them anymore?"

"No, *I* don't want them anymore," I said.

"Listen," she said, leaning closer, "I had this inspiration. What if Chip and I took the girls for a weekend, give you and Frank a chance to get away together, just the two of you. . . ."

I held up my hand to stop her. "It's over, Jeannie."

"But after ten years together," she said, "and the girls . . ."

"Jeannie, seriously," I said. "I want to sell these ties, but beyond that, I'm here because I need to start working again."

When Jeannie first opened the shop, two years before when her daughter Phoebe started school full-time, she asked me to be her partner. I'd wanted to but Frank had been against it, arguing that Amanda still needed me at home, that he was busier than ever at the law firm. So I'd settled for filling in on the occasional afternoon or weekend, plus contributing style ideas, all for occasional and not very lucrative pay.

"Sweetie," Jeannie said, looking pained. "There's not really any money."

"But you said sales had doubled from last year." Starbucks had brought a lot of new foot traffic to

Jeannie's block. And the shop looked gorgeous, all decked out for spring, with antique white linens and copper pots of orange tulips and a new shipment of painted furniture that I loved, each piece costing approximately my entire living budget for the coming year.

"I know," she said. "It's better. But still. I mean, if you wanted to put in more hours behind the cash register I could use the help, especially with summer coming, but I could afford to pay you only maybe seven bucks an hour."

I calculated. Even if I worked forty hours, which amounted to just about all the hours the store was *open* every week, I would gross less than $300, take home under $250. Live in Homewood on $1,000 a month, total? During the Frank years, I spent that much on restaurants and movies.

"But if we were partners, maybe we could work out something for more money," I said, talking quickly in an attempt to stay composed. "If we expanded the business . . ."

Jeannie shook her head. "I work more than I want to now," she said. "Listen, if you come up with some brilliant expansion idea I'd love to hear about it. I'd love for us to work together, you know that. But all I really want to do is arrange things in pretty little groups and have an excuse to go to the flea market."

"I understand," I said, blinking fast, smoothing the ties across the pine table so I'd have something to look at besides Jeannie's too-smug face. Jeannie didn't have to worry about money because she had Chip, whose year-end corporate bonus was worth more than most people's salaries. And until Frank left, I'd luxuriated in that kind of financial backing, too. "Of course. That makes total sense."

"But with child support," she said. "With alimony . . ."

"No," I said. "No, there's not going to be as much of that as I thought." Telling Jeannie about Frank's new yoga career was going to have to wait for a moment when I was feeling more of a sense of humor about my change in fortunes.

"Oh, honey," Jeannie said. "I'm sure you're going to figure out something great. You always managed to find a gig, make the money you needed, pay the rent."

That was the person I wanted to be again, that girl with the fuck-you attitude who slung burgers and beer on and off for years at Declan McGlynn's bar, who modeled shoes and sewed pillow covers and carted the lights around on shoots for music videos. Yes, I'd been a mom back then too, but I'd been a mom like Madonna (with a lot less money) or Jennifer Connelly (without the Oscar-winning career)— urban, sexy, with an even better figure than I'd had pre-baby and a kid who thought it was normal to eat goat cheese salads in sidewalk cafes and sleep till noon.

Could I be that woman again? Was she still in there somewhere, beneath the sneakers and the khakis and the ten o'clock bedtimes?

"I know what we should do," Jeannie said. "I think it's time."

I had no idea what she was talking about. She went to one of the painted cupboards, the biggest and most beautiful and most expensive one, dark blue decorated with the palest pink roses, and turned the brass key that unlocked the top panel. From its depths she extracted something rectangular, brick-sized, wrapped in a piece of pale lavender silk. I recognized that silk. It was the same silk as always, and within it, I knew, were Jeannie's tarot cards.

Jeannie had brought those cards to Miss Forster's with her from Pittsburgh, she'd taken them to Barnard where we roomed together and then to the apartment in the East Village where she and I lived before Marco moved in. For years she read the cards for me nearly every day, but the last time I'd let her read them was the day I finally decided to move in with Frank, the day after the night I slept with my longtime boss, Declan McGlynn. The cards had been so decisive that day: Move in with Frank, they said. You'll marry; you'll have a beautiful child. And as it all came true, I never wanted Jeannie to tell my fortune again. If there was something besides this in store for me, I felt, I didn't want to know it.

"No," I said.

"Oh, come on." She pushed Frank's ties aside, carefully unfolding the silk that encased the cards, and began shuffling them in that stiff way that was so familiar. "The moment is right. You need to know what's going to happen next, don't you?"

"Jeannie, really, no," I said, laying my hand on top of hers, unsure myself why I so adamantly did not want to go forward with the reading. It was just for fun, right? I didn't really believe in fortune-telling, did I? But maybe that was the problem. Maybe I had believed in the cards too much last time, and followed their advice when I should not have. Because from this vantage point, the advice to choose Frank was clearly and seriously *wrong*.

"How are you going to know what to do?" Jeannie asked.

She was serious. And maybe when the question was whether to go out with John or Jim, or whether to head uptown or downtown on Saturday night, asking the cards had been a good way to decide. But not now, not when the issue was what to do with the rest of my life.

I laughed, grateful finally to have something that brought me back to the good mood I'd been in when I first walked through the door. "I'll just have to decide for myself," I said.

"You're not going to leave Homewood, are you?" A worry line creased Jeannie's otherwise flawless brow.

Okay, that possibility had crossed my mind. As I'd

shoveled out Frank's junk, I'd fantasized about moving to a cabin in Vermont, a flat in London, a shack on a beach in Tahiti—somewhere glamorous and exciting and far, far away. And if it had just been me, I might have even done it. I certainly would not have stayed in this sleepy suburban town, where everybody was married, it seemed, where everybody did what was expected from one year to the next. Frank had dragged me here kicking and screaming, and it seemed wildly unfair that now I was stuck here while he was back in the city, which he'd always claimed to hate. But to my daughters, this was home, and they needed that stability. And maybe I needed it, too. If only I could figure out how I was going to afford it.

"Jeannie, don't worry, I'm not going anywhere," I said, laying a hand on her firm, freckled shoulder.

At that moment I felt a gust of wind from the direction of the shop door, and in swept Barb Rogers, Homewood's premiere realtor and Jeannie's neighbor on her stretch of shopping street. With her Dorothy Hamill haircut, corduroy skirts, and shoes that looked good to go on the golf links, Barb bore little resemblance to Jeannie's typical moneyed-and-stylish customer. But Barb, an unlikely collector of items ranging from dolls to World War II memorabilia, was one of the shop's biggest spenders.

Blinking into the dimness of the interior, Barb took a minute to recognize me. "Oh, Kennedy," she said finally. "I've been thinking about you. Now that you're on your own, are you going to sell that big house of yours?"

"No," said Jeannie.

At the same moment, I said, "Yes."

The notion of selling the house had occurred to me before, of course, as a component of all my European and Tahitian escape fantasies. But now I saw a different way to do it.

Jeannie was looking at me with a hurt and baffled look on her face. "You just said you were going to stay in Homewood."

"I am," I said happily, excited at my sudden ability to glimpse, if I held my head at exactly the right angle, a short stretch of my road ahead. "I'm going to sell it and Barb's going to help me find something cheaper right here in town."

CHAPTER *three*

The next time the girls were scheduled to spend the weekend with Frank in the city, Maya refused to go. Rather than confront him with this news on the telephone or at the front door of my house, giving him the opportunity to use his lawyerly wiles to talk us out of it, I volunteered to meet him at the Museum of Natural History to do the handoff. This was exactly the way I put it—"do the handoff"—careful not to either mention or not mention Maya.

Still, Frank was mistrustful, seeming to think I must have a powerful ulterior motive—murdering him, maybe—for braving the drive into New York. Spending my teen years at a girls' boarding school, then college and most of my twenties in Manhattan, I hadn't learned to drive until we moved to Homewood and never progressed far beyond piloting the

Volvo—or the Vulva, as Maya called it—around town or along the back route to the mall. Any highway or city driving had always been handled by Frank.

By the time I reached the museum, my stomach was in a knot from the drive, and the tight black T-shirt I'd worn in a nod to cool—the attitude, not the temperature—was patchy with sweat. I was so wobbly that I had to take off my high-heeled sandals and walk barefoot, Amanda's hand clenched in mine, down the hot dirty sidewalk. Still, I was proud. I may have felt like throwing up during the entire trip down Route 3, through the Lincoln Tunnel, and up Tenth Avenue. I may have been the slowest car on the road, all the other vehicles swerving around me and blaring their horns, but I'd done it, I'd made it, and that alone was an enormous accomplishment.

Frank was already waiting in the museum's lobby, sitting on a bench near the curled tip of the dinosaur's bony tail, checking his watch. His hair might be bleached and spiky, he might have given up his suits and ties for jeans and suede jackets, but he still checked his watch every thirty seconds.

"Where's Maya?" he said right off the bat, peering around me and Amanda.

"She's not coming."

"Why not?"

"She didn't want to, Frank."

"And you let her stay home?"

"What was I supposed to do, hog-tie her and haul her in here? She's taller than me now, Frank. She's even taller than you."

"Oh," he said. "Now I get why you offered to drive in here. You were covering for Maya."

His brilliance was dazzling, especially to him. "Let it go, Frank. If it's anybody's fault that she doesn't want to see you, it's yours."

Frank stiffened. "I really do not want to get into this with you in a public place. Is that why you wanted to come here? To confront me?"

"Frank, I don't want to confront you. It's not always all about you, okay?"

He blinked. "Then what's it about?"

"Nothing, Frank. Maybe I just have something I want to do in the city."

He looked at me suspiciously. I did have another reason for being in New York, but not one I had any more intention of sharing with Frank. I wanted to go down to my old neighborhood in the East Village and hunt for Marco, or rather for Marco's ghost, or maybe for his ghost within me. I didn't really expect to find him still there, but then again, I'd never been able to return to that neighborhood, so inextricably was his presence linked for me with East Ninth Street and Avenue A and Tompkins Square Park. Given Maya's quest and my promise to help her, this seemed like a logical first move.

And then there was my own quest to let go of the past, as Frank had put it, and figure out what I was going to do with my life. I'd been thinking a lot about my years in New York, about the choices I'd made and hadn't made back then, and I was curious to revisit some of my old haunts in search of the ghost of my younger self, to figure out whether she still existed somewhere inside me.

"Do you have a date?" Frank asked. "Is that why you're so dressed up?"

Amanda picked that moment to jump up on the bench beside him and hop away from us, and I couldn't resist the impulse to lean into the opening beside him.

I put my lips up close to his ear and whispered, "Losing you has turned me into a lesbian."

He jerked back in alarm and stared at me as if he'd always suspected it, that close friendship with Jeannie and all.

"What I'm doing here is none of your business, Frank," I said. "I'm ready now. I'm leaving the past behind."

"That's fine," he said, as if I'd been waiting for his permission. "That's appropriate. Come on, Amanda." He stood up and seemed to be aggressively not looking at me. "What would you like to do today, sweetie pie?"

Amanda flung herself across his back. "I want to go to the Planetarium. Okay, Daddy? Please?"

"Sure, pumpkin," he said, darting his eyes toward me. "Then later we can meet Sunny for dinner."

Score one for the asshole yogi.

"I'm going, Frank."

"When will you be home?"

"Later."

"Who's staying with Maya?"

"Maya's been baby-sitting for other people for three years, Frank. She doesn't need anyone to stay with her."

Frank seemed about to keep arguing with me, but then he just sighed. I held my arms out to Amanda and she leaped into them. I hugged her for a long minute, savoring the feel of her narrow chest against me, attempting to make the closeness last, for both of us, all weekend.

"Okay," he said. "Now, where exactly are you going? Because if you're heading downtown you can take Central Park West only as far as . . ."

"Living my own life, Frank, remember?" I interrupted, stepping into my shoes and beginning to back away. "That means without you."

Driving in the city was easier, I discovered, than zooming along the highway, given that the traffic never moved faster than twelve miles an hour. And it was thrilling to be here on my own, my first big solo outing since Frank had left me, the first time I'd really taken advantage of the freedom of my Amanda-less weekends.

I parked my car as soon as I got below Fourteenth

Street, in a lot way over near the Hudson River, and started walking east, toward my old neighborhood. I'm back, I thought, as I threaded my way through the narrow lanes, Jane and Bedford and Leroy, streets whose individual characters I used to know so well but that now seemed indistinguishable from one another. I skirted the north edge of Washington Square Park and then made my way up to the bustle of Eighth Street. Getting ready for this venture at home, even talking about it to Frank at the museum, I'd been nervous, afraid even, worried about all the ways New York had changed and the ways I'd changed, too. But now I was overcome with relief that the city was still itself, and however much I had changed it still offered me the same kind of excitement it always had.

It was green and warm, a perfect spring Saturday, and the sidewalks were jammed with NYU students and kids from the suburbs, with slim and gorgeous young couples and prosperous-looking older ones. As I aimed eastward, my old rhythm of walking in the city overtook me and my feet moved fast, faster, till I was weaving my way gracefully in and out of the crowd, the fastest one in the pack. I'm back, I'm here, I'm still alive, I thought over and over, in time with my step.

Jogging across Astor Place, hugging the curb along St. Marks Place, making this trip I had made so many times over so many years, I felt as if I were journeying back a month in my life with each step, back back back to the time when I worked at Declan McGlynn's bar, when I was rushing home to Maya, when Marco lay in bed waiting for me, when Jeannie and I were young girls. Wild girls, yes, with our ripped fishnets and our one-night-only boyfriends and our joints in the morning. But innocent nonetheless.

But if I felt like my old self, I was aware that I didn't look like her, even in my tight black pants and high heels. On the streets of Homewood, I would have been the hottest babe in town, but here I didn't merit even a glance.

The farther east I traveled, the younger most of the other people in the street became. Most of them looked barely older than Maya. Tattoos abounded: spider webs on necks, Chinese characters on skulls. And piercings everywhere. Vintage in highly creative combinations, the same thing I wore when I lived here, picked from the mountain of rags—torn jeans and satin bed jackets and beaded sweaters and frayed patchwork quilts, all jumbled together and towering nearly to the ceiling—that filled the store on First Avenue.

The rag store was gone now, I discovered when I reached First Avenue, replaced by a shop that seemed to specialize in erotic greeting cards. So was the newsstand, the place where they mixed the great egg creams. That had become a tapas bar. And the tea shop where the ancient Chinese man once stood guard over his hundreds of dusty tins had been transformed into a Starbucks.

I had a strange sense of being in a city that was utterly familiar yet with all its lines and colors rearranged, like a place in a dream. It was like a movie version of the neighborhood where I'd lived, with an entirely new cast of characters to replace the faces that had seemed as fixed as the street lamps or the cement stoops: the shiny-cheeked Dominican man who'd owned the fruit stand on the corner, the tall red-haired designer who'd sewn clothes in her Tenth Street storefront, old Mrs. Persky who'd leaned from morning till night, bed pillow cushioning her elbows, on the sill of her third story window.

Gone, all gone. Only I was the same. Or was I? I stopped before an empty shop, really just to look at my reflection in the darkened windows, and realized with a start that this was where Dobson's antique and design business had once been. Frank had never liked it that I was a waitress; he'd been ashamed of dating a nonprofessional, I think, though that just made me more determined to continue working at Declan's. Declan and I had massaged our initial flirtation into a close friendship, and he let me work as much or as little as I wanted, so I overlooked the aches in my legs and Frank's objections and kept waitressing.

And then, pressured by Frank to make a commitment, pressured by Frank to quit my job and do something more intellectually stimulating, I slept with Declan. Okay, it wasn't all Frank's fault: I'd wanted to sleep with Declan from the first time I'd seen him and took what seemed like my last-ever opportunity. And it was wonderful, the sex better than it had been at the beginning with Marco, better than it had been with anybody before—or since, for that matter. But Declan was a heartbreaker, a charmer who loved women, which made him an excellent friend and an awful boyfriend. And Frank was Mr. Stability, offering me marriage and a home and security for my child. The choice, sexual thrills aside, seemed obvious, even without the guidance of Jeannie's tarot cards.

So I left my apartment and my job and never saw Declan again. I moved in with Frank and I began working for Leo Dobson in this very shop. Dobson had moved uptown several years ago, I seemed to remember reading in some decorating magazine, and while he was brilliant and had beautiful taste and taught me a lot, he was a horrible man, cranky and mean for the sake of being mean. Even Frank, who was left cooking macaroni and cheese for Maya many a night while Dobson kept me late at some apartment he was working on, lugging a chair back and forth, back and forth across a room, finally urged me to quit. And then I got pregnant with Amanda and we moved to Homewood and this former life of mine might as well have happened on Mars.

I felt dreamlike now, too, wandering north on First Avenue lost in these thoughts, then turning east on Ninth Street, the block where I'd lived. My street was lined with shops and restaurants where once there had been only tenements, though my building still looked the same, exactly the same. I had to crane my head all the way back to see the three windows on the top floor that had been mine.

I couldn't believe I walked up that far each day. Or didn't. Maya was born at the beginning of the winter and through all those first months of cold and ice and snow and motherhood I stayed upstairs in my nightgown, too daunted to think of dressing myself and the baby in her snowsuit and hauling us and her stroller down five flights to the street to—do what? Go to the bodega and get her carriage stolen when I carried her inside to buy milk?

That apartment had so many roaches that the first summer I lived there, before I knew better, I lifted a potholder from where I'd hung it on the wall to find its underside so covered with bugs that I screamed and sailed the thing out the window and down onto the blacktop. When Maya was a baby, Marco set the legs of her rickety crib in coffee cans half-filled with water, a roach-foiling trick he'd learned at his mother's knee in Puerto Rico.

I'd met Marco sitting on the stoop of my building, on the third step from the bottom, and I turned around and sat there now, exactly as I had that long-ago night. Feeling the cool of the stone step against my bottom, the memories came quickly, out of my control, as if they'd been trapped in the air above the steps and I could access them only by being right here. It was a summer night and I was my nineteen-year-old self, sucking on one of the cherries I'd just bought from the Dominican fruit stand. And there came Marco, pushing his bike and walking his dogs.

"Hey, baby," he said. "Give me a cherry."

He was lean but muscled, almost tall, with dark straight hair, with those near-Asian eyes that I still saw every day when I looked at Maya, thin lips. I held out my little brown paper bag full of soft dark cherries to him.

"What's your name?" he said. It wasn't really a question. "You live here?"

Thinking about the way I felt about him then terrified me still. It was always beyond reason: I didn't understand it then, from that very first moment, and I didn't understand it now. That experience made me believe absolutely in the power of scent, pheromones, whatever it is that makes you see someone and have to have them. I would go out in the street looking for Marco and I would always find him, drawn by some mystical power of—I won't call it love. Desire. Back then, I was much more likely to believe that this sort of attraction carried some global meaning: We were meant for each other, made for each other. Now, I thought it was just sex.

But even if it was sexual and not spiritual, Marco and I had had a powerful connection, one I hadn't allowed myself to consider for years. It was as if all the bad that had happened had erased the good. Or maybe, to summon the strength to push him out of my life, I'd had to harden myself against all the things I'd once loved about him, all the things that might make me let him back in.

Yes, he had failed to show up on Maya's birthday, yes, the drugs had made him an unreliable father and a hopeless partner, but now I felt that I had created a barrier that had been close to impossible to climb over, even for a man without Marco's problems. I'd moved uptown with Frank, never listed my name in the phone book, never even written it by the doorbell, not left a forwarding address when we moved to New Jersey. So who knew whether Marco had tried to stay in touch with Maya, whether he even wanted to. I hadn't truly given him the chance.

I stood up from the steps as if in a trance and began walking toward Tompkins Square Park, the place where Marco always hung out, day and night, with his drug buddies. I felt now the way I did back when I first knew him and went looking for him, felt the pull of him nearby, along with the push toward him within me. Now it wasn't only Maya who wanted to see him; I did, too. I'm sorry, I wanted to say. I hope you're all right. I hope that in making it better for myself, I didn't make it too much worse for you. For Maya.

But I was afraid that I had, or that life or drugs had. I flashed back on the image that had come to me that night as I was talking to Maya, the only image I'd held of him for years: junkie Marco, homeless Marco.

Then, from the haunted air of this street, came another image: Marco on a night a few months after we started living together. It was late, we were walking down the street kissing, stepping into the shadows to touch each other beneath our fall clothes. Very quickly, very expertly, he slid his hand down the front of my jeans and slipped a finger inside of me.

"Someday," he whispered, "I'm going to put myself inside you as bare as this finger, and I'm going to come and come, and I'm going to make us a baby."

Maybe it was this Marco I was more afraid of seeing again, I thought, as I crossed Avenue A and stepped with trepidation into Tompkins Square Park. I prepared myself to see him, but the person I expected to encounter kept morphing in my mind like a cartoon monster, and my imagined reaction was just as elastic, from horror to relief to anger to friendliness.

Meanwhile, on Planet Earth, it was Saturday afternoon and the spring sun was shining and the benches and paths were populated by students reading and parents with toddlers, by rollerbladers and hobbling grandmas. Sexy Marco, electrifying Marco, the Marco whose baby I was so thrilled to have—he was not there. And neither was the other Marco, the father of my nearly grown child, the beast I had created or the man he had become.

CHAPTER *four*

After my nonencounter with Marco, I was exhausted, ready to strap myself back into the Vulva and inch my way home. But the resurrection of so many memories had left me curious about one more place, one more person, from my past. I wanted to go see Declan McGlynn's.

All the change in the East Village had prepared me to find McGlynn's transmogrified as well, or gone, replaced by a designer boutique or a restaurant serving up comfort food. That's exactly what I thought had happened when I wandered around and around the narrow streets of the western end of the Village without finding the place, confused by all the new shops and nearly convinced I must have passed the building in its new incarnation without recognizing it.

But then I turned left where before I'd turned right, and went down a shaded lane that looked

wholly unfamiliar, and suddenly there it was, looking precisely like its old self, albeit with scaffolding
nearly obscuring the building's brick walls. Above
the rough planks that formed a roof over the first
story of scaffolding, I could barely make out the
gold letters that spelled McGlynn's.

Was it possible that Declan might still be here,
equally unchanged? Oh God. I brushed my hair
back from my face, gave thanks that I'd worn the
figure-hugging T-shirt, licked my lips. The attraction
I'd felt for him when I first met him, when I first
started working at the bar, had dissipated in the face
of his many high-drama romances, and my own
high-drama romance with the jealous Marco, and
our developing friendship, and the need to maintain a
professional relationship as well as keep my job.

But then I slept with him, and all those years of
friendship went out the window and I thought of him
now only as an ex-lover, as an incredible fuck, as a
fantasy who'd fueled hundreds of orgasms in the time
since last I'd seen him. Oh God. I pressed my nose to
the blackened window, which would give me, I knew
from experience, a perfect view of the bar and whoever was behind it. And there, drawing a Guinness
from the ancient brass tap, was my fantasy.

I could just walk away, leaving him none the wiser.
I could go home, clean my closets to get my house
ready to sell, go to a movie with Maya, work on creating my future.

Or I could go through that door. Say hello. Have a beer, revisit my past.

Frank had had a moment like this, hadn't he? I'd never thought of it before, but of course, he'd run into Sunny at the Oyster Bar, where they were each having business lunches. They'd kissed hello, a warm kiss, but one on the cheek. Later, leaving the restaurant, they'd exchanged cards. And then there had to have come a moment when he called her. Or she called him, and he responded. A moment when the kiss moved from the cheek to the lips, when the touch moved from the shoulder to the breast. A moment when he said yes.

So that's what I was doing, too: saying yes. But only to venturing down the sidewalk and into the bar. Yes to standing blinking near the jukebox, its lights glowing pink and yellow. It had always been dark in McGlynn's but the scaffolding made it darker still, shadowing the deep brown wood of the floors and the tables and the walls. The old brass clock, set twenty minutes ahead, still ticked over the bar, and the ancient cash register gleamed gold and silver beneath it.

Yes to crossing the room and taking a seat on one of the ancient wooden barstools, where I had an excellent view of the back of Declan McGlynn.

His light brown hair was longer and softer-looking than it had been ten years ago, threaded through now with gray, and his clothes, a rich brown cashmere sweater and charcoal wool pants, looked softer and more expensive, too. He seemed if anything larger than ever, his shoulders straighter and broader, and he moved as slowly as always as he made change at the cash register, with the same gentle tilt of his head.

He didn't notice me, though he turned half in my direction and I could see his face in profile, the pale skin, the smile that looked the smallest bit sad. One of the men sitting at the other end of the bar said something and he turned in their direction and I heard him laugh. He walked to the tap near them and drew two more Guinnesses, an endless process, as I well remembered, and then set coasters on the bar, and then set down the beers.

I sat and watched, in no hurry for him to recognize me. The last time I was here, sitting at this bar, I wore a tight red-and-orange-flowered dress, unfashionably short. I'd told myself I was there to ask his advice about whether I should move in with Frank, knowing all the while that if I did ask him he'd say no: He'd met Frank and didn't like him. But instead of talking to Declan about Frank, I went and sat with him in the darkest booth in the darkest corner of the bar, sliding in on the same side of the table as him and kissing him until I knew I couldn't stop. I climbed the stairs to his apartment right above the bar, and when he said "Take off your clothes"—just like that: "Take off your clothes"—I unhesitatingly pulled my dress over my head and stepped out of my panties and then unhooked my bra. We made love in the living room, with me sitting on top of him on the sofa, and then we went to the bedroom and made love again. This is what it's about, I thought at the time. This is what all the fuss is about.

In the middle of the night, I woke up to find Declan's arm curled around me, moonlight filling his apartment, and thought of Frank, who seemed to only want the best for me, and felt overcome by a tsunami of guilt and remorse. It had been so wrong of me, in every way I could think of, to sleep with Declan. Where would he be tomorrow? Where would I be? I could not see how one night of wonderful sex could lead to anything I needed.

Now, from down the bar, I realized Declan was staring at me. I smiled, and he kept standing there, leaning against the dark wood, staring at me through the darkness, puzzled.

"Excuse me," I called to him.

He pushed himself upright and started walking slowly toward me, a smile playing at the borders of his lips.

"Excuse me," I said, grinning now. "But do you still have 'I Can't Get Started' on the jukebox?" That was my song, the one I always played when I sat at the bar sipping a beer after my shift, the song I would never let him remove whenever the jukebox man came around to update the music.

He let out a whoop and a laugh and came clear around the bar, lifting me right off my barstool and twirling me around.

"Well, I'll be fucked," he said. "I thought I'd never see you again. How long has it been?"

"Nine years," I said. "Nearly ten."

"God, Kennedy, what kept you away so long? No, never mind, don't say anything." He stood there, his arms around me, smiling down at me. Then he leaned over and kissed me full and hard on the lips, a romantic kiss of the kind I had not experienced, I realized even as it was happening, since I'd last experienced it with him.

Sitting there, telling Declan about marrying Frank and having Amanda and living in Homewood and splitting up with Frank, I was thinking how wonderful it felt to be with someone who saw me not as Frank's wife or Amanda's and Maya's mom or Frank's ex-wife or the woman who worked in Jeannie's shop but just as me. To Declan, I was the sum of my laughter and my insights and my ideas and aspirations, not merely an appendage of half a dozen other people.

And he was that to me. The feeling I'd had about him earlier—that our one night of sex had superseded our years of friendship—faded away and I remembered how much I liked him, mourning all the years I'd let pass without him in my life. I could blame that on Frank, but if I'd insisted on continuing my friendship with Declan, Frank would not have tried to browbeat me out of it the way Marco might have done. No, turning my back on our friendship had been completely my doing. And now, I thought, I was here with him again, with another chance to set our friendship back on its track.

The bar was doing well, Declan was saying, but I was focused not so much on his words as on the slow way his hands moved as he talked, in the same rhythm as always, and how his voice sometimes sounded totally American and sometimes, with some words, as if he'd never gone beyond the borders of County Clare. He'd added food and bought the building, and he was undertaking some major renovations now. About time for a change.

"Oh," I said, alarmed that McGlynn's might fall victim to the kind of wholesale reconstruction that had rendered the East Village so foreign, "I've always loved this place just the way it is."

Looking around the room, I remembered people who had not so much as crossed my mind in years: Harry Murphy, the retired cop who tipped all the waitresses with crisp $20 bills. Phil and George, the aggressively hetero brothers who owned the gay sex toys shop. Veronica, with her long black hair and white skin and pastel cigarillos, who came in to drink after finishing her own shift tending bar at a dive around the corner on Seventh Avenue and would routinely ask Declan if he wanted to go into the kitchen for a blow job. "Oh," she lamented to me at least once a week, "if only he would ever say yes."

"Well," he said. "You haven't been standing here looking at this place for the last ten years. I'm ready for a new view." The brick needed repointing, and the roof was threatening to leak, and the building desperately needed to be painted inside and out, so why not keep going? When it came to the interior, he could do a lot of the work himself—long ago he'd worked as a housepainter, and then he'd bought some other buildings along the way, downtown and out in Brooklyn, when prices were softer before the last housing boom, and fixed those up. He enjoyed it, liked it better, if the truth be told, than running the restaurant and bar, had even considered trading in the old place and starting his own renovation business, though he thought he'd give this a try first.

"So do you still live upstairs?" I asked him.

"Same place."

"Are you working on that, too?"

"In progress," he said.

Without thinking, I said I'd love to see it. It was only when I was climbing the stairs to the apartment, Declan's large figure looming ahead of me, that I flashed back on the last time we'd done this. I'd spent the past nine years regretting having slept with him. I'd just sat downstairs wishing we'd stayed friends, vowing that from now on we would be friends again. And now here I was walking up the stairs behind him, wanting more than anything to reach out and touch his ass.

*   *   *

As soon as he shut the door behind us, Declan kissed me. On the lips. Deliberately. Way beyond hello.

"Wow," I said, rocked by a surge of longing so intense I felt dizzy. "Whoa."

"No?" he said.

"No."

He stepped back. I looked around the apartment, or attempted to look around, trying to give credence to why I'd originally asked to come up here. I'd wanted to see the renovation, wasn't that it? Twelve-foot-high plastic sheeting covered the walls, heavy brown paper carpeted the floors, power tools lay in heaps, sprinkled with plaster dust, and most of the furniture, or what I assumed must be furniture, was covered by paint-spattered drop cloths. Totally boring, compared with the man who was standing beside me.

I looked up at him, remembering what had gone through my mind when I was standing on the sidewalk, peering in at him through the window.

"Yes," I said.

He reached out and touched my hip, and I froze in fear, feeling suddenly like the virgin I hadn't been since I was fifteen and first did it with that blue-eyed boy in the woods behind Miss Forster's.

"I don't know," I whispered.

"I have to ask you," he said, taking my hand and enclosing it in his two large ones. He led me over to a sofa-like shape, pushed the drop cloth aside, and pulled me down so that we were sitting beside each other. "Why did you leave that night without saying anything?"

I was stunned, being called upon to come up with an explanation for my long-ago behavior. "You know I was already with Frank then," I stammered. "I felt guilty. . . . I was worried about Maya. . . . I just felt . . ."

"It was still dark," he said. "I heard the door close and I kept lying there, sure you couldn't have really left, and then when you didn't come back I threw on my clothes and ran out into the street looking for you and I couldn't find you. I walked all the way over to your place and you weren't there."

"You went looking for me?" I'd never imagined that, not for a moment.

"I thought I must have done something terrible to make you leave like that," he said. "And then when I didn't hear from you, and I finally called you, and you didn't call me back—I just couldn't think what I'd done to make you leave."

"Oh, God, Declan," I said. "It wasn't you."

"So what was it then?" he said. "Why did you disappear and never so much as get in touch again?"

"You know, it wasn't all my fault," I said, pulling my hand from his. "You were not the kind of guy I wanted to get involved with."

"Why?" he said, looking sincerely baffled.

"All the women, Declan! Every month, a different one, calling at midnight, wanting you to come over, crying at the bar when you broke up with them."

His fair skin colored. "I wouldn't have been like that with you."

"Why the hell not?"

"Because I was in love with you."

I sat there with my mouth open, and then I started laughing. This was the very thing that made him so goddamn appealing to women, and so deadly. He was always in love. He would never leave them. Until the next one came along.

"Come on, Declan," I said. "We were friends! You were my boss! We weren't in love!"

"So what was that night, then?"

"That was incredible sex," I told him. I considered how far to go. "The best," I finally admitted.

His face broke into a grin. "The best? You're putting me on now."

"You're not going to get me to say it again," I said, blushing.

"Well, you were the best for me," he said. "That night was the best for me. And we'd known each other a long time. You weren't just another girl for me to fuck."

"But you weren't about to offer me a stable life together either!" I cried, exasperated. "You were a bartender, you worked all these crazy hours, I had this little kid I was trying to support, and I felt like it was time to be sensible. And there was Frank, wanting to marry me."

He sat there for a moment, not quite looking at me, seeming to think.

"Is that what you're looking for now?" he said finally. "To get married again?"

I let out a laugh that sounded more like a yelp. The answer to *that* question, at least, seemed extremely clear to me.

"Never," I said. "Absolutely not. No way."

"Jaysus," he said, sitting up straight, the Irish taking over his voice. "That sounds pretty fucking absolute."

"You know I look at my mother," I told him, "getting married five times, sometimes marrying one guy the day after she divorced the last one, and I don't want to be like that." I shivered. "I never wanted to be like that, which was one reason I wouldn't marry Marco and resisted for a long while marrying Frank."

"Okay, I get it, you don't want to get married again," he said. "You're going back to being the wild independent girl I used to know."

"Absolutely," I said, with more certainty than I felt. I forced a small laugh. "I'm going to be the female you."

He studied me for a moment, and then he leaned in close and kissed me. And then he kissed me again. And again. His hand went to my face, trailing down my neck and then starting down the slippery slope toward my breasts. I could feel my nipples springing to attention.

As recently as an hour ago, I might have said I wanted sex about as much as I wanted to put fresh sheets on my bed, or as much as I would like to wrap my mouth around a nice hot chocolate chip cookie. But now, relaxing back on the sofa, feeling my legs fall open, it was all I could do to restrain myself from ripping off my panties and hurling myself onto his face.

"Take off your clothes," I murmured.

His hands stopped moving and he looked at me in surprise.

"What?"

It never occurred to me that he would not remember. That I would have to explain. "You said that to me last time, when we came up here. You sat in a wing chair and looked at me and said, 'Take off your clothes.' "

"Which chair?" said Declan. He stood up and pulled me off the sofa too, leading me by the hand across the crunching paper, skirting the piles of tools, to a chair-type form. He sat there and smiled up at me.

"Like this?" he said. And then, making his voice sultry, "Take off your clothes."

I laughed.

"Go on," he said. "Take off your clothes."

I reached down and began to lift my T-shirt.

"Faster," he said. His face was serious now.

I yanked the T-shirt over my head and tossed it across the room.

"Come here," he ordered, opening his arms to me.

I took a step toward him and then stopped.

"Take another step," he said.

I took another one, a small one.

"You may take three giant steps," he said.

I laughed. "Mother, may I?"

"No, you may not. You may take one baby step."

"Did you play this in Ireland, when you were a kid?" I asked, taking my small step.

"You didn't say 'Mother, may I.' "

"Oh, damn."

"There's a penalty for that."

"What kind of penalty?"

"Come here," he said. "Come over close to me."

I walked over to him and he reached out and took my hand and tugged me toward him. I let him pull me onto his lap so that I was facing him, straddling him, a leg on either side of his hips. He ran his fingers under the wire along the bottom of my bra until his hands met between my breasts, where he moved to unhook the bra, looking questioningly at me. I unhooked it myself and pulled it off. He reached up and rested his hands on my breasts and then ran a thumb over each nipple. I arched toward him and moaned.

"Do you want to?" he asked in a soft voice.

Did I want to breathe?

He edged forward on the chair and then all at once he stood up, lifting me with him. I wrapped my legs around him and he walked toward his bedroom, still holding me. He set me down on the bed and while I lay there he pulled his sweater over his head and unbuckled his belt and unzipped his pants and stepped out of them. Then he stood there, naked, looking down at me. He reached down then and tugged at the waistband of my pants, finding the zipper and pulling it down and then sliding my pants all the way off. I didn't say anything, just moved to make it easier for him.

He pulled off my panties and stroked my thighs, the outsides and then between my legs. I closed my eyes and arched toward him. It had been so long and I was overwhelmed by how much I wanted it. It had been years, really, since I'd actively wanted sex. After Amanda was born, it hurt, and I was exhausted, and fat, and I avoided Frank. And hardly ever enjoyed it on the rare occasions when I felt as if I couldn't keep avoiding him. So I always chose sex without ever really wanting it.

But I wanted it now. If Declan hadn't taken off my panties, I would have taken them off myself. Rolled the condom onto his penis. Guided him into me.

That's when I stopped thinking and just started moving. Stopped deciding and started doing. Heat seemed to be emanating from the walls and we were slick with sweat, able to roll and leap on the bed in a way that defied gravity. At one point I thought, He does this all the time, and then deliberately pushed that thought out of the way. A little while later I thought, The other girls are all better than me. But he leaned in at that moment and began kissing my neck and I was transported again. I felt the sides of my face begin to tingle and had the sense that I was about to fall—to pee, to slide over the edge of the waterfall, to lose all control—that signaled I was close to coming, and then there it was, oh there, oh God, oh.

We lay there, entangled, for a few minutes, and then Declan pulled away from me. I heard water running in the bathroom, maybe the shower. Lying there gazing at the ceiling, I let myself drift, listening to the bits of conversation that drifted up from the street— "and then I go" and "wait, wait"—providing the background music of city life. It had gotten dark and I had to hold my wrist in front of my face for a minute before I could see what time it was, thinking of Maya at home alone, and then I relaxed. Not too late.

After what seemed like a long time, Declan emerged from the bathroom in a gust of steam, his hair wet and combed back, his pants already on, buttoning a fresh white cotton shirt.

"Where are you going?" I asked him, expecting him to answer, "Back to work," or maybe, "Out to get us something to eat."

But instead he said, "California."

CHAPTER *five*

California.

Wow, California. California's supposed to be great this time of year. Have a wonderful time.

Not: What are you going to do there?

Not: Who are you going to see?

Not: When are you coming back?

Not: Will I see you again when you do?

I was the female Declan now, right? I was my former self, independent and sexy, scornful of marriage and commitment. Remember?

I'd walked away from Declan the first time around because I'd been looking for a stable relationship, not great sex, not even a kind of soul mate meeting of the minds, which we'd come closer to as friends than Frank and I had ever come as husband and wife.

And so I'd had my stable relationship, and look where that had left me. Now I was going to go for the sex, the fun, and screw security. I would create my own security, depend only on myself. That's what I'd done when I'd turned down my mother's money, that's what I'd done when I'd kicked out Marco, and it had served me well. Independence allowed me to make my own decisions, to live the way I wanted, and I was ready for that again.

Not that Declan was offering me anything but independence. California, he'd said, without further explanation. And: That was lovely, darling. Can I let you out when I go?

I had to say one thing, fantastic sex seemed to have dramatically improved my driving skills. Many of the inhibitions I'd felt driving into the city earlier that day seemed to have vanished as I headed back to Homewood, sailing through the tunnel, merging and passing on the highway with ease.

The Vulva started vibrating and I saw with a jolt that the needle of the speedometer was bearing up on 80 as I neared my exit. Easing off the gas and edging toward the right lane, I thought again of what Declan's arms had felt like as they slipped around me. How it had felt to squeeze my legs around his waist, for him to push into me. I felt as if I'd had a massage, a sauna, a swim in an ocean of perfect waves. And all I wanted was to do it again.

When I pulled into my driveway, the house was dark but I could see a light glowing in Maya's top floor window. Walking into the front hall and then halfway up the stairs, I called her name: nothing. Maybe she'd fallen asleep with a lamp on. I always warned her not to do that. It could be dangerous, it could start a fire. I walked all the way up both flights of stairs and, saying her name softly now, pushed open her door. But her room was empty.

I hadn't seen a note downstairs—if she went out, she was supposed to leave a note, and in any case her curfew was midnight, twenty minutes ago—but I hadn't turned on a light or really looked. I trudged back down the two flights, kicking off my heels in the hallway outside my bedroom and clicking on lights as I went. But there was no note on the hall table, our usual spot, and nothing on the white board in the kitchen.

Where was she? It wasn't like her to be late. It wasn't like her—until recently, anyway—to go out at night at all. But now, at the end of her sophomore year, she'd suddenly thrown off her baggy sweatshirts and was heading to school in skimpy tank tops. She'd begun going out at night, coming home late in cars full of kids, driven by a kid. She'd become, in other words, a teenager.

I didn't know how to be the mother of a teenager. My own mother spent my adolescence partying with her new artist husband at the Venice Bienalle and in Kensington and Barcelona—anywhere they were paying millions for bad American art—while I smoked pot and read Jane Austen at Miss Forster's. I got drunk on sangria, lost twenty pounds then gained forty, bonded with Jeannie as well as dozens of other girls I never saw again, drove too fast with boys who were drunk on sangria, failed chemistry and scored an 800 on my verbal SATs, faked an asthma condition to get permanently excused from gym, catapulted out of my dorm room on a bed sheet, and woke drenched in sweat at least once a week in the grip of a horrible nightmare—and my mother sat out the whole thing on another continent.

My friends at school, Jeannie included, thought my mother was unspeakably glamorous and cool and that I was incredibly lucky to have so much freedom. I pretended to agree with them, but secretly I hated her for going off to live an exciting life when she should have been taking care of me. Yet when she returned from Europe, divorced the artist, and tried to start telling me what to do again, I compulsively did the opposite, dropping out of Barnard, taking up with Marco, working in the bar.

"My daughter's in the restaurant business," my mother would say when introducing me to one of her friends.

"I'm a waitress," I'd correct her.

"Her husband is Spanish."

"He's Puerto Rican," I'd say, "and he's not actually my husband."

I knew that, even though I'd had Maya so young, I'd been a better, more involved mother to her than my mother had been to me. But the older Maya got, the more at sea I felt about what I was doing, about exactly what being a good mother entailed. I poured myself a glass of water and sat in the living room, gazing at the front door. I stood at the window, staring at the black and empty street. I paced. I picked up the phone and felt it grow warm in my hand, without any idea whom to call.

Maya kept a list of her friends' numbers tacked to the wall in her room near her phone, so I could go up there and call them, one by one. Maya would hate that. But she was now over an hour late. Maybe I should just call the police, check that there hadn't been any accidents. No, that would be worse. I could just imagine her coming home to find the cop cruisers, lights revolving parked in front of the house. Then she'd *really* hate me.

But it didn't matter if she hated me, did it? I mean, I was the mother, my job was to take care of my child, and that meant making sure she was home when she was supposed to be, finding her if she wasn't there, doing what it took to keep her safe, not worrying about whether she liked me. I told myself all this as I climbed the steps to her room, as I stood at her desk, dialing Annie's number, the first on the list. Finally, a sleepy voice, a man, answered.

But Maya wasn't there, Annie's father told me. In fact, Annie was home with strep and hadn't seen any of her friends in days.

I stood, looking down at the street, feeling

chilled, feeling terrified. Now I knew I had to do
something, but I was even less sure what. Call
Frank? I hated to admit it, hated to feel it, but I
wished Frank were there. Frank was great in a crisis.
Was this a crisis? If I sometimes erred in being too
soft on Maya, Frank never confused parenthood
with friendship, unflinchingly laying down the law
and seemingly having the power to make Maya toe
the line when she'd whine and wheedle with me. But
Frank was the last person she'd listen to these days. I
was on my own.

I knew: Maybe she was at Haley's. Haley had been
one of Maya's closest friends for years. Fumbling with
the list, I found Haley's number and dialed. When
she—or someone—answered the phone, a sense of
relief washed over me. There was a party going on.
Obviously, that's where Maya was.

"Is Maya there?" I shouted.

And then had to shout it again when the girl on
the end couldn't hear me.

"Maya!" I yelled. "I'm looking for Maya!"

That's when she, the real Maya, touched my arm.

I jumped and it took me a minute to put everything together: Maya standing beside me, wearing
only her pale blue tank top and green striped panties,
the open closet door.

And the boy, the tall thin boy with long, straight,
dark blond hair, dressed only in jeans. His chest was
bare and his skin was pale and he stood there, silent

and still as an apparition. And then he came toward me with his hand extended, saying hello.

"Jeremy!" Maya cried, slapping the hand he held out. "Don't shake her hand!"

Jeremy looked confused. "Why not?" he said.

"Maya, what's going on here?" I asked.

"Jeremy's just leaving."

Jeremy scooped his gray T-shirt from the floor, where I hadn't even noticed it, but he kept standing there, holding the shirt and looking from Maya to me and back again.

"Maya," I said. "I want to know what's going on. Where were you two?"

"We were in the closet," Maya said. "Duh!"

"What were you doing in the closet?"

At that Maya snorted and shook her head. "You are really thick."

"You shouldn't talk to your mom like that," Jeremy said, startling me.

When I looked at him to see whether he was channeling someone else's voice through his teenage boy's body, he shrugged at me, as if to say, What are we going to do with her?

"Get out of here, Jeremy," Maya said, pointing toward the stairs. "I mean it."

Slinging his T-shirt over his shoulder, he gave me a nearly unnoticeable wave and disappeared down the stairs.

"Why were you so mean to him?" I said to Maya.

"Everything I learned about dealing with men," she said, "I learned from you."

"God, you are an unbelievable brat."

"That's what Frank says."

"This is not about what Frank says, all right, it's about what I say." I was shouting now, my heart pumping fast and my temper boiling over. "You are not supposed to be up here hiding in your closet when I am not home, okay? You're not supposed to be hiding in your closet at all! If you're seeing this boy and you want to bring him home, talk to me about it! Introduce him to me!"

"I don't want to introduce him to you," Maya said calmly. "I just want to bring him up here and fuck him."

I imagined it then, saw my hand reach out and slap her hard across the face. But I managed to restrain myself from doing it in real life, thanks undoubtedly to relative calm bestowed by the three orgasms I'd had earlier.

"Maya," I said through my teeth, balling my hands into tight fists at my sides and then releasing them again. "It is not okay for you to bring that boy—or any other boy—up to your room and, as you put it, fuck him. You have a five-year-old sister living here, you have me living here, and it's just not appropriate to be having sex with strange boys under our roof."

"He's not a strange boy," Maya said. "His name is Jeremy Reiner. He goes to my school. His mother died when he was in eighth grade and his father married his math teacher."

"Maya," I said, feeling as if steam were about to come from my ears. "It's not just Jeremy I don't want you having sex with up here. It's anybody."

"What should I do?" Maya said, smirking. "Have sex with them in cars?"

"Jesus, Maya, you are so totally out of line. That does it, I swear. You are going to be going to school, and coming home, and that is all you are going to do, you hear me? You will not be allowed to stay here alone on weekends."

"Well, I'm not going to Frank's," she said, crossing her arms over her chest.

"Well, you're not staying here," I said, crossing my arms too. "And I'm not going to give you the opportunity to be alone anywhere with that boy, or any other boy. You are too young to be having sex, period."

"What do you think I am, Mom, stupid? Don't worry, I'm not going to get pregnant like you did."

I actually did reach out then, and stopped just short of hitting her, instead grabbing at her tank top and snapping the strap.

"Jesus," she spat, batting my hand away. "Where were you tonight, that made you so freaked out about sex?"

I didn't say anything, just turned away.

"I guessed it, didn't I?" she said, a note of wonder in her voice. "You were also out fucking some guy."

CHAPTER six

It was a miserable week. Maya would not speak to me, coming home from school each day precisely on time and heading directly to her room, slamming the door so hard the windows rattled downstairs. I tried talking to her about what had happened, I tried apologizing, I even tried threatening her further—I swear, young lady, you will be grounded until college!—but nothing got any response. She was just blank, as if I didn't exist.

Then, when I wasn't worrying about her, I was worrying about Declan. It was difficult to maintain my attitude of light-hearted party chick when I was feeling so dismal about Maya. And I was feeling pretty dismal about Declan, too, imagining him romping on a California beach with some Sunny-like creature. I wanted to be cool, I genuinely was not looking for commitment, yet I found myself fantasizing about him as incessantly as if I were the one who was fifteen. Was he thinking about me too? Would I hear from him? If I didn't, should I call him? And when, dear God, was I ever going to get out of this goddamn house and have sex again?

So I was surprised and delighted when Declan called me on Friday afternoon and asked me to go out with him on Saturday night. I asked, very coolly, I hoped, how his trip had gone, and he answered, equally coolly, that it had been fine. We talked about where to meet (McGlynn's, of course) and hung up. And then I panicked about what I was going to do about not only Amanda but Maya, too. In the old days I would have left Maya to take care of Amanda, even letting her have a friend over to keep her company once Amanda was in bed. Now obviously that was out. I couldn't hire another teenager to baby-sit Maya, and I couldn't leave them with Jeannie because she was going to be away for the weekend.

That left my mother. She'd been inviting us to visit for weeks now, anyway, so this was a good opportunity to combine her need to see us with my need to keep Maya under constant surveillance.

I spent most of Saturday minding Jeannie's shop, Maya and Amanda hanging out in the back room, and then late in the afternoon I drove out to my mother's place, only twenty minutes away, but on the far side of the line that separated suburbs from country.

The lawn leading up to Highlawn—my mother

had the kind of place that merited a name—really was high, stretching from a grove of oaks and birches along the road nearly a mile up a green and treeless expanse to the crest of the hill. The modern house—built by my mother after she tore down the ancestral brick mansion left to her by Murray, her fourth, richest, and nicest husband—was perched like a spaceship on the highest peak of a verdant but otherwise unpopulated planet. Building this house was the smartest move she'd ever made, she contended, because not only did it gain her a far superior (in her singular view) place to live, but it had provided the means for her to meet Stanislav, her current husband, who'd worked as a welder on the steel and glass box.

Stanislav must have been banished to the local sports bar, because Mom stood alone by the huge frosted glass door, waving to us as we wound our way from the grove up the long curved drive.

"I don't see why I have to stay here," Maya grumbled from the backseat.

"You have got to be kidding."

"I'm old enough to stay home alone."

"Apparently you're not."

"Jeremy is nice, Mom."

"Good," I said. "Invite him over for dinner."

She heaved a huge sigh and was silent for a moment. Then she said, "You know, I can screw up your relationships, too."

I looked at her in the rearview mirror, but she was

staring out at the trees. "What's that supposed to mean?" I said.

"Nothing."

"Maya?"

"I said *nothing*, okay?"

Maya reverted to the stony silence of the past seven days. Amanda, meanwhile, was bouncing, literally, in her seat.

"Do you think Gram will let me try on her dresses?" she asked. My mother had an entire room built expressly for the storage of her wardrobe, including a little wing for old ball gowns, along with their matching furs, shoes, and tiaras, the only relics from her past she deemed worthy of preservation.

"Probably."

"I like the pink one with the rainbow diamonds. Which one do you like best, Maya?"

Maya didn't respond.

I saw my mother, tiny and blond, grin and wave even more frantically toward us, as if directing an airplane into its hangar.

"You'd better shape up," I told Maya, as I smiled and waved back at my mother.

"No, *you'd* better shape up."

Had my mother ever engaged in this kind of nursery school banter with me? I sincerely doubted it. She more often dictated from on high, or seemed too distracted up there to notice what was happening on my lowly level.

I got out of the car and bent down to kiss my mother—I'd been taller than her since seventh grade—and felt nearly overcome by her Chanel No. 5, the perfume she'd worn as long as I remembered. Smelling it, I was Amanda's age, kissing her good-bye in the Pierre Hotel, where we lived at the time with Hal McAndrew, her lounge singer second husband whose last name I took since my own father had died before I was born. They went out, I remembered, six nights a week. The **seventh, u**sually Sunday, Hal went to his private gam**bling club w**hile Mom took to her bed with a stack of newspapers and magazines and the remote control. I was allowed to sit beside her to watch the *Walt Disney Hour,* when we ate our consommé supper on side-by-side bed trays.

Mom still liked to conduct what she called our "girl time" in bed, so when Amanda scampered upstairs toward the wardrobe room, we followed, climbing the open steel staircase to my mother's bedroom, where space-age blinds tuned out all daylight and the air-conditioning hummed on low all year long. My mother settled on the white and gold bed, patting the embroidered silk cover, inviting me to lie down beside her. To my astonishment, I saw that Maya had followed us upstairs—I'd expected her to retreat to the den and Stanislav's big-screen TV—and was hovering in the doorway.

"What are you standing there for, girl?" my mother said. "Come over here and brush my hair."

This was one of my mother's upside-down ideas of maternal behavior; it would never have occurred to her that the proper order of things would be for *her* to brush *Maya's* hair. When she was little, Maya had always savored this duty, but now she approached the bed slowly, as if walking to her doom. I settled back on the bed, staring at the gold brocade canopy overhead, curious to know why she had chosen to stay with us instead of wafting off on her own.

"So," my mother said. "Who's this man you're goin' out with tonight?"

I sputtered, shocked at being confronted this directly and quickly.

"What makes you think I'm going out with a man?" I said.

"Instinct," my mother cackled. "Something in your voice, some kinda gooeyness. Am I right?"

"You're right, Grandma," Maya said, running the brush through my mother's blond hair.

"How do you know she's right?" I said, looking intently at Maya.

"Oh, I don't know," she said airily, not meeting my eye. "Some gooeyness in your voice."

"No, Maya, I want to know what you're talking about," I said sharply.

"Land's sake, leave the girl alone," my mother said. "She's not even able to brush properly with you talking to her like that."

We were all quiet for a moment, and then my

mother said, "Come on now, Kennedy. Just tell us who he is."

I was saved from having to answer by the *clop clop clop* of small feet in sky-high heels. There was Amanda, grinning in a black chiffon cocktail dress, floor-length on her and cut so low the elastic waistband of her little underpants showed in its decolletage. I started to laugh but then saw her face fall.

"Don't you think I look beautiful?" she said.

"Oh, absolutely," I assured her, carefully controlling my expression. "Very beautiful."

"Divinely sensual," my mother said.

"What's sensual?" asked Amanda.

"It means sexy," said Maya.

"Is sensual good?"

"Absolutely," said Maya.

Amanda grinned and, hiking the dress up above her bottom, clomped back into the wardrobe room.

"Okay," my mother said, when she was out of earshot. "Spill."

I thought about refusing to say anything, or lying outright, but either of those options might make things much, much worse. How could I have any credibility with Maya about honesty and ethics if she found out I'd lied to her, or if I even so much as evaded the truth?

Though a dollop of evasion was obviously on the menu.

"He's an old friend," I said.

"What do you mean, an old friend?" my mother

asked, narrowing her eyes at me. Her expressions had become much more difficult to read since the advent of Botox, her anti-aging treatment of choice. "Is this man a former beau of yours?"

Beau? No. I could call him a lot of things, but beau wasn't one of them.

"Because if he is," my mother continued, "I can tell you right now that you're making a big mistake. Huge. Nothing good ever comes of fooling around with the past."

My mother lived by this anti-past credo. She had never gone back to the town of her Oklahoma girlhood, had refused after her mother died to visit her own father—all I knew about him was that he was, in her words, "a drunk"—and had never after her divorces again seen any of her ex-husbands.

"It's always better," she continued, "after a breakup to move forward, start fresh, find somebody better. Onward! I always say. Upward!"

"Maybe I have found someone better," I said. "I mean better for me now."

"But if you're resurrecting a man from your past," Mom said, "and believe it or not, I have tried that on desperate occasions, then you're picking someone who sees you as you *were*, not as you are or as you will be."

"Gee, Mom," I said, "I don't think there's any need to get so philosophical about this. It's just one night, for God's sake."

"One night! Kennedy, that is another thing you've

got to learn. There is absolutely no point in your engaging in a short-term affair of any kind at this point in your life. You have dinner, you have sex, if it's good, you marry him."

"Mom!" I cried, rushing to cut her off. But I was too late; Maya was already laughing.

"Da daaaaah!" Amanda had reappeared, dressed in her favorite pink sequined gown, complete with rhinestone tiara. I remembered my mother wearing that dress during the Hal era. She'd seemed like a fairy princess to me, that magical, that distant.

"Darling," my mother said to Amanda, "be a love and get Grandma her cigarettes."

"Since we're doling out advice," I said, "you should quit smoking."

"And you should start wearing lipstick and a Wonderbra," my mother said.

"And you should stop giving me advice."

"But I'm your mother," Mom said. "I'm supposed to tell you what to do."

"I don't think so, Mom."

"Oh, really?" said Maya to me. "Then how come you're always trying to tell me what to do?"

"That's different, Maya. You are fifteen years old."

"That doesn't mean you get to ruin my life."

As neatly as she might have reached for a cigarette, my mother reached back and shackled Maya's wrist. "Don't disrespect your mother," Mom said.

"But she's torturing me."

"I don't give a rat's ass if she's stickin' hot coals in your eyeballs. She is your mother and you will honor and obey her."

That sobered us all up for a moment. As annoyed as it made me to listen to my mother trying to direct my every move after she spent virtually my entire childhood in benign neglect, I couldn't very well continue to tell her to back off when she'd just given Maya such a stern lecture on parental respect. Especially since it was a lecture I felt that Maya so sorely needed.

Finally, though, the silence began to create a kind of tension of its own and, thinking of what Mom had said to Maya, I felt a laugh bubbling up in my throat. "Hot coals in her eyeballs?" I said finally, a loud chuckle escaping into the hushed room.

"I was thinking fast!" Mom said, beginning to laugh, too. "I was trying to make it dramatic!"

Only Maya was not amused. "You know, don't take this as some big diss, but you two are really hypocritical. I don't see what's so wrong with me having a boyfriend when you had, like, a hundred of them, Grandma. And when Mom has one, too."

"You have a boyfriend?" my mother said.

At the same moment I said, "I do *not* have a boyfriend."

"Oh yeah?" said Maya. "Well, maybe you better tell him that. He's all, Oh Maya, I knew you when you were just a wee lass, and Oh Maya, tell your Mom I'll see her tonight."

Wee lass: That tipped me off that she wasn't bluffing. I felt myself color, my face hot.

"When did you have this conversation, Maya?"

"I'll tell you if you let me see Jeremy."

"Who," my mother said, "is Jeremy?"

"Maya, I swear, if you don't tell me everything right now, you will not see Jeremy for the rest of your life."

"This morning, all right?" Maya said. "He called this morning, while you were in the shower."

"How could you not have told me?" I said.

"Chill. I'm telling you now."

"Will somebody please let me know what is going on?" Mom said.

"My mom's boyfriend called, and I neglected to tell her."

"I am completely lost now," my mother said. "Who is this boyfriend?"

"Don't worry, Grandma," Maya said. "You'll have a chance to meet him very soon."

I bolted upright, my eyes wide.

"What's that supposed to mean?"

"He's coming here," Maya said, not meeting my eyes, twirling the brush through my mother's hair. "That's why he called. He said he was going to be out in New Jersey at his wine distributor's or something and he would pick you up at our place to take you out on your big date in the city. But I told him we were coming out here, so you could dump me and Amanda off. And then I gave him the directions."

I leaped off the bed, my heart ricocheting against my ribcage, stalking toward the window and then back to the bed again.

"Here?" I said, frantic. "He's coming here? When?"

"Don't bug, Mom," Maya said, swiveling her wrist very slowly so she could see her watch. "You've got like . . . five minutes."

"Five minutes!"

I was wearing a not-so-sexy gray T-shirt and an even-less-sexy pair of khakis. But they'd have to do.

" 'Bye!" I cried, grabbing my shoes from where I'd kicked them off beside the bed and heading for the door. "Be good for Grandma! Don't wait up!"

Barefoot, I flew down the steel staircase and out the front door and down the steep lawn toward the woods, certain that my mother and Maya and probably Amanda, too, were standing at Mom's bedroom window, watching me run. I had just made it into the birch grove and over the bridge when Declan roared up the dirt road in his old BMW, nearly running me down. Flagging him down, I jumped into his car and made him back up all the way to the highway. I was determined not to allow my mother and kids to catch so much as a glimpse of his taillights.

chapter *seven*

Hurtling in Declan's car along the highway toward the city, I felt anything but cool. I was still shoeless, for one thing, and sweaty from careening down the hill. And I was seething at Maya for being so devious for no reason I could divine beyond wanting to screw me back. Plus, I was all atwitter in Declan's presence despite my firm resolution to be otherwise.

"So where is Homewood from here?" he asked.

"South," I said vaguely.

"It's right around here, isn't it?" he said. "I was looking at a map before I drove out here. Isn't this your exit coming up?"

He flipped on his signal and moved over into the right-hand lane.

"You don't want to go to Homewood," I said, thinking, Oh, no. Anywhere but there.

"Oh, but I do."

"Really. There's nothing there."

"It's where you live, isn't it?" he said, looking over at me, a smile playing at his lips. His pale skin seemed to be just a shade more burnished after his week in California. "I'd like to see the town where you live."

"It's completely boring," I said.

But he didn't seem to agree, taking the Homewood exit and then driving slowly through the streets while I slunk down in my seat, certain that if I sat up straight I would encounter everyone in town I'd ever met. He commented on the big trees and the lush lawns, the wide streets and the charming houses.

"Where's your place?" he said. "I'd love to see it."

"Absolutely not," I said, visualizing Mrs. Husk and Patty Putnam next door coming out to gawk at the hunky guy I was bringing home. Distributing a neighborhood newsletter with the front-page bulletin that Kennedy Burns was once again having sex.

Declan shot me a surprised look and I realized my reaction might have been a bit harsh.

"My place is a mess," I said, even though it was tidier than ever, thanks to my week spent in lockdown with Maya. "Aren't we going into the city?"

"I thought we'd have dinner out here."

"Oh God," I said. "Terrible idea. Awful restaurants out here."

"Really?" he said, looking amused. "I'd be curious to see what you think is awful. Just for professional reasons, of course."

We had reached the downtown, just around the corner from Jeannie's shop, and he'd slowed to a crawl.

"What about that place?" he said, indicating the new French bistro opposite Starbucks that all of Homewood had been buzzing about.

"I heard the food is terrible," I told him. "Besides, you can't get in without a reservation on Saturday night."

"Terrible food and capacity crowds," Declan mused. "Amazing."

"Listen, Declan," I said. "I'd just rather go into the city, all right?"

He stopped the car. "Why is that, darlin'?" he said. "Do you have some problem with us being out in your town together?"

"No," I said. "No, of course not."

"You're sure?" he said. "Because I get the distinct feeling you don't want to be seen with me."

"That's ridiculous," I said, though of course that was exactly what I was feeling. Everyone I knew in Homewood was aware, naturally, that Frank had left me. They all knew I was living alone with the girls in the house I'd shared with Frank, and they probably also knew, thanks to Barb, that I was planning to stay in town but was considering putting our house on the market. That was all fine, the price of small town life. I just didn't want them to know I was having sex with a large Irish bar owner.

But not as much as I didn't want Declan to know that I didn't want them to know.

"Okay," I said, "if you really want to eat dinner out here, I'll take you to the one place in Homewood that really does have great food. It's just that . . . I hope you like Ethiopian."

Declan laughed. "Ethiopian," he said. "Homewood must be more sophisticated than you've led me to believe."

"Not really," I said.

Especially given that almost no one in Homewood ever went to the Ethiopian restaurant, which was my ulterior motive for taking Declan there. Plus, the restaurant fronted onto a parking lot instead of the street, which made it highly unlikely that we would run into anyone on our way in or out. This, I figured, would be a win-win situation: Dinner in Homewood without having to confront anyone from my real life, followed by wild sex at his place in the city where, once again, I wouldn't have to confront anyone from my real life.

The restaurant, as I had hoped, was quiet and nearly empty, and so dark that even if Jeannie had been sitting across the room she wouldn't have recognized us, hunkered down in a corner booth. Once I felt assured that we were hidden from sight, I relaxed and began telling Declan about the food, which really was excellent, pointing out items I liked on the menu.

He, however, was quiet, and seemed to grow only

more quiet as the meal progressed. We had caught each other up on the big events of the past nine years the other night; now we were left with the day-to-day. What had I talked to him about when we worked together? He had always been easy to talk to: an attentive listener, especially for a guy, who always was ready with a gentle comment that nonetheless pierced the heart of any subject. But we had been just friends then, I reminded myself. Now we were—something else.

"So how was California?" I said, in my desperation bringing up the one subject I'd declared for myself off-limits.

"Fine," he said, not looking at me, picking at his spicy lentil stew.

What did you do there? I thought again, for the hundredth time. Who did you see?

"Good weather?" I asked.

"Oh, sure. Fucking fabulous weather." He balled up his napkin and threw it on top of his food.

"Don't you like your dinner?"

"I never knew there were so many ways to serve lentils," he said, and I might have laughed, but he wasn't even smiling. He fished a crumpled pack of Lucky Strikes from a pocket and lit one. I'd forgotten that he smoked, but now I remembered that he always only had one after each meal. I guess that meant, as if the dirty napkin left any doubt, that his meal was finished. I didn't have the heart to tell him that restaurants in New Jersey didn't allow smoking, though the owner seemed to be deliberately looking the other way, apparently unwilling to alienate his only customers.

"So tell me," Declan said, blowing out a stream of smoke. "How long have you and Frank been apart?"

"I guess it's—" I counted in my head "—nearly five months now. Since right after Christmas."

"So you're divorced? Separated? What?" Declan said.

"Well, nothing officially, I suppose."

Thinking about it now, I remembered that Frank was supposed to draw up the papers through his law firm, and that he'd never gotten around to it, which had gone right over my head since I hadn't been in any rush to push the divorce forward. And now that I was interested in getting our situation resolved, it looked like I'd have to seize control of it myself, except I had no idea where to start.

"So this split," Declan said, "or whatever you want to call it, do you think it's going to stick?"

"What do you mean?" I was on edge now, and although I'd quit smoking with much difficulty when I'd gotten pregnant with Maya, I had the urge to snatch the cigarette from his fingers and inhale the nicotine down deep enough to calm my churning stomach.

"Do you think you and Frank might get back together?"

"Ha!" I cried, delighted to find myself suddenly back on solid ground. "No way. Not a chance in the world."

"But you two were together a long time," Declan said. "You have a child together."

"I'm not the one who left him."

"Exactly," Declan said, picking a piece of tobacco from the tip of his tongue then, looking around the table for an ashtray and not finding one, carefully stubbing his cigarette out on the edge of his plate. "That's why I thought you might be hoping for a reconciliation."

"Maybe I was, for a while," I said carefully, feeling as if it were important to be honest. "But not anymore."

I felt my cheeks redden then, and gave thanks that the restaurant was so dark. I didn't want him to think that I'd given up on getting back together with Frank because of him. I'd given up when Maya told me Frank had introduced the girls to Sunny, hadn't I? More than a week before I even remembered that Declan still existed.

"But don't you think it's important," he said, "for parents to try to make things work if they have a child? Don't you think it's better for the child?"

"Of course it's better for the child," I said. "Theoretically. If there's any chance the parents can create a good relationship. It just doesn't always happen."

"But if there were any chance," he said. "If Frank presented himself before you right now, and said he wanted to be with you again, and asked you to reconsider, don't you think you'd owe him that chance?"

I shook my head. What was he getting at? I didn't

want to talk about Frank with Declan, much less muse together on the possibility of Frank begging me to get back together.

"I don't think I owe Frank anything," I said, slapping my hands on the table, trying to signal in a friendly but absolute way that the subject was closed. "Come on, let's go do something fun."

Declan, however, remained subdued as he paid the bill and ambled behind me out of the restaurant. I tried to pick up the pace out the door and across the parking lot. From the corner of my eye I thought I saw Barb but I turned my head away and walked more quickly, waiting for Declan with my head down at his car. He didn't speak until we were on the street again, driving away from the downtown.

"Which way?" he said.

"The way we came in," I told him. "Down Main and then left on Elm and then straight up until you hit Route 3, which will take us all the way into the city."

"No," he said. "Which way to your house?"

"Oh," I said. "I don't think it's a good idea for us to go to my house. It's a mess, like I told you, and I don't have any air-conditioning, and I was thinking maybe we could have a drink somewhere in town before . . ."

"No, darlin'," Declan said gently, interrupting me. "I'm going to drop you home. Unless you'd like to bring me back to your mother's."

It was as if he had slapped me, and despite my

most strenuous efforts to stay cool, I felt tears spring to my eyes.

"It's just that I'm so tired," he said, still in the gentlest of voices. Why did he feel as if he had to appease me? He'd had a lot of experience, I remembered, with rejecting women, and with mopping up the results. "This jet lag . . ."

But California jet lag—I knew because Frank had frequently traveled to his firm's L.A. office, so he could tack on a visit to his parents—made you sleepy in the morning, not at night. Well, I wasn't going to be one of those girls going into McGlynn's pleading with Declan to give me one more chance. I wasn't going to let him do that to me.

"Home is good," I snapped. "Turn right here. Then left here. Then straight. Okay, it's the tan one, up there on the left."

As soon as he pulled up in front of my house, I had my hand on the door handle, ready to get out.

"Okay," I said briskly, pulling the cloak of protection tight around me. "Well, it was fun running into you again. Maybe we'll meet in another ten years."

I had one foot on the curb and was stepping out of the car when Declan put his hand on my arm and said, "Kennedy, wait."

I hesitated, but I would not look at him, much less sit all the way back in the car.

"I'm sorry," he said, "that our timing's always been so lousy."

I was about to snap that yes, I was sorry, too, and to huff out of the car and slam the metaphorical door on our relationship. Then I thought: I don't believe that. Maybe the timing had been bad when we met, or when we first slept together, but right now it felt just about perfect, with him still single, and me newly free from Frank. If he wasn't interested in getting more involved with me, or if he just didn't like me enough to pursue a relationship, then fine. But I wasn't going to let him get away with blaming it on timing. Or on me.

"My timing's fine," I said. "It's you who's cutting this short."

"I think you're the one who's not ready to be in a relationship," he said. "I think you're the one who's pulling away."

"That is not true," I said.

"Then why didn't you wait for me to ring your mother's doorbell? Why was Maya totally unaware that you and I were supposed to see each other tonight?"

"Maya, my mother," I said, not knowing where I could possibly begin, "that's all very complicated."

He sighed. "Life is fucking complicated."

I let myself relax back into the passenger seat and I turned to him. He was staring out the windshield at Mrs. Husk's house and at the silhouette of her now leafed-out cherry tree. He looked so bleak that I thought maybe I had been too quick to assume he wanted to get rid of me. Maybe I had given him the wrong impression and it was up to me to explain.

"Declan," I said, reaching out gingerly and touching his shoulder. "You're right, I didn't tell Maya about you, I didn't want you to meet my mother, I didn't want to bring you here, but that's not because I want to be with Frank again or because I don't want to be with you."

He looked at me hard. "What is it then?"

I took a deep breath and let it out, a sigh that consumed all the air in the car. What was it indeed? The smallness and psychic narrowness of the town, the quick judgments of my mother and my daughter, my uncertainty about where things were going with him, my resolution to be cool—how to reduce all that to something that could be explained, comprehended?

"It's so new," I whispered finally. "I'm scared."

He continued to stare at me, weighing my words, it seemed, and then he leaned over and kissed me, a soft kiss involving only lips, which could have been a friendship kiss, or a good-bye. But having told the truth I was stripped of my protective shell, and the touch of his lips went straight to the heart of me. Without considering, I flung myself across the gap between the seats and against him, pressing my breasts to his chest and kissing him as if it were the last chance I'd ever get. Which I was afraid it might be.

"I want you completely, can't you see that?" I cried,

all notions of restraint vanished, cool a concept that very obviously didn't apply to me. "Don't you know that I'd fuck you right here if you'd let me?"

Inside the house, there was a moment when I hesitated in the face of its lingering Frankness—Frank's beige sofa, Frank's walnut bookcase, the bed where I'd slept with Frank—but then I remembered: Declan doesn't know that, doesn't see that. And I don't care. When he started for the stairs, I took his hand and led him into the living room to my black velvet couch. I was already pulling my T-shirt over my head, unzipping my khakis, reaching for his belt.

"Wait," he said.

He stepped back from me and sat down.

And then: "Go on. Do it. Take off your clothes."

The room was dark, the lights off and the curtains closed.

"You won't be able to see," I said.

"I'll be able to see."

There weren't many clothes left to take off. I stepped out of the khakis. Then, standing there in my underwear before him, already so turned on, I took off my panties, leaving only the bra. He leaned back, watching me, breathing deeply, beginning to touch himself through his pants. I pulled the cups of my bra down so that my breasts were bare and pointed straight out.

"My God," he said.

I put my hands over my breasts.

"Come here," he said, holding out his arms. "Come here to me."

"No," I said. "Now you. Take off your pants."

I stood there watching while he pulled down his zipper and then wriggled out of the pants, letting them drop to the side of the couch.

He reached for his underwear but I started laughing. "No," I said, teasing him. "Your socks next."

"Sorry, darlin'."

The socks were off, then he sat up and yanked his shirt off, and then he stood up and took off his underwear. He turned around and faced me.

"Lie down," I said.

He lay back down on the sofa and slowly, slowly, I walked over to him, the tips of my fingers still on my breasts. When I was above him, I reached down and ran my fingers over my stomach down through my pubic hair, then slipped a finger inside myself.

Groaning, he reached up, grabbed my hips, and pulled me down hard so that in a flash I was sitting on him, his cock all the way inside me with one thrust.

And then he was my fantasy and my reality at the same time. We were making love and I was fantasizing us making love as we did it, each stroke creating an image of a stroke that made me push more hungrily against him. I moved on top of him until I collapsed onto his chest in exhaustion, my heart pounding though I was still aching for more. Then, holding me, he rolled us off the sofa onto the carpet and he took over, and it was all I could do to lie there with my legs splayed willing him deeper and deeper into me. Finally, I drew my legs up and hooked them over his shoulders so that it felt as if, each time he bore down, he was reaching someplace within me that seemed to exist only for him.

And then suddenly I needed to take charge and I rolled him over again and pinned him down, my hands pressing his wrists into the carpet, and moved my hips around and around and around in a dizzying spiral. I was charging forward now, not holding back except in one way: I wanted to cry out "I love you" but I stopped myself. Stopped myself over and over. I love it, I thought. That doesn't have to mean I love him.

Collapsed on top of him, his heart banging in my ear as I drifted in and out of sleep, I felt as if I'd been living the past ten years as a head with no body, or a will with no impulses, and now the situation had flipped and I was all nerves, all lust. I'd believed this experience was gone from my life forever, and more disturbing, I hadn't cared.

My skin was slick and my legs were tingling and I felt my breath slow as his hands stroked my back. We drifted off to sleep like that, his penis still inside me, and I didn't wake up until we had slipped apart. I pulled two pillows and an afghan down from the sofa and arranged them under and over us and fell back asleep in his arms. And only woke up again when I heard the front door open.

She didn't see us at first and I hoped she might not. I held very still while Declan slept on, giving thanks that he didn't snore. It was evident immediately that Maya wasn't alone and I wanted to know what was going on.

"She won't be back until tomorrow afternoon," Maya said. Then she snorted. "When I'll be with her."

There was silence, then a weird smacking and breathing sound that I soon realized was kissing.

"Not here," Maya said. "Let's go upstairs. We can use my mom's bed."

"No, God!" said a boy, Jeremy I presumed. "Gross!"

"My bed's too small," said Maya.

Jeremy laughed. "I know," he said to her. I heard a zipper. "Let's just do it right here."

I leaped to my feet, yanking the afghan off Declan, startling him awake and into combat mode. He rolled over and sprang to his feet, scrambling for his clothes.

"All right," I said, striding toward them, the afghan wrapped toga-style around my body. "Hold it right there."

Maya screamed. Jeremy said, "Holy crap."

"What the hell are you doing here?" I said to Maya.

"What are you doing here?"

I ignored her question. "You're supposed to be at your grandmother's."

Maya tossed her head. "Grandma and Amanda were asleep. I didn't think it would matter if I left."

"You didn't think it would matter? Making a secret plan with your boyfriend, having him sneak out there and pick you up . . ."

"He didn't sneak out there," Maya said.

"You mean Grandma knew he was there?"

"No," Maya said, looking sheepish for the first time. "I took the car."

I was stumped. "What do you mean, you took the car?"

"Your car, I took it," she said, enunciating too clearly. "I drove it from Grandma's to Jeremy's and then we came over here."

"But you don't know how to drive," I said, stupidly.

"Apparently I do," said Maya.

"You are in trouble like you never imagined existed, young lady," I yelled, not sure whether I was more floored by her slipping away from my mother's or driving the car or coming here to have sex with her boyfriend. Or just by how thoroughly I seemed to have lost any control of her. "You have broken the law, and you have defied your family, and you are behaving in a totally unacceptable way."

"Listen to yourself!" Maya cried. "Look at yourself! Jesus!"

At that moment, Declan appeared from behind me, pants safely belted, putting one hand on my shoulder and reaching out with the other.

"Declan McGlynn," he said, shaking first Jeremy's hand, and then moving to shake Maya's. She crossed her arms and ignored him.

"This is nice," she said. "Very nice."

"Maya, you are on thin ice here."

"*I'm* on thin ice? I'm not the one who's naked. I'm not the one who's been doing it on the living room floor."

"And I'm not the one who's a child!"

"I am not a child! This is my home, too, and I want to be able to bring Jeremy here."

"Oh, honey," I said, taking a step closer to her. "You can bring Jeremy here."

Maya quickly stepped away from me. "I want to sleep with him here, okay? I told you that. Not bring him here for milk and cookies!"

"Maya," Declan began. "I think what your mother is saying . . ."

She didn't even acknowledge him. "You know what, Mom, I don't have to put up with this shit. If you won't let me be with Jeremy in my own house, I'm going to go live somewhere else. I'll go live with my father, my real father. You hear me, Mom? I can go live with him, because I know where he is."

CHAPTER *eight*

"Do you think he's going to be nice?" Maya asked me. I'd let her take the day off from school and we were heading west, into rural New Jersey, to the Greenmarket Nursery, where reportedly we would find Marco watering rhododendrons, fertilizing dogwoods, and lining up potted pansies. Maya might as well have been holding a gun to my head. If I wanted to keep her connected to me, I had no choice but to take her to see her father—and to be supportive about it. In exchange, she was holding off on giving me a hard time about Declan. Deal.

Since I'd had my doubts that Marco was even alive, I'd barely allowed myself to speculate on the issue of his congeniality. I couldn't even decide whether I wanted him to be nice or not. Of course, Maya wanted him to be nice, the perfect father of her fantasies, and I wanted her to be happy. But if he turned out to be a jerk, I'd have less reason to fear that Maya would go to live with him, as she'd threatened on Saturday night. There was no way, after all these years of raising her by myself, that I was going to let her go live with him, nice, not nice, whatever. But as I'd discovered on Saturday, what I let her do and what she did were often two different things.

When it came to Jeremy, we'd negotiated an arrangement that she seemed willing to abide by for now. He was welcome in the house, they often vanished up to her room, but he was not permitted to sleep there overnight. The idea of my teenage daughter having sex I could maybe learn to accommodate—I'd started having sex when I was her age, after all. But just as I was not ready to host Declan for overnights, neither did I want to share my morning coffee with Maya and her adolescent lover.

"His wife sounded nice," Maya said finally. Our exit loomed. I flipped on the directional and felt my hands grow moist and my stomach knot.

"I can't believe," I said, "that he's married." What I meant was: I can't believe any woman would put up with him. What I meant was: I can't believe that the junkie who nodded off over his toothbrush had been reclaimed.

"No, she sounded really nice. She didn't even ask me who I was—I had this whole story prepared about how I was from Publisher's Clearinghouse and I was calling to say that he had won a thousand dollars but I had to give him the news myself so he could confirm his identity."

I laughed. "A thousand dollars?"

"Well, I wasn't going to say a million. What if she fainted or something? So anyway, she just gave me his work number."

"But you didn't want to talk to him first."

She wanted to check him out, she said. See what he looked like before announcing herself as his daughter. Which was all right with me, since it injected a little caution into the enterprise and also gave me a role in their meeting and thus a teaspoonful of control.

I shook my head. "I can't believe he has a job." Aside from his Wall Street trader scam, Marco had always been more of a freelance kind of guy.

"I think he's, like, the owner."

I made a left at the stop sign at the end of the exit ramp and then a right; almost instantly, we seemed to be deep in the woods. What the hell was Marco doing in the woods? When I knew him, he went for years, literally, without leaving Manhattan. He went for months without going above Fourteenth Street, without seeing a tree that didn't have an iron fence around it. Once, we went to the Poconos for the weekend, and he spent our single afternoon there staring at a car race on TV, his back to the window so that he ignored even the *view* of nature.

"This is less than half an hour away from our house," I said.

"I know," Maya said. "That's why it took me so long to find him. I was looking in New York, and it turned out he was in New Jersey all the time. Isn't that amazing?"

Oh yeah, amazing. I loved knowing Marco was barely across the county line.

Maya plucked at one of the embroidered flowers on her white blouse. I'd had one almost exactly like it back when Marco and I were together. When I wore it, he told me I looked Boriquan—Puerto Rican—the highest compliment.

Ahead on the right, there was a clearing and suddenly there was the nursery—called Greenmarket Nursery, yes, but underneath that the sign said Rivera's Trees and Plants. I was amazed; he was the owner indeed. Well, he had always had a lot of entrepreneurial spirit, doing very well in the drug-selling business, I had to admit, before he got addicted and I discovered where all that money had really been coming from.

We pulled into the dirt and gravel parking lot, parking in front of a long low red and dark green building, flowers massed along its front porch. As far as we could see to the left, there were flowers spilling from pots, giving way to rhododendrons and azaleas, and in the distance larger trees stretching all the way to the horizon. I reached over and took Maya's hand, and was pleased and surprised when she didn't pull hers away.

"What's it like?" she said. "For you, I mean."

"You mean seeing your dad again after all this time?"

"No," she said quietly. "I mean seeing Declan. What's it like to hook up again like that with a guy you knew before?"

I was very conscious of the feel of her dry warm hand, of wanting it to stay relaxed, for her fingers to stay curled softly around mine.

"It's nice," I said. "Like going back, finding all the things I used to like so much and had almost forgotten. And discovering new things, too."

"What about the bad stuff?"

"What do you mean?"

Her hand tensed, then pulled away. "I mean the bad stuff," she said impatiently. "There must have been bad stuff, or you would have kept seeing him before, right?"

"Are you thinking about your dad?" I asked gently, the theoretical bad stuff about Marco much more alive for me than anything that might be wrong with Declan.

And then just at that moment, nearly right in front of us, he emerged from the building, a blazing magenta azalea in each arm.

I knew him instantly. Although nearly seventeen years had gone by since the day we met, he looked more like the Marco that had taken a cherry from me on my stoop than he'd looked at almost any time since. He was muscled again, and lithe, his skin brown from the sun. He was wearing a T-shirt and jeans, as he had been that day, and his big hands were splayed across the clay pots just as they had once spread across baby Maya's back and bottom as he paraded her through the East Village. The sight of him, so alive, so familiar, made me gasp for breath.

It took me a moment to recover myself enough to reach over and take Maya's hand again, squeezing it as I pointed toward Marco with my chin. "There he is."

She looked startled, as if she'd had no idea what he was going to look like. And then I realized, yes we had pictures of him, but only a few, and they were snapshots, paler and smaller than they make them now, and Marco was always in the picture with me and usually baby Maya, too. All she'd ever seen was a tiny half-obscured face.

"He's so old," she whispered, staring intently as he set down the azaleas on a bale of hay.

It made me laugh out loud—if we hadn't had the windows up and the air-conditioner still running, he probably would have been able to hear me—to hear her say he looked old precisely when I'd been thinking how young he seemed.

"Not so old." I calculated. "He'll be forty next winter."

"His wife sounded young."

Wife: I bet, I thought. But whoever she was, hearing about her existence gave me an unexpected stab of jealousy.

He stepped back and surveyed his azalea arrangement, making a fast little nod of his head the meaning of which I knew very well: I like what I did. Then abruptly he turned and disappeared around the side of the building where all the flowers were.

"Shit," I said, scrambling to open the car door. "We don't want to lose him."

I began walking as fast as I could toward where Marco had vanished but then I realized Maya was not with me. Looking around, I saw her standing a few feet from the car, looking as if she was about to cry. I doubled back to where she stood.

"What is it, honey?"

"I don't know," she said. "Maybe this is a big mistake. He has another family now. He's not going to be interested in me."

I put my arms around her, forgetting until I was already holding her that this kind of public display had not been permitted since third grade. But this time, she didn't push me away. "You're his daughter," I said, smoothing her already-smooth hair. "You're beautiful. You're smart. You have a right to be here."

"Do you think he's going to be happy to see me?" Tears teetered on her lower lids.

"You know, he always loved you," I said, wanting to reassure her without setting her up for disappointment. "But what's really important is that you follow through on this thing you've been wanting to do."

She nodded and sniffled and then pulled away from me, wiping her cheeks with the back of her hand. "Okay," she said finally. "Let's go."

He wasn't among the flowers. He wasn't in the greenhouse. We trooped back to the front of the building and looked inside, but he wasn't there either. I wanted to have them page him, but Maya wouldn't let me. "I don't want him to be on guard," she said. "I want to take him by surprise."

We went back past the azaleas and the perennials and the herbs, up the dirt road into the field of potted trees. The sun was beating down but the ground was muddy. I felt the mud ooze up the sides of my feet and between my toes; Maya's shoes kept getting stuck and she finally took them off and walked barefoot through the field.

Finally, we reached the end of the dirt road, where the field of trees turned into forest. We hadn't found him and there was nowhere else to go. We turned around and looked back toward the nursery. That's when we saw the truck.

It was an old truck, dark blue and squeaky, kicking up a spray of mud behind it. It slowed as it neared us and we stepped back off the dirt road. Then it stopped and the driver, Marco, leaned out.

"Can I help you?"

"Marco."

It took him a minute, not because he didn't recognize me, I think, but because he couldn't believe it was me.

"Mary Mother of Jesus."

He stepped out of the truck and looked hard and suspiciously at me, as if he thought I might not be real, and then he did something I had not, in all my imaginings of this meeting, expected. He walked over and put his arms around me and held me close, kept holding me and holding me and holding me.

"Marco," I said finally. "There's someone here who's been looking for you."

He turned and looked at Maya. "It can't be," he whispered.

"It is."

She stood there shyly, uncertainly, not making a move toward him. But then, with even more energy than he'd embraced me, he took two quick steps and threw his arms around her and hugged her tightly. Over his shoulder, I saw her face turned toward the sky, smiling.

"My-my," he said. I'd forgotten: That was what he'd called her when she was one, when she was two.

"Dad," she started to say. Then, "Marc—" Then she just hugged him back.

"What are you two doing here? You can't imagine how many times I thought about this, how many times I'd see somebody from the back, or I'd see a little girl . . ." He stepped back and looked at Maya. "But you're not a little girl anymore."

She shook her head no and looked pleased that he'd noticed.

"You're a beautiful young lady," he said. "As beautiful as your mother." He laughed a little. "More beautiful."

"She looks like you," I said.

He squinted, studying her. "Like my mother," he said finally, "when she was a young girl, in Río Blanco, the rain forest. That's half your heritage, you know that? You speak Spanish?"

"*Un poquito,*" Maya said. "I'm taking it in school. Mom was making me do French but I switched."

Right about the time she started looking for Marco, I figured. And just this week she'd announced that she was dropping Burns, Frank's last name, which she'd voluntarily adopted when we moved to Homewood, and reclaiming Rivera.

"*Bueno,*" Marco said. "You can practice with me. Oh, wait till Tina hears about this."

"Tina?" I said.

"A nurse," Marco said. "You believe that? A young girl, working her first job, when they brought me in there. To, you know, the place where they helped me fix that problem I had."

"You mean the drugs?" I said.

Marco shot me another look I knew: Shut up.

"It's okay, Marco," I said. "Maya knows about that."

He raised his eyebrows. "You told her?"

"I didn't have to tell her. She'd picked things up over the years. She figured it out."

"You think it's right," he said, "a young girl should know something like that about her father?"

I was aware of Maya standing silently on the margins of the storm that suddenly seemed to be gathering over me and Marco and I realized how familiar this felt, too. It had always been me and Marco fighting, or not fighting but circling one another in anger, or even in passion, and Maya who'd been left out. It had been a relief, after Marco was gone, to be able to shine all my attention on Maya. And part of what I'd found appealing about Frank was that, if things were tepid between us, they were also calm, and Maya was an equal member of our circle rather than the outsider to a tempestuous romance.

If Maya was going to have a relationship with her father again, that dynamic had to change. I didn't want to be part of it, even in a make-believe way, and I didn't want to impose it on her again either.

"It's not a question of right or wrong," I said, trying to keep my voice calm, soothing. "She understands it's a kind of illness, not something you did to try and hurt her."

"Of course I wasn't trying to hurt her," Marco said angrily. "I would never hurt her."

"I told her that," I said, searching desperately for a change of subject. "So that's great. You're with somebody, with Tina."

"Officially married," Marco said, holding up his ring finger as evidence. "Five years. Two kids. Both boys."

Boys like you couldn't give me, was what I heard. As crazy as he'd always been about Maya, he'd hoped for a son. Six sons, he always said he wanted to have, which would have been enough to send me screaming to the hills if the drugs hadn't done it.

"Good for you," I said.

"Yeah, look at all this," he said, spreading his arms and surveying the land all around, most of it, as far as we could see, part of the nursery. "This could have been yours, Kennedy, think about that."

I did think about it. Me and Marco, Marco and me, out on the farm with Maya and all her little brothers. Was there any way I could trace a line from there to here? Could I see myself, nursing Marco, as Tina apparently had, back to health and well-being? No, obviously not, I hadn't even tried, hadn't known where to begin. It had seemed easier back then, far easier, to give up and start fresh.

But then I became aware of Maya still standing there, silent, watchful, and I thought, for her it would have been better if I could have found some way to stay with Marco. She must be thinking: I wish this were mine, I wish this belonged to the three of us, together.

"Maya's been so excited to meet you," I said.

"Yeah?" He put an arm around Maya's shoulder, pulling her close, but his attention stayed trained on me.

"What about you?" he said. "Whatever happened with you and what's-his-name?"

"Frank," I said. "I married him."

"And divorced him," Maya said quickly.

"Not divorced yet," I said.

"Oh yeah?" Marco said, raising his eyebrows, another level of interest seeming to register on his face. "So you're a free woman again?"

"Since December," said Maya. "Frank dumped Mom right after Christmas."

"It was a mutual decision," I said.

"It was not," said Maya.

"Maya, please. You don't know everything."

"Yes I do."

"Kids," I said, making an attempt to smile at Marco, to show him we were in this together. "You know how teenagers are these days."

"No, I don't," he said. "You kept me from seeing my daughter since she was six."

"Oh, come on, Marco, I never stopped you from seeing Maya. You were the one who had problems. You were the one who stopped showing up."

"Oh, yeah, like I really felt wanted around you and the stiff, your Park Avenue lawyer boyfriend, husband, whatever. Then I came trying to see Maya and found out you were gone, disappeared. How do you think that made me feel? That was it for me. That was bottom."

"You were close to bottom a long time before that,

Marco," I said. "Don't you dare try to blame all your troubles on me."

"Stop!" Maya yelled. "Stop it right now!"

Everything was silent for a moment.

Then I said, "I'm sorry. I'm sorry, Maya."

Marco didn't say anything. I had the urge to prompt him to apologize to Maya—I could tell she was looking toward him, waiting to hear that from him, but he didn't say anything, just kept standing there looking pissed-off, kicking at the dirt with his work boots.

"Mom warned me about you, but I didn't believe her," Maya said finally. "I thought you were going to be happy that I found you."

At last, he looked her in the eyes.

"I am happy," he said. But he kept frowning.

"Then act it! Jesus!"

Marco turned to me. "What kind of language is that?"

And here I'd been feeling proud that she hadn't said Jesus fucking Christ. I put up my hands and turned away, walking a few yards away through the mud.

"Okay, I'm happy," I heard Marco say. "I mean it, I'm very happy."

"So your wife," Maya said, "she knows about me?"

"Sure she knows. I wanted to find you, for a long time. I just didn't know where to look."

"I'm right here," Maya said.

It was quiet then and I imagined that he put his

arms around her, that he kissed her on the cheek, that they held each other for long enough to begin to make everything all right.

"So," I heard Maya say finally, "can I, like, come to your house?"

"Of course you can come to my house. Sure you can come to my house. It'll be a party."

"So, when?"

"I don't know. You have school? You're a kid, of course you have school. I work long days on the weekends, Saturday and Sunday, but maybe I could take a little time off, come and get you after school one of these Fridays."

I swung around. "I'll bring her to your place," I said.

"I can get her," Marco said.

"He can get me," Maya said.

"No," I said. I may have realized that I had to step aside if Maya was going to develop a relationship with her father. But my first job, as it had been back when I'd kicked him out of our life, was still to protect her. Yes, I admit it, I wanted to see his house, his boys, his wife. But mostly I wanted to make sure my daughter was safe, at least as safe as I could keep her at this point in her life.

"That's my one condition," I said. "I bring her to you."

CHAPTER *nine*

"It's a wreck," Barb the realtor said.

Jeannie and I were working in the shop, packing up everything left over from early spring and Easter—the painted eggs and the bunny ornaments, the magnolia buds and the wooden flats of grass that Jeannie trimmed with scissors—and Barb was keeping us company.

"But it's $200,000," I said to Barb. "Nothing in Homewood is $200,000. I may actually be able to swing that."

"It needs another $200,000 worth of work," Barb said.

"Maybe I could do some of it myself."

Barb shook her head. "This isn't a project for an amateur," she said. "Especially a lady amateur."

"Barb!" I said, slamming down the silver egg-shaped candy mold I'd been holding. "That was beneath you!"

Barb looked sheepish. "I know," she said. "I'm sorry. I just don't think it's the place for you, Kennedy."

"Let me decide that," I pressed her. "At least take me to see it."

She rolled her eyes and shook her head. "I'll give you the address," she said. "Drive by. Then you can decide whether you want to take the next step of making an actual appointment. Mrs. Glover was very clear that she didn't want a lot of people trooping through the house."

"I don't know why you want to rush into this," Jeannie said. "Summer's coming, the girls are going to be home full-time. You should take it easy, wait till fall to figure out what you're going to do."

"I don't have until fall," I said impatiently.

I was shocked, now that money was so tight, to discover how much we had been spending to live our "normal" middle-class suburban life. Maya was used to ordering whatever she wanted from J. Crew, we'd always belonged to the pool club, and we had two cell phones plus super digital cable. But now, we had to trim not only these extras but the essentials as well. I'd begun clipping grocery coupons, the Vulva was going to have to last another 100,000 miles, and there was no way, even if I'd wanted to, I was going to be able to afford to stay in the house I'd shared with Frank.

"Come on, Jeannie," I said. "Come look at it with me."

"I'm trying to get out of here so I can get to the

mall before Phoebe's out of school," Jeannie said. "I've got to get shoes for that thingie at the golf club. Why don't you come with me?"

Once upon a time, I would have, happily. Jeannie was proud of her position as the golf club's style renegade, even if their definition of forward fashion was a pair of Chanel mules. I couldn't afford to spend like that anymore, but what's more, I was getting excited about the idea of living more frugally. I was rediscovering how independent I'd felt in New York simply because I was willing to live minimally. It may have been the age of excess, I may have enjoyed being a guest at lavish parties and enormous beach houses, I may have combed thrift stores for real cashmere and Hermès, but what I loved most was living a life I could easily afford.

Jeannie, however, had never been a fan of the thrifty lifestyle, especially not when she'd been forced to live it. It came from growing up poor, she said; she was terrified of finding herself back at vinyl wallets and Cheerios for dinner. Whereas I, growing up with a mother who'd married—and married and married and married—for money, was more terrified of selling my soul.

"Can't," I said now. "Spending freeze. Besides, I've got to work so you can leave to shop, remember?"

"If you two want to just drive by the house real quick, I'll hold down the fort," Barb offered, looking thrilled at the prospect of half an hour alone in her favorite store. "The place is right nearby."

I felt grateful for her offer, partly because I was

anxious to see the house, and partly because I wanted a little time alone with Jeannie. It seemed she was always sailing out the shop door the minute I showed up to take over, and when she was there, I was forever rushing off to be with the girls or do some job to get my old house ready to sell. Normally, we might have planned things so that we'd have at least a little overlap at the store, but I was aware that Jeannie was making a lot of plans to give me maximum hours on the payroll. I was also aware that I was avoiding her.

I'd missed my initial and best opportunity to tell her about Declan. I might have called her right away, that first night, if it had not been for the crisis with Maya. And then there had been my fear that maybe my fling with Declan would last only that one night. I didn't want Jeannie asking me every day if he'd called, and then clucking in disapproval when he didn't.

But then I did see him again. And expected to keep seeing him. And never caught Jeannie up on my news.

She drove now, piloting her silver M-class through the streets of lower Homewood as I read off Barb's directions.

"God," she said. "This house is in the ghetto."

I laughed. "Don't be ridiculous. Homewood doesn't have a ghetto."

But okay, to the people who lived on the town's richest streets with the biggest houses, as Jeannie did, maybe this part of town did look a bit shabby. Brick apartment buildings stood beside Victorians that had been converted to offices; aluminum-sided multi-family houses squatted next to tidy restored bunga-lows. Most of Homewood's non-white families lived in this neighborhood, as did its young people and its old people and its artists and musicians, and the dads who'd been kicked out by their wives, and the couples with no kids, and the single moms. Come to think of it, maybe it was the rest of town—where almost everyone was white and married and well-off—that was the ghetto.

"Now I know why I never come down here," Jean-nie said.

"I was just wondering why I didn't come down here more often," I said. "I guess I've never had friends who lived in this part of town."

But maybe I needed some new friends, I thought. The friends I'd had with Frank were not, for the most part, interested in continuing the relationship. Even Jeannie, I knew, no longer invited me to every dinner party or cocktail party she threw. I was not hurt so much as lonely, eager to connect with other people who had kids but not spouses, who were living the suburban life but without big bucks.

"What was that street name again?" Jeannie said. "Willow-something? I don't think I ever heard of that."

"Barb said it was a little street, just a dead end. Oh, look, look, she said it was just past this church."

In fact the church, which featured one of Home-wood's handful of homeless people sleeping on its front steps, was one of the town's architectural treasures, built of limestone and boasting a slate-shingled steeple that rose high to a fairy tale–style peak. This was not one of the stylish congregations in town, but the church itself was certainly the most beautiful.

Willow, just Willow, Lane turned off to the right after the church. It was not much of a street, six or seven closely spaced houses along each side, seeming to dead-end in a thicket of thorny bushes.

"Barb said number 24," I said, looking at the paper where I'd scribbled the directions and the address. "But the numbers end at 22 on that side, and 23 on this side. I don't think there is a 24."

And then the bushes shook, and a wooden gate, its paint long weathered away, seemed to open from within them, and out from the wall of green stepped an old lady with her back hooked over into an upside-down U, so that her head was bent toward the ground. She was pushing an empty wire grocery cart, its wheels wobbling and squeaking, and she moved so slowly it was difficult to imagine that she would make it as far as the church on the corner, never mind all the way downtown, by nightfall. As she passed Jeannie's car, she swiveled her head and, pale blue eyes looking directly through the passenger window into mine, gave me a huge smile.

"That must be the house, in there," I whispered to Jeannie, when the old lady had finally hobbled out of earshot.

"I think she's a witch," Jeannie whispered back. "The house is probably made of candy."

"No," I said. "She looked nice."

"You're going to end up like her if you buy this house," Jeannie said.

I was wounded. "Maybe I want to end up like her."

We both got out of the car and stood there for a moment, waiting to stop being annoyed at one another, and then I edged forward. It was impossible to see beyond the green without pushing open the gate, and so this I did. A small white cat darted from within and dashed down the street.

"Oh shit," I said. "I didn't mean to do that."

"Next will be a fire-breathing dragon," Jeannie said.

I opened the gate further and there, tucked deep within the property, through a tangle of rosebushes and daylilies and uncut maple saplings, stood the house. A wisteria vine as thick as the beanstalk Jack might have climbed twined up the side of the house and along a pergola, its purple flowers fat and ripe and fragrant even from here. Even from across the entire garden, it was easy to spot the cracks that veined the stucco walls, to see all the shingles that were missing from the roof.

"Oh my God," I said. "It's beautiful."

"It's a nightmare," said Jeannie.

"I love it," I told her.

"Oh no," said Jeannie.

"Can you imagine what it could look like with a little work?"

"A little work?" Jeannie gasped. "How about a Swiss bank account and a team of big strong men?"

I thought of Declan, the work he was doing on his place, the work he might help me do out here. Here was my opening to tell Jeannie about what had been going on between us, and this time, I thought, I'd better steel myself and run through it.

"I know a big strong man," I said.

"Oh really?" She raised her perfectly shaped eyebrows at me. "I didn't know there were any big strong men in Homewood."

"He's not in Homewood." I said, trying to keep my voice nonchalant. "He's in New York."

Jeannie was looking at me with genuine interest, and skepticism. "Surely you don't mean Frank?"

"Frank's doing yoga, not bodybuilding," I laughed. "No, I'm talking about Declan McGlynn. Remember him? The Irish guy who owned the bar where I used to work?"

"The one you did it with that time," Jeannie said.

It was all coming back to me. Jeannie had already been married to Chip at the time, was already living in Homewood, was encouraging me toward making more of a commitment to Frank. She'd been scandalized by my sleeping with Declan, and had only felt okay about it once she came to view it as the event that tipped me toward marrying Frank.

"Let me remind you that he'd also been my boss and friend for five years before that," I said. "But the thing I really want to tell you is, it's happening again."

She looked blank.

"The sex," I said. "With Declan."

"Hold on, I'm not following you." She stood there frozen, her mouth hanging open. She was wearing enormous Chanel hoops—gold intertwined Cs—and even these weren't moving. "You mean you're sleeping with this Declan person?"

"No big deal," I said, stepping back into the cul-de-sac and slamming the gate to the cottage shut.

"No big deal." Jeannie started nodding very fast, the Cs bobbing along with her head. "You have sex with some . . . stranger, and you call that no big deal. Come on." She beckoned with her hands. "Tell me everything."

There had been a time in our lives when we dissected every element of our sexual encounters: length, width, endurance, orgasm intensity, technique, overall satisfaction rating. But that had ended with our marriages, and with Chip off-limits, I didn't have any desire to offer up Declan for Jeannie's erotic entertainment.

"It's great," I said. "I really like him."

"'It's *great*'? You expect me to be satisfied with 'It's great'? I want details! Specifics! Is it great like when it's your anniversary and you're staying in a hotel without the kids? Or is it great more like when you use that magic vibrator thing with the rotating dildo?"

"Jeannie!" Sunday nights with the *Sex and the City* girls aside, I seemed to have really lost my appetite for shared raunch.

"Give me a break!" she cried. "You're the only one having sex here. The least you could do is tell me about it."

I was stunned. "You and Chip don't have sex?"

"You know what I mean! Every couple of weeks, if I can avoid him for that long, we grope around under the covers and I basically hope it's not going to take too much time——which it usually doesn't, so at least I get some satisfaction."

I did know what she meant. That's the kind of sex I'd had with Frank. And would have contentedly kept having in exchange for his steady paycheck, if he hadn't up and left me. But hearing about it now from Jeannie, thinking about that dreary sex life stretched out endlessly into her future when I had been reminded that the world offered so much more, I felt terrible for being so secretive with her.

"It's scary how much I want it," I told her, a revelation as peace offering. "I'd forgotten how incredible sex could be."

Jeannie studied me for a moment. I couldn't decide whether she was about to tell me to go fuck myself or to ask me to reveal more.

Finally she said, "Good for you."

"Really?" I asked, surprised. "I thought you'd tell me I should find somebody else like Frank, or like Chip, who could offer me security, forget the passion."

"That is what I think you should do," said Jeannie. "That's what I would do if I were you. But there's also something to be said for a great cock."

I was about to protest that Declan also had some positive qualities out of bed. But then I thought, why bother? If he wasn't offering me marriage, a seven-bedroom center hall colonial, and a cut of his half-million-dollar paycheck, Jeannie would not be impressed.

"So what's it like," she finally said, "having a big strong man in your bed, saying Yes yes yes?"

"He's not saying Yes yes yes," I admitted.

"Oh yeah? What's he saying?"

I had to think about that. And then it became clear. "Maybe maybe maybe."

Barb fumbled with the lock as I stood with Declan on a slab of bluestone that was nearly overgrown with weeds, what counted for the step up to the house's front porch. I had driven by the place at least a dozen times in the days since I'd been there with Jeannie, and now I was finally going to get to see inside, with Declan in tow. I squeezed his hand.

"Thanks for coming," I whispered.

"You're welcome," he whispered back, returning my squeeze.

This was the first time I'd seen him in nearly three weeks. He'd call me every few hours, and then I wouldn't hear from him for days. I wouldn't call him, telling myself that was being cool. Then I'd call him, telling myself that was being cooler. He worked all the time, and I tried not to feel insecure about all the women who paraded through the bar, within his easy grasp. Whenever I wasn't working at the shop, I was stuck at home supervising Maya, which I hoped might make me seem busy and mysterious, though all it made me feel was oppressed. The fact was, I wouldn't have been able to see him even if he'd asked me, which he hadn't. Needing his advice on the house gave me an excuse to ask him.

There was only one twist to this get-together. One big twist. I'd arranged to have Amanda play with Jeannie's daughter Phoebe so I wouldn't have to drag her along with me, but then, as I was leaving my house to come over here, Jeremy showed up. Because Jeremy and Maya still weren't allowed to be at the house alone if I wasn't there, I'd brought them with me. Maya would have been content to wait in the car, but Jeremy wanted to see the place and now seemed so eager to get inside that he was trying to help Barb with the lock.

"I hope the owner doesn't mind this crowd trooping through," I said.

"Mrs. Glover isn't home," Barb said, the key finally catching. "I came and got her and brought her to the senior center myself, poor thing. She's lived here for nearly fifty years and she can't see anything that's wrong with it. She's just crushed when everybody doesn't love it the way that she does."

The door swung open and my first impression was that winter was locked inside the house, still chilled despite the warmth outside. And every surface—the dark wooden floor, the hall table, the gilt mirror—was coated with a thick layer of dust.

"Sorry," Barb said. "It's difficult for Mrs. Glover to clean."

"Jesus—Miss Havisham," said Maya.

"I don't mind," I said. I was already drifting away from Barb and Declan and Maya and Jeremy down the hallway and into the living room. It jutted out from one side of the house so that it had floor-to-ceiling windows on three sides, three down each of the long walls and two flanking the fireplace at the room's far end. There was a beamed cathedral ceiling, and dark wooden floors that sloped crazily in unpredictable directions. The walls and ceiling were threaded with cracks; plaster lay in cat-sized chunks on the floor. And oddly, since the owner was still living there, the room was empty.

"Where's all the furniture?" I called to Barb.

She appeared from somewhere behind me, Jeremy at her side. "She has a place in Maine where she's moving in a few weeks, as soon as summer starts," Barb said. "A lot of her stuff has already been shipped."

"So she's ready to close," I said.

Barb shot me a sharp look. "Your house isn't even on the market yet."

"This room is awesome," said Jeremy.

I looked at him appreciatively. "I agree."

"Kennedy," Declan called from somewhere behind us. "I need to show you this."

Where the kitchen must once have been was a huge old iron sink, big as a bathtub, with its rusted faucets lying in the basin. A monstrous old stove stood away from the wall, revealing a thick layer of mouse turds on the linoleum—or rather, where the linoleum used to be. Now it seemed that the pattern was totally worn away, replaced by something that looked like dried mud. There were no cabinets, no countertops, and the overhead light was dangling from a lone frayed wire. The only functioning appliance seemed to be an ancient refrigerator that was humming loudly and throwing off the scent of gas.

"It's hooked up to a propane tank," Barb informed me.

"I didn't even know you could do that."

"Mrs. Glover doesn't hold with electricity," Barb said. "The house has it, but she doesn't like to use it."

"The kitchen does need a bit of work," I said, looking around.

Declan flashed me a look of alarm. "A bit, I'd say. It seems as if there was a leak under the sink that never got fixed and rotted away the floorboards. And another one," he pointed overhead, "from what's probably the bathroom upstairs down through this light fixture. This entire ceiling may have to come down."

"But hey, Mrs. B., I put in one of those IKEA kitchens with my dad, and it wasn't too bad," said Jeremy. "And have you seen the dining room in here? It's got this cool picture painted right onto the wall."

He meant the mural, a scene of old Amsterdam and its canals that wrapped all the way around the room, covering the entire four walls above what looked like walnut wainscoting.

"Look at this, Declan," I said. "Isn't this amazing?"

"It is beautiful. Though it would be difficult to restore the plaster where it's cracked along the edges of the mural."

"I don't mind that," I said. "It adds charm. What do you think, Maya?"

She was still standing in the front hall, leaning against a wall, a sour look on her face. "I think it's a rat hole," she said. "Can we go now?"

"Oh, come on, Maya, this place is bangin'," said Jeremy. "Come and see this."

She rolled her eyes but she pushed off the wall and joined him where he seemed to be leading the tour. There was a tiny sunroom beyond the dining room, and a "flying staircase"—that's what Barb called it— that led up to the second floor, where there were three small bedrooms, painted pink and yellow and green like candy mints, and a single bath. In the bath were a big old pink tub, a big old pink sink, and a pink toilet that seemed to be losing water from its base.

"There's what's wrong with your kitchen ceiling," Declan said.

"It might need a new roof, too," said Barb.

"Slate," said Declan. "That's going to be expensive."

"My mom would have loved this place," Jeremy said.

"Oh," I said. "Did your mother like old houses?"

"Ghost houses," Maya muttered.

"Yeah," Jeremy said happily, apparently not having heard. "She was always dragging me around to open houses and estate sales and she was always putting up wallpaper and stuff like that. She and my dad, they redid our whole house."

"I should look at the pipes in the basement," said Declan. "And the furnace. And I bet it's all covered by asbestos. I think you're looking, just for the plumbing and the heat, at another $30,000 at the very least."

"Electricity?"

"This is old knob and tube. Not what you really want, but probably not worth fooling with. If the squirrels and the mice . . ."

"So what are you saying?" I interrupted. I felt annoyed that Declan seemed to be wrecking the reverie of appreciation I was sharing with Jeremy. "That I should just forget the whole thing?"

Declan and Barb exchanged a look.

"Kennedy," Barb said finally, "I know Mrs. Glover has this fantasy that some nice young person—some nice young woman, just like she was half a century ago—is going to come along and fall in love with this place. But the fact is that the only one who can or should undertake this kind of rehab is a developer with a whole crew of guys who can just sweep through here and do it over for a profit."

"That's exactly what I'm afraid is going to happen!" I cried. "Some rich developer is going to buy this house and polyurethane the floors and plaster over the mural and paint over the woodwork and put in some stupid modern kitchen and then resell it for a million dollars."

"But that's who has the resources to undertake this kind of job," Barb said.

"I have resources," I said. "A lot of the problems here look bad but they're really just cosmetic, cleaning things out, patching and painting, sanding the floors, weeding the garden. And I've got taste. I've got very good taste."

"Kennedy," Declan said. "Taste is not going to do it. There are the mechanical problems. And then with the level of deterioration here, the dust—it's not going to be a matter of slapping a coat of paint on the walls."

"But you could help me," I said, any thought of holding back on this request vanished in the face of how much I loved the house, how much I wanted the house. If I sold my place I'd have enough money, if I educated myself I could undertake the work, and if Declan helped me I could actually make it happen.

"I don't know," he said. "You're not being realistic about the amount of time and energy involved."

"I'll help you, Mrs. B.," Jeremy said.

I appreciated how sweet Jeremy was being, but all my attention trained on Declan. "So you're saying you wouldn't help me?"

He sighed deeply. "I'm not saying I wouldn't, I'm just saying it's not practical. I've got the bar, and I live on the other side of the river, and I wouldn't be free to spend very much time here, even in the best of circumstances. You'd be on your own a lot of the time. I know you love the place, but honestly, darlin', it's too much work and you don't need this kind of headache with all the rest you've got going on in your life."

Barb was across the room nodding in agreement.

"Can we leave now?" Maya said. When nobody answered her, she turned on her heel and walked outside. Jeremy had been listening to us intently, but now he followed Maya.

"So you're telling me not to take it," I said to Declan.

He hesitated. "I don't want to make this decision for you."

"But I asked you here to give me advice," I said. "I want you to tell me what you think I should do."

He hesitated again. But finally he said, "All right, if you want my opinion, I think you should walk away."

"Okay," I said, sensing the house already receding into the netherworld of roads not taken. "Then I'll walk away."

CHAPTER *ten*

Maya was going to Marco's for her highly anticipated first weekend with his family, Amanda was visiting Frank, and I was getting to spend an entire two days and a complete night with Declan at his place and at his invitation. But first I had to hand-deliver Maya to her father.

"You don't need to come to the door with me," Maya said as we pulled up in front of his place, which was huge and white and perched atop a hill high above the street, seemingly reachable only via a steep staircase. I couldn't stop staring at it. There must be a lot more money in azaleas than I would have guessed.

"Oh, no," I said, reaching into the backseat to take her suitcase hostage. "I'm coming to the door with you."

"You're not coming to the door with me."

"If I don't go to the door, you're not going to the door."

Maya muttered something and then huffed out of the car, running up the steps—there must have been at least a hundred of them—to the front door. I scrambled to catch up with her, and was so out of breath by the time we met at the top of the stairs that I couldn't say anything else to her, even if I'd been so inclined. She was already ringing the bell.

Someone I at first guessed was the baby-sitter but then realized must be Tina answered, a baby on her hip. Even given her thick makeup she looked astonishingly young, with her long blond hair and tight white jeans.

"Maya!" she cried, in an accent as thick as Carmela Soprano's. "C'mere. Gimme a hug."

Maya did as she was ordered. Then, releasing my daughter, Tina turned to me. "C'mere," she said, beckoning me too into a hug redolent of perfume and hairspray. Her thin arms were surprisingly strong. "We both had his babies, I figure we could be close."

"My mom was just leaving," said Maya.

"No, I wasn't."

"Your mother can come in for a minute," said Tina to Maya, in that firm but friendly tone I had always aspired to but never achieved. "You can put your suitcase in the room at the top of the stairs, the pink one."

Maya went upstairs and Tina led me into the pristine white and gold living room, setting the baby, who looked like a miniature Marco, on a white satin crib quilt spread on the carpet. Over the fireplace was a family photograph as large as an ancestral portrait. "Diet Coke?" she asked. "Or maybe you're hungry? You want some eggplant?"

"No, thanks." Outside the wall of sliding glass, across the backyard with the pool and over miles and miles of trees and suburbs beyond, the skyline of Manhattan seemed to float in the haze. "Wow, this is some place."

"I didn't want to leave the city," Tina said, "but Marco with his trees—you know how he is." Not really, I thought. She seemed to be looking for something in the backyard and suddenly she tilted her head back and opened her mouth, bellowing, "Marco! Company!"

"Oh," I said, suddenly feeling nervous. "Is he here?"

"Sure he's here. You think I'd let him invite his kid and then disappear?" She looked at me as if I might be as crazy as Marco probably claimed I was. "Marco!"

I didn't hear him coming until he was in the room, padding barefoot on the thick carpet, his strong tan legs sticking out from white shorts.

"Oh," he grunted. "So you two have met."

"Of course we met," Tina said. "What did you think I was going to do, ignore her?" Ig-naw huh. "You're a moron, you know that, Marco?" Just as I was marveling that she could talk to him like that, she tripped in her hot pink beaded mules over to him and pressed her full body against his, kissing him some-where beneath the ear.

"Do me a favor, hon," she said. "Change Ryan's diaper, wouldja? Where's Marco Junior?"

Marco looked vaguely toward the sliding doors. "We were out in the yard."

"You left Marco Junior in the yard by himself with the pool right there? What are you, out of your mind? I'm tellin' ya. Men!" She looked back at me as she headed for the door. "Nice meetin' ya," she said. "Don't worry about Maya. She'll be fine."

And then Marco and I were alone in the room, except for the cooing baby on the floor.

"I'm just waiting to say good-bye to Maya," I told him.

"To tell you the truth," Marco said, "I never wanted to see you again."

I felt my back stiffen. "I can take Maya and go."

"Not Maya," he said. "You."

Shaking his head, he crossed to the white and gold credenza, opened one of the top drawers, extracted a disposable diaper and some wipes and dropped to his knees on the carpet beside his baby son.

"Who's a handsome boy?" he said, leaning close to the baby's face and shaking his head some more, but now for the baby's benefit. "Who's Daddy's handsome boy?"

"He looks just like you," I said.

"All my kids look like me," he said, still addressing the baby.

"You've really changed," I told him, thinking not at that moment of how much he'd changed in the global sense but of how willing he was at this stage to undertake diaper patrol when with Maya he felt his only duties were providing and playing.

"People change," he said, wiping the baby's bottom then slipping the new diaper on with an expert's touch. "Most people. But you haven't changed."

This I was surprised to hear. I felt as if I'd changed so much since the time we were together, I was surprised he was even able to recognize me.

"I haven't?"

"Not a bit."

He was still on his knees but had gathered the baby into his arms and was sitting up straight now, looking up at me intensely, in the old way, and I felt myself drawn into his force field.

"I thought about you all the time," he said, "for years."

Outside, I could hear Tina calling Marco Junior, and then the reassuring sound of the child's whine. Marco got to his feet and moved closer to me.

"Until I met Tina," he said. "But now, since the day you showed up at the nursery with Maya, I'm thinking about you again. I can't help it. I'm thinking about you."

He was so close now I could smell the baby's sweet hair. I had been thinking about Mrs. Glover's house, I had been thinking about my kids, I had been thinking about money, I had been thinking about Declan. But I had not been thinking about Marco, not when I had any control over it, though sometimes, when I was lying down to go to sleep, his face as it had looked that day in the field of trees appeared to me.

"You're a married man," I said, trying to make light of it, to put an easy barrier between us. "Our relationship's in the past, over."

"I don't know," he said. "You're standing in front of me right now. Maybe I should have married you."

He reached out then, with the hand that wasn't holding the baby, and touched my hip. Despite my higher intentions, I felt my body spring to life under his touch.

"Wow, are you two getting back together?" It was Maya, suddenly right beside us and grinning. "All my dreams are coming true."

Quickly, I stepped back.

"I was just telling your father to take good care of you," I said.

"Oh, he will," Maya said, with complete confidence. "This is a beautiful house, Daddy."

Daddy. Yipes.

"Thanks, sweetheart. But I bet you got a beautiful home, too."

She shrugged. "It's okay. Mom says we have to move."

"Oh yeah?" He raised his eyebrows, focusing once

again on me. "You're not going to disappear on me again, I hope."

"I'm looking for a cheaper place in Homewood," I assured him. "Money's a lot tighter since the breakup with Frank."

Marco threw his head back and laughed. "So the big-shot lawyer left you high and dry, huh?" he said. "I guess you woulda done better with the poor Puerto Rican."

"I have to be going," I said. "Maya, if you need anything . . ."

"I know. Call you in New York."

"New York," Marco said, considering. "What's in New York?"

"Mom's new boyfriend," Maya said. "Hey, you probably know him. She used to work for him back when you two were together. Declan or something like that."

I felt myself turning red, as if I had done something wrong. Marco had always been jealous of Declan, had always suspected that something was going on between us, accusing me, during his periodic rages, of sleeping with Declan back among the canned goods and untapped kegs. Through the glass doors, I could see Tina and Marco Junior nearing the house. Everything was conspiring to let me know it was time to make my getaway. Giving Maya a quick hug, I moved to the front door. Marco moved in behind me to open it. And then, just as I began to shift my focus to where I was going rather than where I was leaving, just as a gust of fresh air cooled my face and filled my nostrils, I felt Marco's hand make stealthy but unmistakable contact with my backside.

CHAPTER *eleven*

When the alarm rang on Sunday morning it was still dark, and I hurried to shut it off, intending to rise as silently as possible, to sneak off to the flea market and slip back into the apartment before Declan was even awake. But as I moved to leave the bed his big hand reached out for me and pulled me back toward him.

"Where you going?" he mumbled.

"The flea market."

"Come here," he said, pulling me close, his warmth and bulk enveloping me. "Stay with me."

"I told you," I said, gently removing his hands, wanting to stay in bed at least as much as he wanted me to. "I promised Jeannie I'd do this and all the best stuff goes early."

He humphed and curled back into the covers, but when I returned to the bedroom after brushing my teeth and dressing behind the closed bathroom door, I was startled to find him out of bed and pulling on his pants.

"What are you doing?" I asked.

"I'm coming with you."

"You don't have to do that."

"I know," he said cheerfully. "I want to."

It had been a wonderful weekend. Declan had taken off all day Saturday and we'd tramped through the city, visiting his favorite bars and restaurants, drinking a cappuccino in one place and eating a pastrami sandwich somewhere else, stopping in for just a taste of the roasted peppers or a martini or a cupcake with a giant frosting rose on top. Then despite all we'd eaten, he'd insisted on cooking me dinner, but by the time it was ready we were tangled around each other in bed, making love for the second of three times.

I couldn't believe our weekend was already half over. But I was happy, walking up Sixth Avenue in the dark, holding my flashlight and feeling the wad of cash Jeannie had given me pressing against my thigh through the front pocket of my jeans, that he had decided to come along.

"You know, all my years in New York, I've never done this," he said, as we reached the corner of Twenty-sixth and Sixth, where the markets congregated in open-air as well as indoor parking lots.

"Oh, it's great," I assured him. I'd started coming

here when I lived in the East Village, sometimes carting baby Maya along in a Snuggli or her stroller, and later I learned to judge quality and negotiate well from trailing around after Dobson. During the Frank years, Jeannie and I would escape our families some weekend mornings and come here together, buying for the shop or our houses. This was the first time in nearly a year I'd been here.

Declan let me lead the way and at first I hurried, worried he'd get bored, but after a while I found I was the one who had to slow down for *him*, he was becoming so engrossed in the displays. We were attracted to different things: When I stopped to choose a striped canvas I thought might be good for pillow covers, he picked up some old fishing gear. He looked at cocktail shakers while I sifted through silver spoons. We moved along companionably, finding our own pace without feeling much of a need to talk. Or much of a need not to talk.

This weekend, I'd been rediscovering the connection we'd felt all those years when sleeping together was just a fantasy, one we thought would never come true. I was thrilled to find we were still able to spend hours in each other's company without struggle, drifting from long calm silences to animated conversation and back again. With Jeannie I'd always had the animated conversation, with Frank I'd had the calm silence, but with Declan I had both.

As we moved through the stalls I kept buying—a

Blue Willow platter and a hammered copper bowl, a cross-stitched tablecloth and a hooked rug, a 48-star flag and some rhinestone sunglasses I knew Jeannie would snatch for herself. Everything I bought Declan insisted on carrying. I stopped to hold an onyx and sterling pendant to my throat and noticed that Declan's burden of bags had grown so large that he wasn't able to look at anything for himself.

"Oh, I'm sorry," I said, dropping the pendant and tugging at the bags so he would give me some of them. "We have enough. We should go."

"Why don't you get that pendant?" he said. "It looked pretty on you."

"Oh, no. Jeannie doesn't carry jewelry in the shop—it's one of her rules—and I can't afford to buy anything for myself."

"Let me buy it for you," he said.

"No, no. I couldn't." I'd seen the price on the pendant: over $400. But still, I was pleased that he'd offered.

"Come on," he said. He set down the packages and picked up the pendant, holding it again to my throat. "This goes on a chain?" he said.

I nodded. "Most people would wear it on a long one."

"But it looks beautiful like this, near your face."

I could feel his fingers against my neck, and it was that I wanted, more than the jewelry.

He was already reaching into his own pocket, taking out a wallet, extracting five crisp hundred-dollar bills for the pendant.

"You should bargain," I whispered.

"Okay," he smiled, looking at the gray-haired man who was minding the stall. "Will you throw in a short little chain, maybe this one?"

He threaded the chain through the pendant and very carefully, with me holding my thick hair off my neck, fastened it for me.

"There," he said, stepping back to survey the effect. "Now it's official."

I felt myself color. "What's official?"

"We're officially going out."

In the cab on the way back downtown, we began kissing. Even though the sun had just come up, we behaved as if it were dark, touching each other, pressing against each other so that by the time the taxi pulled up at Declan's door, we couldn't wait to pay the driver, grabbing our bags and rushing upstairs and into bed.

It may have been the wonderful start to the day that made me slip. Or how relaxed I'd grown having the whole weekend together. Or maybe it was the heat of the cab ride, or the locket, the locket that made me feel more secure.

It happened while we were making love, and I was moving above him, and leaning down over him, my breasts rubbing up and down against his chest, and I felt like I was about to come, felt that excitement and suspension for the longest time, and it just came out. I said, "I love you."

Softly, more a breath than a statement, but he heard it. He froze. I stopped moving and held my breath.

"Heat of passion," I said.

He seemed to relax a bit, his hands moving up to my hips again.

"You don't mean it?" he said.

"No, no, of course I don't mean it. I mean, I love you, as a friend, but I don't love you, as in *love* you." I laughed nervously and shifted my position, feeling our bodies slip apart. I was babbling, making things worse every second. "I'm sorry."

"You don't need to be sorry, darlin'," he said. "I'm the one who's sorry."

"Why are you sorry?"

He sighed deeply. Then, very gently, he eased himself out from under me, turning on his side to face me and propping his head on his hand. "There's something I've been putting off telling you."

I sat up straight, hugged the sheet around my body.

"In California," he said, "there's someone else."

That was so unexpected, even after all my suspicions, that I went silent for a minute.

"You mean someone," I said at last, "as in another woman?"

A beat. And then: "Yes."

"Wow," I said, getting up from the bed, pulling on

my panties and then my shirt without really thinking about it. It just seemed imperative that I hear this clothed. "Going all the way to California, it must be serious."

"It is," Declan said simply. His face was still calm, unperturbed. I stepped into my jeans, zipped and buttoned them, and then stood there waiting, I wasn't sure for what. Waiting to believe this was real.

"I didn't know you were going to walk into the bar that day," Declan said, animated now, his composure finally falling away. "I had no idea I'd ever see you again. I didn't plan for things to happen this way."

So whose plan had this been? Certainly not mine. I'd already had one man leave me for another woman this year, and that was all I could take. More than I could take.

"I can't do this," I said.

From what I knew of Declan's promiscuous history, I thought he was going to argue with me, to try and persuade me that his seeing a woman in California didn't have to interfere with us seeing each other in New York. But instead he said, "I know."

"You've got to choose," I said. "Me or her." Still thinking I had a chance.

But he took a deep breath and said, "Her."

CHAPTER *twelve*

I flew back to Homewood, pushing the Volvo as hard as it would tolerate, coming up fast behind too-slow cars and flashing my lights to force them out of my way, the bright June sunlight assaulting me the whole trip west. When I got to town, I did not go home. I did not go to Jeannie's. Instead, I went directly to Mrs. Glover's.

Just being inside the gates of the house made me feel calmer, hopeful again that the world might offer me some goodness. I did not believe that everything happened for the best—could not accept that murder or starvation, for instance, were somehow more positive than the alternatives——but I nevertheless took comfort in reminding myself that leaving Declan, Declan leaving me, cleared the way for me to buy this house. And maybe buying the house was the thing that would ultimately make me happiest.

I knocked on the front door, which caused a shard of ancient black paint to splinter off onto my knuckles, and it was so silent within, and I waited for so long, that I began to think that Mrs. Glover must have already left on her daily eight-hour grocery run. But then finally I heard some distant shuffling, and then a surprisingly strong voice calling that she was coming, she was coming, and then the door creaked open and there was Mrs. Glover, peering up at me from below.

"You're the woman in the fancy car," she said.

I smiled weakly. "It wasn't my car."

"Glad to hear that." She stood aside, admitting me to the front hall. Anticipating this moment, I'd been half afraid of what I'd see, worried that maybe the place *would* seem overwhelmingly dilapidated to me, or not nearly as attractive as it had that first day. But the opposite was true; the house seemed more beautiful than ever, and I felt more sure of what I wanted to do.

"I love your house, Mrs. Glover," I said.

"Yes," said Mrs. Glover. "It's a beautiful house. Well worth loving."

"I want to buy it."

"You want to buy it?" Mrs. Glover said, looking at me suspiciously. "The realtor people didn't tell me anything about you. They brought around some big-shot developer wants to fix it up, telling me it needs a fancy new kitchen and a marble bathroom or some such, and I say that's just a load of malarkey. It's been a fine house for me, and it will be a fine house for someone else, exactly as it is."

I didn't know about the "exactly as it is" part. The mouse turds in the kitchen, for instance, would definitely have to go. But I agreed that this was not a house that should be transmogrified into some cookie-cutter suburban palace. It just needed to be coaxed back to its own unique brand of glory.

"I want to live here, Mrs. Glover," I told her. "I'm a single mother, I've got two daughters, and I'm looking for a place I can afford to buy on my own."

"Single mother, hmmm?" Mrs. Glover said. "I was a widow when I moved here in '52. Two kids, husband killed in the war, finally saved enough to get out from under the in-laws' thumb."

"God, that must have been hard," I said. "I'm separated."

"Oh," said Mrs. Glover, reaching out to pick up a thin leather-covered book that had been lying on the hall table and very slowly lowering it into a box at her feet. She was packing, I realized, and at this rate filling this single box was going to consume the entire day. "I thought you might have been one of those types today who think you don't need a husband to have a baby. Doesn't matter. I bought this place on my own and it feels right that I should sell it to a woman on her own. How much will you give me?"

The asking price was precisely $200,000—no canny $199,900 for Mrs. Glover.

"$200,000?" I said.

"Oh, keen negotiator, eh?" said Mrs. Glover, chuckling. "All right then. Sold."

I would have loved, at that moment, for us to shake hands or hug and move off, equally satisfied, toward our separate destinies. But I had to tell Mrs. Glover there were a couple of other issues we needed to discuss.

"Here's my problem," I told her. "I'm not going to be able to close on this place before my own house is sold. But the day of the closing, I'm going to need to move in here with my girls because I can't afford to rent something. Which means—" I winced here, anticipating her protest "—I've got to start fixing the place up this summer, before I technically own it."

"What are you going to do to it?" she said, picking up a piece of junk mail and letting it loft down toward the box where it landed on top of the book. "You're not going to carpet the floors and put in some goddamn granite countertop, are you?"

"No, no," I said. "Nothing like that. It's just, with a small child, I'm going to need to patch the walls, and fix the leak in the toilet, and clean it up a bit." I was obviously unequipped, as well as disinclined, to undertake a major rehab. I didn't want to queer the deal when she'd just said she wanted someone to buy it who loved it exactly as it was. But I also had to be honest with her—as well as make the house livable.

"You're not trying to trick an old lady, are you?" she said.

"No, Mrs. Glover. I'm just me, trying to find a way to buy this house that makes both of us happy."

"Okay," said Mrs. Glover, her voice suddenly crisp and sure. "Here's the deal. You ante up ten percent. Then as soon as I leave for Maine, you get access. You do what you want, but no wild colors, no goddamn plastic windows or additions sticking out into the garden. Got it?"

"Got it," I said.

"Then, come September 1, if your house isn't sold or you fail in any other way to close the deal, all bets are off." At this, she swept the rest of the junk mail and newspapers and paperbacks off the hall table and down into the box where they landed with a crash, raising a mushroom cloud of dust.

I hesitated, then finally I said. "I'm not sure what you mean by that."

"I mean if you can't finalize the purchase by the beginning of September, our agreement is over and I keep your deposit and any value you may think you can claim from the work you've done."

"And I get?"

"Zilch," she said. "Zip. Zero."

"Okay," I cut her off. I liked Mrs. Glover, but I no longer felt sorry for her, not a bit. "I get it."

"So do we still have a deal?"

If I looked left, I could see into the living room,

where the light was flooding in as if it were a clearing in a fairy tale forest. And then, if I looked to the right, I could also see into the rudimentary and largely non-functioning kitchen. I put my hand to my throat, trying to decide what to do, and it was only then that I realized the pendant Declan had bought me early that morning at the flea market was still around my neck. I snatched my hand away as if I'd touched a flame.

"All right," I said to Mrs. Glover. "We have a deal."

Things galloped ahead after that. I spent the week doing the final work necessary to get the house I owned with Frank on the market—touching up paint, scouring bathrooms, storing all remaining junk in the attic and basement. By Friday they hammered the FOR SALE sign on the lawn, with an open house scheduled for Sunday. I promised Frank I would split the profits on the house with him, which delighted him, given that his own income had been considerably downsized. But even though he was studying and teaching yoga full-time, he was still officially on a leave of absence from the law firm, meaning that on the books it looked as if he still had a generous income, so he agreed to co-sign for my mortgage. Though I'd been dipping into my half of our savings account for living expenses, and needed to take out more for the down payment, there was just enough left to underwrite the basic work I needed to do to move the girls into Mrs. Glover's house by September. It wasn't going to be fancy, maybe it wasn't even going to be completely finished, but our new home felt at least within reach.

The girls and I hid out at my mother's for the weekend—I let Mom think her advice had influenced me to stop seeing Declan —and by the middle of the following week we had a buyer for our house. That gave me just enough time to get an ad in the paper advertising a yard sale for Saturday.

The night before the sale I woke up, as I did most nights, at three and then lay there for more than an hour, obsessing over whether I should have done something differently with Declan.

But what could I have done differently? It wasn't as if I'd had much room to maneuver. He was the one who'd been involved in another relationship, he was the one who'd set limits on what could happen between us, and he was the one who in the end had chosen something else. Someone else.

Who was she? What was it about her, about Sunny, that made Declan and Frank prefer them to me? Should I be sexier, sweeter, smarter, thinner, tougher? Did I choose the wrong men, and what kind of man should I be with instead, or were all men simply jerks? Were all relationships doomed to failure, or was it just my relationships?

I fell asleep only after forbidding myself to agonize over these issues any longer, and then woke up at seven, exhausted and deranged, to the buzzing of the front door. It was Frank, arrived to take Amanda into the city. But instead of going upstairs to fetch Amanda, he dropped to his knees before a carton of his old records—the Circle Jerks, Suicidal Tendencies, The Ramones—that I had left near the door for the sale.

"You're not selling these, are you?" he said. He was flipping through them, pulling almost every one from the box. "These are very valuable."

Maya, who'd promised to spend the day helping me, had materialized from the kitchen, coffee cup in hand.

"Maya," Frank said, "you might want some of these."

"I will never," she said, "want any of your lame-ass records."

She had started speaking to him again, but that didn't mean she was being nice to him.

Maya and I went to work but it seemed that the more stuff we tried to lug outside, the larger Frank's pile grew. Besides the records, he'd grabbed back tennis rackets, golf clubs, skis, books, shirts, even a pair of his old underwear that had somehow escaped the charity bag.

"Where are all my ties?" he asked me.

"Oh, for God's sake, Frank. Give it a rest."

Finally Frank left with Amanda and as much of his old crap as he could carry, leaving Maya and me to finish setting up the sale unperturbed. Even after I'd carried out everything I planned to sell, I kept seeing other things I decided to add to the mix. There was a little twig stand I'd bought for four dollars at a flea market that I'd imagined in my new house, at the top of my flying staircase, sitting in the sun that flowed through the hall window, maybe holding a vase filled with full-blown pink roses.

But that stand was worth a hundred dollars—at least that's what it would sell for in Jeannie's shop. In the Frank era, a hundred dollars was nothing to me: I'd drop that much without thinking on clothes Maya would end up not even wearing; I'd spend it on a bad movie and a worse dinner or forget it in a purse I stopped using. But now a hundred dollars represented something closer to what it meant in the days I lived on Ninth Street and came home after working an entire night at Declan's with that much in my bag. With a hundred dollars I could buy enough paint for an entire room. I could rent a floor sander for a day. I could pay someone to hook up a washer and dryer.

I grabbed the twig stand and ended up also taking out a pair of old oil portraits and some McCoy jugs and a cross-stitched linen tablecloth and a pair of Hitchcock chairs. I carried out a little needlepoint footstool and a spatterware jug, seven pink deco parfait glasses and three rag rugs.

"Wow," said Maya. "You're getting rid of everything."

"I figure anything we don't sell I can always bring back inside."

"Oh, for God's sake, Mom. Once you go through all the trouble of hauling it out here you might as well dump it." She peered at me. "Why are you wearing that rag on your head?"

"It's keeping the hair off my face." I'd come across the orange bandana when sifting through old clothes; I'd used it to tie my hair back when Maya was a baby and now it made me feel girded for battle.

"I don't want to say anything," Maya said, "but you look like an insane person."

I looked down at myself. I did have on a weird assortment of clothes, gathered from the depths of my attic trunks. I was wearing a shirt printed with fishes given to me on a beach in Mexico by a traveling Frenchman and a pair of baggy plaid shorts that had once belonged to my mother's dead husband Murray.

Suddenly, a man with a gray goatee was wending his way through the furniture we had so artfully arranged in the backyard, stopping to sit on Frank's beige sofa and trying on one of Frank's old sport jackets. He was totally ignoring me and Maya.

"Excuse me," I called, "but the sale doesn't start for half an hour."

"Tell that to them," he said, jerking his thumb back toward the street. Two women, one fat, one thin, had parked at the end of the driveway and were heading our way. Across the road, old Mrs. Husk emerged from her house, a rumpled plastic bag dangling from her arm. Patty Putnam from next door, in full tennis whites, stepped out of her back door, tow-headed toddler on her hip, and waved at us.

"Oh my God," I said to Maya. "I'm not ready for this."

"Don't sweat it, Mom. I think we've got everything out here."

"No," I said, seized with panic. "I mean any of it." Sorting through everything, tagging it and carrying it outside had seemed to take forever; suddenly it was all moving too fast.

The gray-bearded man approached Maya holding out a Tiffany dish, one of Frank's corporate Christmas gifts, along with a ten dollar bill. Maya grabbed the money and stuffed it in her denim carpenter's apron, a twin of one I was wearing, remnants of my tenure at McGlynn's.

"Don't be ridiculous," she said to me. "What would you want to hang on to this junk for?"

"I'm afraid it's a big mistake. Maybe I shouldn't be selling this house."

"Too late," Maya snapped. The fat woman was holding a lamp and her friend was holding the cord, looking around the yard as if she expected to find somewhere to plug it in. "Time to look to the future. Onward and upward."

"You sound like Grandma." I tightened my bandana.

"Gram knows how to move on with her life. I want to be just like her."

And not like you, was the implication. But hey, five husbands aside, maybe Maya would do better in life emulating my mother than me. I may not have approved of my mother's values, but she was the one who lived in a mansion with a nice hunk of a husband and several million dollars in the bank, while I was alone and broke.

I was in the process of trying not to let that realization make me feel suicidal when we were set upon. At least that's what it felt like to me: a pack of wild animals eviscerating the life I had built with Frank. As overwhelmed as I felt by the crush of the crowd, as steadfast as I was in refusing to part with anything for less than my asking price, Maya was hawking our wares as aggressively as a carnival barker. You want to buy that T-shirt? Take three. Instead of one book for a quarter, pay a dollar and fill this whole bag. I'd wanted two hundred dollars for the beige couch; I caught her unloading it for thirty-five.

"What are you doing?" I said. "You're giving it all away."

"If you don't give it away now, you'll give it away later. Plus look." She pointed to the bulging pockets of her apron. "I've got about five times as much money in here as you do. I want us to make maximum bucks so you can fix up that dump you're going to make us live in."

I wanted to make maximum bucks, too, wanted to

rejoice in dispensing with all my worldly goods, to achieve that sense of lightness and freedom I'd heard other yard salers describe. I told myself I should be happy that Patty Putnam's kids could use the miniature blue table and chairs Amanda had outgrown, that the English professor who bought seven bags full of books actually wanted to read them. But all I felt was exposed, the shiny scraps from my once-cozy nest scattered by the wind.

I was hungry—I admit that. I was hot, too. And there were the tiredness and anxiety I've already mentioned. But those weren't the only reasons I snapped when the sour-faced woman with the frosted hair approached me carrying the twig stand and holding out a five dollar bill.

"Oh no," I said. "The price on that is $100."

"A hundred dollars! Why would this broken down little thing cost that much?"

In Jeannie's shop, someone might think that. But they'd never say it.

"It's an antique."

"Well, your daughter told me it was $5."

"My daughter was mistaken."

"I'm a lawyer," Sour Face Frosted Hair told me, "and you're legally and morally obligated to sell it to me for that amount."

"Well, I'm a single mother who's too desperate," I said, snatching the stand away from her, "and I want you the fuck out of my sale."

I wanted everyone out of my yard. I stomped inside with the twig stand and then I slammed outside again, clapping my hands and yelling, "Okay! All right! Sale over! Time for everybody to leave."

Maya looked at me in horror but I ignored her, walking around personally evicting everyone who wasn't paying attention to my proclamation. I knew I was on the edge—over it—but I didn't care. It was almost fun. "Move along," I said. "That's right. Get out. No, you can't buy that. Give it back."

When everyone was gone, I single-handedly pushed one of the big old dressers I still intended to give to Goodwill down to the end of the driveway, carrying boxes and chairs and even a couple of old fishing poles out there for good measure. Then I turned over the piece of oaktag we'd hung on the maple tree out front advertising the sale and wrote on the flip side: SALE OVER. GO HOME.

I'd found an ancient pack of Lucky Strikes in the pocket of an old jacket and now I hunted them down, scrounged some matches and popped open a bottle of beer. Then I sat on a lawn chair surrounded by what felt like acres of my unsold junk, smoking and drinking. Maya stood above me, gazing down at me with disgust.

"What is wrong with you?" she said. "You're supposed to be a professional."

"This was personal. I've had it with dismantling my life for today."

"I thought this was what you wanted."

"It is what I want," I told her. "That doesn't mean I'm happy about it."

I sat there alone in my bandana and my fish shirt and my plaid shorts and drank the rest of the beer and smoked the cigarette until it scorched my fingers. Then I had to sit there some more to let the dizziness from the cigarette pass.

Finally, what seemed like a long time later, I got up and carried everything I might be able to sell in Jeannie's shop into the garage. Then I carried stuff I could use in the new house—only what you love, I told myself; only what you love—into the kitchen.

The rest of the stuff I started carting toward the curb. Anyone who wanted to take it, could, and what didn't get scavenged I'd haul off to Goodwill. It was while making one of my curbside deposits that Maya wandered out of the house, Jeremy having materialized with her.

"What are you doing now?" she asked, surveying the assortment of clothing-filled bags and light fixtures and books and broken-down furniture I'd piled near the sidewalk.

"This is stuff to give away. People can just drive by and take it."

"That's really ghetto, Mom."

"I don't care," I said. "This is what I'm doing."

I headed back down the driveway for my next load.

"I'll help you, Mrs. B.," Jeremy said, trotting after me.

I looked at him in surprise. This boy was so eager to please that he was either a secret ax murderer, or in really desperate need of a mother. Back on the sidewalk, Maya rolled her eyes. "Oh, all right," she said. "I'll help, too."

With the two of them walking twice as fast as I was and carrying twice as much, we had the backyard cleared in what felt like minutes. We thought we'd dispensed with everything when Jeremy found a big white plastic bag stashed under a bush.

I looked inside. It was full of Amanda's baby clothes, the tiny grass green sweater and the onesie with the pink and blue duck print and the red velour elf suit, the smocked dresses that my mother bought at Saks and the little faded overalls I'd collected along the way. Maya must have brought it outside to sell when I wasn't looking.

Maya came up beside me and peered into the bag. "What do you want to do with this?"

"I think I'll just take it back inside."

"Mother, would you please let go. Jeremy, take this out to the curb."

"Whoa, Maya," said Jeremy. "That's so harsh."

"My mom's a pack rat," said Maya.

"I sympathize," Jeremy said, hugging the bag. "I still have like, every action figure and Game Boy game I ever owned."

"He keeps them under his bed," Maya said, smirking.

"There's nothing wrong with that," I said. Jeremy really had a very sweet face, so fair to Maya's darkness. "Just holding something you loved at a different time in your life can take you back to your old self."

Maya rolled her eyes again and, humming a sad song, pantomimed playing a violin. As soon as she had our attention, she snatched the bag from Jeremy and trotted down the driveway as the two of us stared after her.

"Don't feel bad, Mrs. B.," Jeremy said. "She really cares about you."

I touched his arm. Even if Maya did aspire to be like my mother, she seemed to already have better taste in men than Mom had ever had. "Thank you, Jeremy."

"Hey, Jeremy," Maya called from the sidewalk. "Let's go."

"We're going to the mall," Jeremy said to me, shrugging. "I've got to look for a summer job. Are you going to be okay?"

"I'm going to collapse," I told him. And then, through the fog that was my mind, I had an idea. "Jeremy, would you like to work for me fixing up the house? I couldn't pay you much, but it would definitely be as much as you'd make at the mall."

He broke into a wide grin and patted me on the shoulder before heading down the driveway, where he leaped—I thought it was for joy—once into the air. When he reached the sidewalk where Maya was waiting, he put his arms around her waist and pulled her hips close to him and then they kissed. I looked away, into the Putnams' yard, and when I looked back they were gone. I was so tired I could have lain down right there on the grass of the backyard and gone to sleep. Instead, I trudged down the driveway toward the house. But rather than going inside I kept walking until I got out to the curb, where I grabbed the bag full of baby clothes and carried it with me when I went inside and locked the door.

CHAPTER *thirteen*

"**O**kay, honey," I said to Amanda. "You can play on the floor here while I work."

I set my flea market fake alligator suitcase, filled with tools I'd collected from yard sales and my new plumbing supplies, down on the bathroom floor, alongside my library copy of *Home Plumbing Projects & Repairs*. Amanda, Barbie dangling from one hand, Ken from the other, frowned and looked at me with serious doubt in her eyes.

"Why is the toilet lying there like that?"

"Don't worry. Mommy's going to fix it."

I thumbed through the book, looking for page eighty-one, "How to Remove & Replace a Wax Ring & Toilet." The leak that had looked fairly minor that day I'd seen the house with Declan had turned out, I discovered during a five-minute consultation with a plumber that cost me $85, to mean that the ring that sealed the toilet needed to be replaced. I was determined to save the $350 the plumber wanted to charge by handling this myself, and had gotten as far yesterday as lifting the toilet up and tilting it onto its side, where it now lay like a wounded flamingo.

"What if I have to go to the bathroom?"

"It's going to be fixed by then," I said. "And if it's not, we'll just pee in the bushes."

I was trying, for Amanda's sake, to sound more confident than I felt. I'd been working on the house for a few weeks, but this was the first major repair job I'd tackled. Most of what I'd done so far had been basic preparation and cosmetics. I'd swept out all the dust and cobwebs, as well as the rodent droppings, and washed down the surfaces I wasn't planning to remove or replace.

In the process of scrubbing the kitchen floor I discovered that the pattern hadn't worn away after all—the floor had just not been washed since probably the Watergate scandal—and under all that mud was gorgeous marbleized linoleum of the kind that went for thousands at the flea market. That happy surprise motivated me to take to the yard with a chain saw, where I uncovered a bed of antique roses and the remains of a fabulous perennial garden.

Of course not all the surprises were good ones. When I scoured the oven, for instance, I discovered that baked grease had been the only thing holding it together. I was planning to put off the tougher jobs until Jeremy returned from his July Fourth vacation with his family. But in a few days I'd be working at the house full-time, and the toilet couldn't wait.

I unpacked my adjustable wrench, my ratchet wrench, a screwdriver, a putty knife, plumber's putty, and a new wax ring to seal up the toilet. I put on my rubber gloves. Still Amanda stood there staring at me.

"You can play right here," I said, "in the hallway. Or in the pink bedroom. I thought that was the one you would probably like to be yours."

Amanda walked on her skinny legs over to the doorway to the pink bedroom and stared at it.

"It hasn't got any curtains," she said finally.

"No, honey. But we'll put curtains in there. Beautiful curtains."

"I like my own curtains."

"Okay, then. We'll put up your own curtains."

In just three days, Frank would be taking her to the Hamptons, with Sunny, for a whole month. Maya had already left to spend part of her summer vacation with Marco. The house was so quiet with just one child, and I missed Maya more times during the day than I ever would have guessed possible, given that it seemed to me she spent most of her time in her room or out with Jeremy or otherwise ignoring me. Feeling what a gap she left in my life made me dread Amanda's being gone, even though much of the time I was with her I felt guilty I couldn't give her more attention, and wished for uninterrupted time to work on the house. I was looking forward to having Jeremy as both a surrogate child and a helper.

"This bedroom doesn't have a bed in it," Amanda said.

"Honey, I've explained this to you." And explained it to her and explained it to her and explained it to her but still she couldn't seem to understand. "We're going to pack up all our own furniture and move it over here and then this house will look just like our old house, only prettier. Now why don't you play here with Barbie and Ken while I get the toilet fixed?"

Since the toilet was already lying on its side, I could skip Steps 1 through 5. My first move was to scrape the old wax and putty from the bottom of the toilet, a not unsatisfying job.

"I'm bored."

Amanda was standing in the doorway again.

"I can't play with you now. Do you want to help me fix this?"

She made a horrified face. "I don't want to get poopy all over me."

"The toilet doesn't have any poopy in it," I laughed. "That's all gone."

"No, thanks," Amanda said. "Can't I play outside?"

One of the things I loved about this house was that, ringed with shrubs and as the last house on a dead-end road, it was a safe place for Amanda to play.

"All right," I said, "but you can't leave the garden.

Gram's supposed to be here in about an hour to get you but try to keep yourself entertained until then."

"Oh-KAY," Amanda said, sounding spookily like Maya.

Oh-KAY. "Turn stool upside down," my book instructed. Stool? Oh, they meant the bottom section of the toilet. Once I figured that out, it took me a while to realize I could separate the tank part from the stool part, and then a longer while to get enough of the right kind of leverage on the toilet to turn it over. The toilet in the picture looked so white and shiny while this one was stained and streaked with unknowable, unspeakable things. My cleaning supplies were still in the back of the car but I didn't want to stop working to go get them.

I'd never known a toilet was constructed in such an obvious way. I guess I'd always thought there were all kinds of sophisticated mechanisms down there, but it was just a porcelain bowl with a hole in the bottom. This doughnut of yellow gunk, like a squishy plastic pineapple ring, was what kept water and all the rest from seeping out. I secured the pineapple to the toilet with a plastic sleeve and squeezed a bead of putty all around the edge of the bottom of the toilet. I had learned to squeeze an extremely tidy bead of putty.

Feeling positively macha, I moved to Step 8. Three or four careful readings made it evident that the next thing I had to do was lift the toilet bowl, flip it over, and set it down precisely on the bolts sticking up from either side of the drain hole. I had to do this without letting the toilet touch the floor, which would wreck my beautiful putty. But I couldn't lift the toilet and turn it over all by myself. Twice it hit the floor and I had to reapply the putty all over again. And now I'd just squeezed out the last of the putty from my tube and was holding the toilet above the bolts, trying to keep it steady with my aching arms while I lowered it slowly on its course toward the bolts.

"Yoo hoo!"

I jumped, and the toilet slipped from my arms, thudding so hard onto the floor I thought it would crash through into the kitchen.

"Jesus, Mother, you scared me half to death!"

"Well, I'm sorry, Kennedy, but I didn't see a doorbell downstairs."

My mother stood primly in the hallway, dressed in a black and white Chanel suit and delicate spectator pumps. She was holding a silver vase filled with pale orange tea roses. "I brought you a housewarming gift," she said, extending it to me.

"Very pretty. I don't suppose you can help me lift this toilet."

"Lord alive," she said. "You have got to be kidding."

"It's not really heavy. I just need another hand to help me flip it and position it over these bolts."

"I am sorry, darling, but I don't do toilets." She brushed at her suit even though she hadn't actually touched anything. "Why don't you have an expert handling this?"

"Because I can't afford an expert, Mother. Did you see Amanda on your way in?"

"Yes, she seemed to be playing happily with her dolls. But listen, dear, whatever plumbers charge, it can't be more than you'd make if you were spending your time working instead of doing this."

"I don't think I'm capable of doing any job that would pay more than plumbers charge," I told her. "Anything legal, anyway."

Fumbling in her purse, Mom extracted one of her long, gold-tipped cigarettes.

"Mom, really, you know I don't like it when you smoke in the house."

"In this house?" Mom laughed drily and lit up.

"Oh, never mind," I said.

"No, don't worry, I'll put it out." Right on the wood floor.

Mom looked around the house. "I don't understand, Kennedy," she said. "How are you going to do this work all by yourself in two months? It needs . . . so much."

"I'm not all by myself, Mother—Jeremy's going to be helping me. And I've got books. I'll just do the best I can. It doesn't have to be perfect when the girls and I move in. As long as I can get the basic things functioning, I can do the rest after we're here."

"Kennedy." My mother hesitated, not a customary

condition for her. My entire being went on alert. "I've been thinking. Why don't you let me give you the money to pay qualified workmen to fix this place up?"

This idea had, naturally, crossed my mind. Though I'd just as quickly dismissed it. But now that she was raising the issue, maybe the time had come for us to loosen up. What had happened over my pregnancy with Maya had been a long time ago, after all, and Mom and I had years since moved beyond any resentment. If I had more money I could hire guys to refinish the floors rather than trying to wield the heavy machinery alone, have a backhoe clear the open part of the yard instead of handling it weed by weed, get the plumber to come in and reset this damn toilet.

I got so lost in fantasizing about how much easier this job would be given money and professional help that I hadn't been focusing on what my mother was saying. But now I tuned back in.

"We could get a crew in here," I heard. "Gut the place. Or better yet, the thing to do might be to knock everything down, start from scratch. It's a fabulous piece of property. We could build a nice modern house back here, maybe even with a swimming pool, instead of trying to resurrect this old dump."

I stared at my mother, dumbstruck.

"You can't not do this, Mom, can you?"

"Do what?"

"See your money as a way of controlling my life."

"I do not want to control your life," Mom said. "I

was just saying, if you would give me the extreme *privilege* of investing in your home, that we could make it a wee bit nicer. I was just offering you a few decorating ideas, that's all."

"And what if I said I'd be very grateful to have the money but I'd still want to do things my way?"

"Well, that would be fine, dear, just fine. I don't know why you think I would presume to tell you what to do. When you brought Frank home that first time, and I could see your whole dreary future stretched out before you, did I say anything?"

My mother had hated Frank from the moment he stepped into the old house when she lived there with Murray. She'd planned an elaborate evening of charades, her favorite game, and Frank had been hopeless at it, attempting to spell out every word with his fingers. Then, when Mom insisted he stick to mime, he lay down on the sofa, shoes still on, and fell asleep. And snored.

"You didn't like him but you wanted me to go ahead and marry him because he had money," I pointed out.

"Remember, I thought you should divorce him, too," Mom said. "I am more often right than you give me credit for. Look at what happened with that bar fellow. I told you not to go out with him, and you admitted I was right about that."

Yes, but I'd lied.

I shook my head. Admittedly, fixing this toilet

was a tough juncture. But most jobs in the house were not going to be that hard. If I needed more money than I'd budgeted—not huge, hire-someone-to-gut-the-house money, but the modest couple of thousand I might need to complete the project as I wanted to do it—I could almost certainly work something out with Frank, or Jeannie.

"Mom," I said, "I just think you and I get along better if we keep money out of our relationship, okay?"

"Oh, for God's sake, you are so freaking pig-headed." And with that she pivoted on her perfect little heel and stomped downstairs.

I heard her calling for Amanda and had just managed to lift the toilet back up and maneuver it halfway over the hole when I heard my mother shriek, "Kennedy! Kennedy! Get down here right now!"

Dropping the toilet, I raced downstairs and out into the hot, bright day.

"I can't find Amanda!" my mother cried.

"I thought you said she was here when you came in."

"She was." My mother pointed to the base of one of the big shade trees. "But she's not there anymore."

Yelling her name, we fanned out across the yard. My heart was thumping and I kept trying to think of the next place Amanda might have gone. Was there a way into the basement of the house? Could she have somehow sneaked past us into the kitchen? Or had she wandered out into the street, into a neighbor's yard? Could someone have come in here? Grabbed her, taken her?

"Good God," I heard my mother say.

Then: "Kennedy. I think you better come over here."

Mom was standing at the far corner of the yard, peering into some rhododendron bushes. She didn't look horrified, so that calmed me, a little. But she didn't look happy, either.

She pointed into the bushes and said, "Look."

Amanda was squatting in there, her little red shorts and pink panties around her ankles, an enormous poop lying on the dead brown leaves beneath her. She was looking up, tears brimming from her eyes, at my mother and me.

"Oh, honey," I said, crashing into the bushes.

"I had to go to the bathroom."

"That's all right." I ripped some leaves from the rhododendron and then felt a nudge at my elbow as my mother handed me some tissues. I took them gratefully, passing them to Amanda. "Let me help you, sweetheart."

"That's just it!" my mother cried. "Why won't you let me help you?"

"I would love you to help me," I said, "if you could get over having to run the show."

"Maybe I'm just worried about the way things are going," my mother said. "It seems to me that doing everything your damn way is just getting you in deeper and deeper doo-doo. So to speak."

"I'm fine," I said, backing out of the bushes and pulling Amanda to me, pressing her damp head against my stomach.

"I don't think you're so fine."

"I'm perfectly fine. Everything's wonderful."

"All right!" my mother said, throwing up her hands. "You're wonderful! The kids are great! The house is perfect! You're doing better without me!"

She reached out her hand and Amanda took it, and then they turned around and my mother stomped away, at least as much as a ninety-five-pound woman can stomp on long grass when wearing leather-soled designer pumps and tugging a five-year-old girl after her. I stood there watching them go, trying to believe that everything we'd both just said was true.

Once Amanda left on vacation with Frank, I began working on the house from dawn until way past dark every day, trying to get as much as possible done while the girls were away. I had a portable floodlight I'd cart from room to room, so I could see what I was doing, but I was eager to get a light fixture hooked up in the living room, where there wasn't even a decent outlet. I'd spent hours patching the cracked plaster on the living room walls and if I could continue working in there after dark I might be able to finish tonight. Once I'd painted that room and refinished the floors, I hoped it was going to look so beautiful it would spur me through the other, more difficult parts of the job.

But like most of the jobs in the house, installing the light took three times as long as I'd estimated. I found I could handle the work—I was strong enough, and certainly smart enough—but I had everything to learn and I was slow. The sun was seconds from setting. Finally, I connected the final wire, screwed on the plastic wire cap, pushed the fixture into the wall, and held my breath as I flipped the switch. There was a momentary buzz, then suddenly silver sparks shot from the wall. I shrieked, covering my ears with my hands, as all the lights in the house blinked off. Then, silence. I must have blown the main fuse. I stood there breathing hard, staring at the new fixture, now hanging from the wall, just able to make out in the gathering darkness that its wires and the plaster around it were charred black.

Outside, the sky flashed and then an explosion sounded, and I screamed again, believing for a minute that the light and the noise were kind of aftershocks from my electrical blowout. But then I realized that the sound was coming from farther away. An explosion? My God. I hopped to my feet and hurried outside, though at first I couldn't really see anything from my tree-shrouded property. A storm? Another flash of light, another boom, and then I saw a sparkle of red in the sky. July Fourth.

I sank down onto the front porch and looked with relief toward the sky. If I leaned back until I was lying almost flat on the porch I could see everything, just above my tree line. I sat there, my eyes glazed and my mouth open, staring, spent, grateful that fate had forced me to stop pushing forward for just one moment.

The fireworks were so loud that I saw the bushes shaking before I heard the rustling. At first I assumed there was an animal, a squirrel or one of the neighborhood cats, in the yard, but then the gate squeaked open and through the darkness of the yard the pinpoint of a flashlight appeared. It hesitated for a moment but then began to move in my direction.

I shielded my eye with my hand like a sailor, trying to tell who it might be. One of the neighbors? Jeremy? Even the possibility of Declan wildly ran through my head.

And then the unmistakable figure of Jeannie, wearing red-striped capris and a star-printed navy blue top, appeared. I'd barely seen her these past weeks, ever since the house mania started. Oh no. I'd forgotten her annual July Fourth barbeque.

"Shit," I said. "I'm sorry. I don't even have an excuse."

"You do have an excuse," she said, plopping down beside me. "Don't worry. Chip's friends were so boring. You would have hated it."

Chip's friends were always boring, and I would

have hated it, but that was because of my own longtime party phobia, attending them as well as giving them. It was only Jeannie's talent for decorating a room and preparing wonderful food and being a gracious hostess that made her parties more bearable than most.

"I'm sure you did your usual beautiful job," I said.

"I brought the best part to you." She extracted a silver cocktail shaker and two glasses from the plastic bag she was carrying. "Margaritas. If you have a blender and some ice I can turn them into frozen margaritas."

"I don't even have electricity tonight."

"Oh my God," Jeannie said. "This *is* Dogpatch. No matter. These are still cold." She drained the shaker into the two glasses and handed me one like an angel welcoming me to heaven. I took a sip and heard myself moan, it was so delicious.

"Thank you," I said.

She shrugged. "Everybody went to the fireworks. I was happy to have an excuse to get away. I've been missing you."

"Oh," I said. "I've been missing you, too."

"For a while there you were around the shop so much, even if we didn't spend much real time together, I got to see you a lot."

"I know," I said. "I'm sorry. This is just taking every ounce of my energy."

"I understand," Jeannie said. "I know."

I was grateful to her for saying just that and no more. We sat there drinking the margaritas and watching the fireworks. As the fireworks began exploding faster and faster, building up to the finale, Jeannie reached over and put her hand on my arm, and it was that hand, after so many days of not being touched by anyone, along with the drink, and the fireworks, and the sparks flying through the living room, that finally made me break down. In front of Jeannie, I could fall apart in a way I couldn't with my kids or my mother, in a way I'd never been able to with Frank or Marco.

"Tell me," she said, when I calmed down enough to make conversation possible.

"It's nothing," I said.

"That doesn't sound like nothing."

"I'm scared I won't be able to handle this," I said. "I'm exhausted. I miss the girls."

"What about Mr. Maybe?" Jeannie said.

"Mr. No." I tried to laugh but didn't succeed.

"So you haven't heard from him?"

I shook my head no.

"Have you thought about getting in touch with him?"

Another shake no. "But God, Jeannie, I miss him so much. Once I started feeling those feelings again, it's hard to switch them off."

"Do you ever think you made a mistake?" she asked, draining her glass. "Asking him to choose?

Do you ever wish you'd just said it was okay for him to see you and her at the same time?"

I tried to wish it, but the truth was I knew I'd never have been able to do it, would have felt even worse than I felt now had I tried. I realized that I could never be what I'd laughingly called the female Declan, that all along I'd been a committed monogamist, if at times one disguised in a vinyl miniskirt. Free and easy, ha. That woman wasn't gone; she'd never existed.

"But even if I couldn't share him, I sometimes regret slamming the door on everything," I told her. "We were friends for a long time before, and sometimes I wish we could go back to being friends even if the other part didn't work out."

"Maybe you should ask the cards," Jeannie said. "I could go to the shop and get them, and you could ask right now."

I was slightly more tempted than the first time she'd offered, but then I realized I didn't need her to read my cards. "I already know what I want to do," I said.

"What?"

"I want to call him."

"So why don't you call him?"

"I will," I said, feeling certain I would, maybe tomorrow, as soon as I figured out exactly what I wanted to say, and got myself in the right frame of mind to say it.

She fumbled in the plastic bag again, and extracted a cell phone.

"Oh, no," I said. "Not now."

"When?"

"Another time," I said.

She thrust the phone more forcefully in my direction.

I looked at the phone.

She held it out to me again.

And then I took it.

CHAPTER *fourteen*

The day Declan promised to come to the house, I made sure Jeremy was there. Then worried that I should send Jeremy away. Then wished I could disappear myself. Then decided I was being ridiculous. Friends, remember, friends, I told myself.

When I called that night with Jeannie, I told him that I had bought the house after all, that the work was going well but I needed his advice on the painting. What advice exactly I meant, I had no idea. I hadn't even actually started painting yet. But I sprung for an electrician to come in and repair the damage I'd done with the light in the living room, I finished plastering, and the morning of Declan's planned visit, Jeremy and I began painting.

Or rather, I'd paint for a while, hop over to the window, and then do some more painting.

"What are you looking for, Mrs. B.?" Jeremy asked.

"Oh nothing," I said, going back to where Jeremy

and I were opening paint cans, fitting sleeves onto rollers. "Just maybe a friend was going to stop by."

What was it going to be like, I wondered, being friends? In New York all those years ago, we'd worked together, hung out at the bar together once my shift was done. So now were we going to go the movies, talk to each other about our lives, our problems? Talk about our new lovers? Not that I was ever going to have one. I didn't think I was ready to kiss another man and tell Declan about it. In the margarita-free daylight, I didn't feel ready for any of it.

"You seem pretty nervous," Jeremy said.

"Oh, no. I'm worried about how to do this."

"So what do we do? Just, like, spread the paint around?"

"You pour it in this tray like this," I said. "Then you take the roller, kind of squish it back and forth, and roll it up the wall. Right?"

Jeremy shrugged. "I don't know. My mom put wallpaper everywhere. We never painted."

I'd never painted either. Frank always paid someone to do every job. We hadn't even owned a paintbrush.

"Is it supposed to look all bumpy like this?" Jeremy asked, frowning at the pearly gray swath he'd just applied to the wall.

I surveyed his work. "I think so. I think it smoothes out when it dries."

"Hey Mrs. B.," Jeremy said. "Do you mind if we listen to some music?"

I actually liked Jeremy's taste in music. A serious musician himself—he was saving money for a new set of drums so he could start a band—he listened to blues from the thirties and rock from the fifties and soul from the seventies, an eclectic mix that Maya nevertheless branded wholesale as "old people's music." When I was a teenager I'd thought so too, but now I found I liked oldies, any kind of oldies. I was dancing while I painted, having forgotten to be nervous, when Declan walked in.

"I can't believe what you've done in here," he said.

Jeremy and I both froze. I made myself turn around slowly to look at him, trying not to think about whether I had gray paint in my hair. Had he always looked this good? Oh God, this had been a mistake. How was I going to manage friendship when all I wanted to do was throw myself into his arms?

"Do you like it?"

"It's amazing. Who did the replastering in here?"

"I did."

So badly, the first time, that the walls were probably an inch thicker than they had been originally. But I'd finally gotten the knack of blending the plaster to the right consistency, learning to gauge the wetness the way you do when you mix up pancake batter or mashed potatoes, and of flicking my wrist just so when I smoothed it on. Besides the toilet, that was perhaps my proudest accomplishment.

"I'm impressed," he said.

"It's been fun," I said, truthfully. "Very satisfying."

"I know you really wanted the place. It's great you ended up getting it."

"Really? I thought you thought it was a bad idea."

"Yeah," he said. "But who cares what I think? This is your life."

Yes, it was. My life, and my children's, and nobody else's, certainly not his. I just wished he seemed a tiny bit more regretful about that.

Declan moved toward me, closer, then closer still, until I began to wonder whether I'd judged the whole thing wrong, thinking that he was about to try and kiss me. But he kept going, moving right past me until he was up almost to the wall, squinting and leaning in until his nose nearly touched the wet paint.

"What are those bumps?" he asked.

"Those are supposed to be there."

"Those are *not* supposed to be there." He looked around the room, then walked over to one of the walls we hadn't started painting yet and swiped his finger across it, examining his fingertip. "You didn't wash these walls before you started painting, did you?"

"Um, were we supposed to?"

"That's your problem," he said. "These walls haven't been touched in years. You've got to scrub them down first."

"All right," I said. "I'll go get some water to do the two we haven't started yet. We'll just have to live with the bumps on the other ones."

Declan shook his head. "The paint's going to peel off," he said. "You've got to scrub this down now and start over completely."

"I don't have that kind of time," I said. "Everything can't be done perfectly."

"This isn't about doing it perfectly," Declan said. "If you don't back up now, this paint is going to be hanging down in great sheets, flaking off and bubbling. I'm not trying to make your life more difficult, Kennedy, but I know what I'm talking about. Come on, I'll help you. We'll probably be done in the same amount of time."

Declan leveled a look at Jeremy. "Are you old enough to drive?"

"Of course."

Declan tossed his keys across the room. "Go to the paint store. I saw one on the main street, driving in. Get some heavy-duty detergent, some Dax. Sponges. Proper buckets." He lifted up one of the rollers we'd been using. "Jesus, look, this is coming apart already. Get some decent rollers, too, would you. Whatever's most expensive. And brushes. Good brushes. Thin ones and thick ones and middle-sized ones."

"Wait a minute," I said. "I can't afford all this stuff. We're going to have to make do with what we have."

"I've got money."

"No."

"Kennedy, don't be so fucking ridiculous." He

handed some crumpled bills to Jeremy. "Get out of here."

"Don't you go anywhere, Jeremy."

"Go on."

"Stay here."

"I'm leaving," said Jeremy.

And then we were alone. Why in hell had I wanted to see him? And how had I ever managed to stay away from him for so long? The six weeks that had passed since that last day felt like an eon, far more time than the nine years we'd gone without seeing each other before. It felt so good just to be in his presence again that I had to remind myself, once more, that I was determined to go back to being friends. We'd done it happily before, when he was with other women, and I was with Marco and then Frank. We could do it again.

"Kennedy."

He stepped toward me. I stepped back.

"I was so glad you called," he said.

"I shouldn't have." But I knew, even as I said it, that refusing him was a luxury I allowed myself because he was there.

"Please. Can't we talk about it? You never even gave me a chance."

"No, you never gave *me* a chance. I thought we were seeing how it would be, just you and me, and it turned out it was never just you and me." I was surprised how much heat I still felt around this issue. I'd asked him here, thinking I was ready to move to a new phase of our relationship, but I felt like I was still standing back in his bedroom, saying all the things I hadn't had the presence of mind or the nerve to say that day.

"It was, when I was with you. This other thing, it was going on before you came back. I didn't know what was going to happen with you."

I held up my hand. "Just don't, okay? Don't make this my fault."

He stood there silently for a moment, and then his shoulders slumped, and he looked completely defeated and helpless. "Okay," he said finally. "You're right. It's not your fault."

"Good," I said, warming to my argument. "Before I say any more, just let me ask you one thing. Are you still seeing her?"

He hesitated for just a moment. "Yes."

Of course, I'd already known that. If he'd stopped seeing her, or changed his mind about his choice, I realized that I expected I would have heard from him. I had been the one to call him. I was the one who, on some level, was still hoping it would work out.

"Kennedy," he said then. "It's not what you think."

"How do you know what I think?"

"She's not just another woman," he said, taking a deep breath. "She's the mother of my child."

The wind stopped moving through the windows, the birds stopped chirping. This did not make sense.

"But you said you didn't have any children."

"No," he said. "I just didn't say I did have one."

"You have a child." I was still trying to take this in.

"She lives in California," Declan was saying now, in a tumble. "Her mother and I were together, five, six years ago, and when she got pregnant, I—I wasn't great. I didn't want to get married, didn't really want the baby. Soon before the baby, before Katherine was even born, Lucy packed up and left me, moved out to San Francisco where she'd gone to school. At first she cut off all contact, but I found myself having a lot of regrets as time went on, wanting to see Katherine, thinking I should have given the relationship with Lucy more of a chance. That's where I was the day you walked into the bar."

"Why didn't you tell me right then?"

"I didn't know what was going to develop with you, Kennedy. I didn't know what was going to happen with them. And then you said you weren't interested in a serious relationship."

"So you were happy to just keep me as a casual thing on the side," I said. "Your East Coast fuck."

"Kennedy," he said, "that's not fair. You were the one who kept insisting it was casual, who kept acting like it was cool if we saw each other, cool if we didn't."

"I thought that's what you wanted," I said miserably.

"And you didn't really feel that way?"

"I did, at the beginning," I said. "And then I tried to because I thought that's the way I should be. But that last night, when I told you I loved you, that was not totally an accident."

He ran his hands through his hair, looking up at my ceiling in what appeared to be agony. "So you meant it."

"What does it matter!" I cried. "You loved *her*! You still love her!"

He took a minute to speak. "Yes, I love her," he said. "How can I help but love her? How can I do anything but take my relationship with her seriously, when our daughter is involved?"

"So," I said, trying to keep my feelings in check, "do you think the two of you will get back together full-time? Get married, maybe?"

"I don't know," he sighed. "The relationship is not without its problems."

"Every relationship has problems," I said lightly.

"Ours didn't." He looked hard at me.

I barked out a laugh. "Oh yeah! It was so problem-free that we aren't together anymore!"

He reached toward me again, and this time his fingers made contact with my arm, the mere touch so electric I leaped away.

"Who's not together anymore?" It was Jeremy. I hadn't heard him come in. We both must have looked alarmed, because his face broke into a grin. "Whoa," he said. "You don't really have to tell me. Here's the stuff you wanted."

"We're not going to be needing it, Jeremy. Put it over there and Declan can bring it back to the store." I picked up the paint scraper and started jabbing at a place where the paint was peeling, like the skin on a sunburned back, from the woodwork around the window. I'd heard all I wanted to hear from Declan, and said more than I wanted to say.

"You really should fix what you did to these walls first, you know," Declan said.

I kept stabbing at the woodwork. "I have my own way of doing this."

"Fine. All right," Declan said. "Just do it with some decent tools, would you?" He took a new scraper from the bag and laid it in my hand. I looked at the price tag.

"Eighteen dollars?"

"You'll feel the difference," he said. "Just the way it feels in your hand will give you more pleasure."

"Oh," I said dryly. "Is this about pleasure?"

"Everything's about pleasure."

"You're supposed to be a Catholic."

"Lapsed, darlin'. Seriously lapsed. All right now. The first thing we've got to do in this room is wash it down. Then you start painting by cutting in the corners and around the windows and baseboards and ceiling. And then you roll the walls out last."

"Too frustrating," I said. "It'll be easier to keep at the little stuff if I can see the whole room painted."

"This is not my *preference*, Kennedy," said Declan. "You do it this way because once you roll out the walls, the room is filled with paint fumes and you can't stay in it. So if you do the small, slower stuff first, then you can roll and immediately leave and let the room dry and when it does, boom, you're finished."

"Oh," I said, impressed at his logic.

"Yes. Oh. Jeremy, put some water—hot as you can get it—in these buckets and I'll mix in the cleaning solution. Then we'll wash down these walls. We'll have to wait for them to dry before we can start painting."

"We?"

"I just want to give you the benefit of my vast knowledge." He smiled a little.

"How did you get so smart?"

"You don't have to be smart," he said. "You just have to be smarter than the paint."

"Well," I said. "I guess you qualify."

"Very fucking funny."

Jeremy brought two of the buckets, filled with steaming water, back into the room.

"You know," Declan said, addressing Jeremy more than me. "I made my fortune as a housepainter before moving here. First, I went to England. I came off the boat wearing five pair of overalls, one on top of the other, and carrying a suitcase full of tinned beans."

"You never told me about the beans," I said.

He shrugged, shook cleanser into the water, mixed it with the wooden paint stirrer. "I used to be embarrassed about it, I guess. But now." He looked up at me, an enormous grin breaking out on his face. "I'm fucking proud of this know-nothing kid who left home all by himself at seventeen with a huge suitcase full of baked beans."

This would have been around the same time I was finishing up at boarding school, thinking my life was miserable.

"It sounds hard."

Declan looked thoughtful. "I guess it was, looking back, but at the time, no, I didn't think it was hard. I was thrilled out of my mind to be saving so much money and getting ready to go to America. And I had my mates with me. It was all Irish fellas then. Now it's Poles. Same deal, with the suitcases."

I dipped a sponge into one of the buckets and lifted it out, steaming in my hands. Then I pressed it to the wall and rubbed up and down, then back and forth.

"No," Declan said. "It's really better if you stick to one direction, all up and down is the best. Same thing with paint. You can't be going every which way. And you can't put it on too thin, but if you put it on too thick you get drips."

"Why does it do that?" I asked him.

"It's the nature of paint," he said. "It's how paint behaves."

"Like you," I said, more to myself than to him. But like my "I love you," it was now in the air.

"What?"

"Like you," I told him. "Acting like you always do. The way you always have."

"I'm not like paint," he said. "I can surprise you."

"I don't think so."

"I surprised you about Katherine."

"Surprises don't count," I told him, "when they're based on lies."

"I didn't lie, I omitted."

"Whatever," I said, one of my favorite expressions from Maya's vocabulary. "I think we've got this painting stuff down now. You don't have to hang around."

"I don't mind."

"Well, I do." What was the point? I was happy for him that he'd reconnected with his daughter, but her existence, the fact that the other woman was her mother, made me feel there really was no hope for him and me. I could admit to myself now that the friendship idea had just been a rationale to see him again. We'd been friends all that time, I knew now, not because we preferred to be friends but because sex had not been on the table. Friendship had been what we'd settled for instead. But I wasn't willing to settle anymore. Not on where I lived, not on what I did with my life, and certainly not on my relationship with Declan. When we let ourselves have it all, our relationship was as good as it got. He was right: We hadn't had any problems. Except that we couldn't figure out how to be together.

"All right," he said. "But I promise, I'm going to surprise you one day soon."

"You do that," I said. Never guessing that he could.

CHAPTER *fifteen*

It was 5:30 in the morning and I'd already been up for almost three hours, first lying awake in bed and then sitting in the living room and then pacing the house, growing more and more frantic. In the middle of the night Frank had called to say there was a problem with Amanda and he was rushing back with her. He wouldn't tell me what it was, even when I insisted. I told myself it couldn't be a terrible accident or else he wouldn't be driving all the way from the end of Long Island to New Jersey, at least a three-hour trip. It couldn't be a disease; he'd bring her back during the day if it were a disease.

At first I calmed myself by thinking that, having ruled out the two worst things, whatever was left couldn't be that bad. But for Frank to wake me up, to drive through the night, to refuse to talk about it on the phone, saying it was too important, too serious: It had to be something major. And if it wasn't the obvious possibilities, the others, when I allowed myself to think about them, were all deeply disturbing. Sexual abuse. Some sort of serious psychological or emotional problem. Night terrors. A refusal to speak, or eat.

Finally, I saw Frank's headlights and I sprinted outside to meet them. He was walking up the driveway, carrying the sleeping Amanda in his arms.

"Is she all right?" I cried. "Just tell me she isn't going to die."

He smiled a little. "She isn't going to die."

"Oh, God, I've been so worried, Frank. What is it? What's going on?"

I held out my arms to take Amanda from him but he shook his head and carried her inside and laid her down on the black velvet couch, the only piece of furniture remaining in the living room.

"Where's the blue afghan?" he said.

"I sold it at the yard sale."

"Is there something else we can use to cover her?"

I ran upstairs and got the comforter from her bed. She looked fine sleeping there on the sofa, tan, her hair streaked blond, almost as light as Frank's.

"She's okay?" I said.

"She's fine."

"So what's the problem?"

"Can I have some coffee? I'm sorry but, you know, I didn't make any before I left and I didn't want to stop."

I looked full at him then. "What?" I yelled. "You woke me up in the middle of the night and I've been sitting here going out of my mind for hours and now you want to drink coffee before you talk to me? What in hell is going on?"

Instead of answering me, he walked out to the kitchen and poured himself some coffee, ignoring the milk—"I'm really trying to stay away from animal products." Then he carried his coffee into the dining room, where he settled himself onto the floor in the lotus position, gazing out the window at the rising sun.

"Frank."

He faced me and I saw he was blinking back tears. I held my breath.

"I left her, Kennedy. It was terrible, out there, and I left."

I was confused. Was this a confessional? Was he telling me he'd left Amanda with Sunny, or worse, alone, because he couldn't hack full-time fatherhood? So now he was bringing her back to me to take care of?

"You left Amanda?"

"I left Sunny, Kennedy! She was just . . . awful with Amanda. She couldn't handle being with her for more than a day or two at a time. And suddenly I saw everything, how wrong it was."

"What did she do to Amanda?" If she hit her, I thought, if she so much as laid a finger on her I was going to hunt her down and kill her.

"Don't worry, Mommy," Frank said. "She didn't do anything to Amanda. It was just her . . . expectations. And the things she said to me when Amanda couldn't hear."

"What do you mean?" I sat down on the floor beside him. I couldn't help it; now that I knew my child was all right, I wanted to hear more about Sunny's failings, about all the ways she was inferior to me.

"Like the first night out there, she wanted to go to dinner at this really fancy place in Southampton. I knew Amanda was going to hate it but Sunny said it was her vacation, too. So we went, and there was nothing on the menu Amanda would eat, but of course she was starving, and cranky, so I tried ordering her plain pasta with butter but then it showed up with herbs sprinkled all over it and Amanda burst into tears and crawled under the table. Sunny demanded that she come back out, then Amanda bumped into the leg of the table, and Sunny's white wine ended up all down the front of her new linen sundress."

I was laughing by that point, picturing it.

"It wasn't funny," Frank said glumly.

"It's funny now."

"Well, that was Day One," Frank said. "And it just got worse. Sunny expected Amanda to tag placidly along to shops and restaurants, and then she wanted to spend hours sitting on the beach reading and got annoyed if Amanda talked to us or wanted me to play with her."

"What did she expect?"

"I guess she thought it was going to be like some happy photograph of a romantic couple on vacation with a cute little kid, where the kid never makes any noise or has any needs of her own." Frank shook his head. "And then the house we rented—you know how expensive places are out there, so this place was astronomical—"

"How much?"

"What?"

"How much was it?"

"You don't want to know."

"Yes, I do."

"Okay, it was $15,000 for the month."

"Jesus." My mouth must have fallen open. I bought groceries only on double coupon day and he was spending $15,000 to rent a beach house?

"We signed the lease before I left the firm," he said. "But it was a shack! That's the point! At least I wasn't the one who picked it out—Sunny found it on the internet—and it turned out to be this tiny little bungalow with practically cardboard walls with two tiny bedrooms that were right next to each other so that I just couldn't get into it. You know."

Ugh. I didn't want to know.

Suddenly his face lit up. "Remember that place we stayed in Martha's Vineyard the first year we were together?" he said.

He really did look younger and more relaxed and

better, even, than he'd looked a decade before, when I first knew him. Now, he looked more like the kind of guy I'd always been attracted to: rumpled, boyish, guys like Declan.

"Maya must have been around the same age Amanda is now," I said.

"Yes, I remember how nervous I was, thinking about spending a whole two weeks with her."

"But it was really fun."

"It was. It was great. I remember taking her into the ocean, holding her as we rode the waves, teaching her to body-surf."

I remembered how thrilled Maya had been, in the rough waves in his arms, and how much attention he'd lavished on her. She'd soaked it up and I, despite my best efforts to resist, had, too. He'd insisted on footing the major part of the expense of flying to the island and renting a car instead of dealing with traffic and ferries, staying in a beautiful inn, eating lobster dinners by the beach. Those two weeks had felt like an aspirin after five years of headache. Of heartache.

"Surfer boy," I said, patting his arm.

And then caught myself. I hated allowing myself to have any kind of positive feeling about him.

"You see," he said, "that's the way I thought this trip was going to be with Sunny and Amanda. I remember that trip being a real turning point for us. I went from being this guy who was dating a woman who had a kid to feeling like the three of us could be a family. You know?"

"Your big mistake," I said.

"No, Kennedy," he said, trying to take my hand. "Don't you see what I'm saying? God, I'm such an idiot. It was Sunny who was a mistake. Don't you see? You're my wife. We're the family. This is where I belong."

I snatched my hand back, appalled.

"This is what you drove through the night to tell me?"

"Yes."

"This is the mystery I've been up since three in the morning worrying about?"

"Yes. Kennedy, I'm sorry. I couldn't sleep. I haven't been able to sleep all week, since Sunny left . . ."

"I thought you left her."

"Yes, I left her, but she left the house at the beach. What I mean is, I broke up with Sunny because I realized I really belonged back here with Amanda. With you."

I stared at him, at his beach-brown skin, at his uncharacteristic shadow of unshaven beard and at his bleary eyes, shining with determination.

"You have got to be out of your mind."

"Oh, Kennedy, please. I don't blame you for being upset. I know what I did to you was horrible. But I love you, Kennedy. I'm your husband. Doesn't that mean anything to you?"

"It meant everything to me, Frank! It was my whole world until the day after Christmas, when you picked up that suitcase you'd stashed in the front hallway and told me you didn't love me anymore, that you were leaving me for another woman."

"I know," he said. "I know. I was insane."

"Insane! I want to know, Frank. When did you put that suitcase in that closet? Was it on Christmas Day? Christmas Eve? Or was it even earlier than that? When you sat with us on Christmas morning, were you counting the hours until you could take the suitcase and walk out the door?"

"Kennedy, that's not fair."

"That's not *fair*? You leave me, and then you call me unfair for *saying* you left me? That's like blaming the victim for screaming when she gets hit."

"Do you think it was easy for me to leave you and Amanda and Maya? It was the hardest thing I've ever done in my life. You picture me sitting there on Christmas morning counting the hours, when really I was in agony."

"Oh, God, I feel so sorry for you. That's awful that it was so painful."

"Kennedy, I don't expect you to feel sorry for me." Once again, he reached for me.

"If you try to touch me one more time, I swear I'm going to bite your hand."

He put his hands behind his back. "I don't know what to say. I'll do whatever you want, I'll say whatever you want, whatever it takes to get you to let me come back home."

"This is not your home anymore, Frank. I think you should go outside, and get in your car, and drive into the city to your own apartment."

He mumbled something.

"What?"

"I said it's not my apartment anymore."

"Oh, so you just *presumed* I was going to let you stay here?"

"I wasn't presuming anything, Kennedy. When I broke up with Sunny I told her she could have the apartment. She'd already given up her own lease."

"Well, go stay in a hotel then."

"Kennedy, please, can't we talk about this? I know you don't owe me anything, but we spent all those years together, and we have a child together, and it's not like we can just walk off into the sunset and never see each other again, even if that's what you want. No pressure, but if you'd just let me sleep on the couch for a few days—"

"Go sleep on Sunny's couch."

"Kennedy, if I ran into Sunny on the street . . ." He took a deep breath, shut his eyes for a moment. "I can't bear her. And I love you. I swear, Kennedy, I love you so much, I love Amanda, I love Maya, please *please* give me another chance. Please won't you just talk to me about it."

"Stop!" I yelled. "Just stop it!"

"Mommy?" came Amanda's sleepy voice. "Mommy, is that you?"

I scrambled to my feet. "Yes, sweetheart."

"Mommy!"

I was in the living room and she was running across the wood floor, leaping into my arms, wrapping her wiry little legs around my waist and clinging to me with a fierceness I'd forgotten.

"I'm home!" she said. "How did I get here?"

"Daddy drove you here when you were sleeping," I told her. "He said you missed me."

"He missed you more," she giggled. "He said we could all be together again. Can we, Mommy? Can we?"

Frank was standing in the hallway. I looked at him, ready to murder him.

"Oh, please, Mommy. That would make me feel like Sleeping Beauty, like I woke up and all my dreams came true."

I kissed my little daughter on the forehead, thrilled to have her back again, safe in my arms, and reluctant to break it to her, quite yet, that this story was not destined to unfold like a fairy tale.

Frank persuaded me to let him sleep on the sofa that night, and offered to stay and take care of Amanda so I could work on the house the next day, and then I let him sleep downstairs again that night; soon we assumed a new domestic rhythm. He held down the fort at home, putting Amanda in day camp only long enough to teach a yoga class or two at the Y, and I worked sixteen hours a day, a total reversal of the way things had been when we were married. We weren't having sex, but we hadn't had sex much during our marriage, either. The only other difference was that now we were sleeping on separate floors.

On one hand, I still wanted him out. But with Amanda so thrilled to have him here, to have us all theoretically together, I couldn't bring myself to force the issue. As long as Maya was still at Marco's, which she was scheduled to be for more than another week, I figured I could let things drift along, take advantage of Frank's willingness to help and in exchange let him crash on the couch until he found a new place.

One night, after a particularly difficult day at the house, I arrived home later than usual to find the house dark and candles sputtering on the dining room table, which was set elegantly for two. Frank was sitting cross-legged in the dim hallway, surrounded by books he had emptied from the walnut bookcase.

"What are you doing?"

"I made us dinner," he said, "and then when you were later than I expected I thought I'd do a little packing for you. It's ridiculous that I'm here all day while you're working and then you should come home at night and pack."

"I appreciate it," I said, "but it's my move, Frank. I

can handle it. Maya will be home soon and she'll pitch in."

"I'm happy to do it. Really, Kennedy. I want to prove to you how much I've changed."

I had to admit, he had changed. He'd always been sweet with Amanda, but now he was also competent. In the old days, on the odd evening when Frank took care of Amanda while I went shopping with Maya or worked at Jeannie's, I'd come home to find the kitchen littered with dishes and food, Amanda's dirty clothes on the bathroom floor and the tub still filled with scummy water, and Amanda awake with her Barbies while Frank snored on the couch. Now, I came home at night to a spotless house, a sleeping child, and often a hot meal. Though, until now, not one that was served by candlelight.

"I'm impressed, Frank," I told him. "Really."

"So what did you do today?" he asked.

"Oh." I waved my hand. "Nothing interesting." I'd avoided talking to Frank about the new house. I didn't want him involved. Here, at least he semi-belonged; that was my place and my place alone.

"No, tell me," he said, another personal first. Never before had he actually persisted in trying to get information about anything that wasn't directly about him. "I want to know."

"Oh, I'm mainly trying to get the kitchen in some kind of order. I mean, I can't do anything too elaborate, but there's nothing in there right now. Jeremy is

helping me put in plain white shelving, a countertop . . ."

"I'm so impressed by how you've taught yourself to
do all this. How you made this happen, all by yourself."

"I started doing it because I had to," I told him,
"but you know, it's really weird, I discovered I love it.
And I'm good at it. I'm actually good at it."

"That's great, Kennedy."

That was probably the longest I'd ever talked about
myself while Frank sat there and listened. I stopped,
figuring my time at the podium was more than up,
but he just kept sitting on the floor smiling and looking up at me.

"Some of my new neighbors stopped by the house
today," I said.

"Oh yeah?"

"Yeah, they were really nice. They couldn't believe
what I'd done to the place—I guess they used to help
Mrs. Glover with shopping and little jobs around the
house, so they knew what kind of shape it was in. The
woman actually asked me if I'd be interested in reno-
vating their kitchen."

"You should do it."

I looked at Frank to gauge if he was serious. "I
don't know. In my own house, if I screw something
up I have only myself to answer to. But I don't think
I'm good enough yet to handle doing this kind of
work for someone else."

"Really, you should consider it," said Frank. "You were always talented at making a place look great. Even that little apartment you had in the city was cute."

"You hated that apartment. You said it was a hippie pad."

"Forget me," Frank said. "I was a jerk. I'm embarrassed by how I used to be, always having to have everything my way."

"And you're not like that anymore?"

"I hope not."

"So what happened to you?"

"Don't get mad," he said, "but Sunny just wouldn't put up with me being that way. I had to change for her. And then I wanted to change for me. And for you."

"Don't say that, Frank."

I was still standing in the hallway, but him forcing me to confront the issue of our relationship, or our ex-relationship, or our maybe-future-relationship, made me feel as if I were about to keel over. Crossing to the dining room, I plunked onto a chair, which jiggled the table so that one of the candles went out.

"Kennedy," Frank said, standing up and coming into the dining room, where he seemed to loom over me, his shadow enormous in the light of the lone candle. "Whatever happens with us, don't you think it's a good idea for us to talk about things?"

All the years we were together, it was me who always wanted to talk, to chew over our relationship, and he who had refused, even getting away with a minimal explanation the day he left. Now it seemed we'd switched roles in this way, too.

"I've thought about it a lot," Frank continued, "what went wrong between us, what our problems were, how I could change to make things work. And that's something I think was an issue, that from the very beginning I insisted on always taking the lead, deciding how everything was going to be, being the Big Daddy."

Yes, that had been true, but at the same time I'd let myself play the little child, dependent on him for everything from money to a direction in life. I often hadn't liked the way things were, complaining about his silence or his long workdays or his repressed emotions or his lack of participation. But I'd let my dissatisfactions stay low-grade and chronic, never pushing them to the point where he'd have to change, or the relationship would, or I'd have to leave. I'd been more content with the status quo, in the end, more afraid of striking out on my own, than I'd been unhappy.

"I'm different now, too, Frank," I said. "I know I resisted making my own life, you were right about that, but now I'm doing it, and I like it."

"You're doing great," he said.

I shook my head firmly. "I can't go back."

"I'm not asking you to go back," he said, edging

in closer and moving behind me, laying his hands on my shoulders, beginning to rub. "But don't you think maybe you could consider going forward?"

His hands felt wonderful on my aching muscles and I closed my eyes, letting my back relax and curve until I was almost leaning against him.

"God, what is that you're doing?" I asked him as he began digging his thumbs into my back up and down my spinal cord and along the bones I thought of as my wings.

"Stimulating your chakras," he said. "Trying to tap into your positive energy."

Immediately I tensed. "You must have me mixed up with Sunny."

"Never," he said, immediately reverting to the conventional massage.

I closed my eyes, and began to relax again, and give myself over to his hands. I kept wanting him to make it easy for me to force him to leave. And instead, he was making it easier and easier to let him stay.

The only thing I couldn't bring myself to do was sleep with him. I mean make love with him. And sleep with him. I found that it was stunningly simple for me to slip back into feeling married to Frank, even given the topsy-turvy new order of things, in every way but the sexual one.

I was not sure what this meant. I thought maybe I just needed a little more time, maybe it was evidence that I was still hurt and angry. Or maybe it was a side effect of physical exhaustion. Or maybe I was one of that legion of women I'd read about afflicted by low sexual desire, though that hadn't been a problem with Declan. But my relationship with Declan had been new, fast, unfettered. Maybe this was just the way it was for couples who'd been together a long time; that's what Jeannie told me, what I'd always told myself. Or maybe this was just something I was going to have to accept about me and Frank.

There were so many other things in favor of us getting back together. There was Amanda, most importantly, as even Declan himself had pointed out, the prime motivation for his own relationship, the main reason he hadn't chosen me. And there was Maya, too, although she may not know it yet. I'd artfully avoided mentioning Frank's return whenever I talked to her on the phone at Marco's, aware that her initial reaction to Frank would almost certainly be negative. But I couldn't help believing that it would be better for her to live with two parents in relatively more financial stability than to live with me alone. The fact that Marco was on the scene meant only that she'd have two fathers to love her.

And then there was me. My alternative if I didn't get back together with Frank was a future on my own, with my daughters, in my charming cottage, all alone. Alone, I realized, was what I'd likely remain. Jeannie had been right: There were no men out here. If I was going to stay in the suburbs—and I'd long ago committed to that—it was better, in every way, to be married.

To be married to Frank? He was, in the end, still my husband, and a lot of the problems I'd had with the relationship before now seemed moot. He was totally involved with the domestic side of our life, and supportive of both my work on the house and my blossoming idea of starting a contracting business. Homewood's first female contractor: I was sure to be a big success, he said. Maybe we both could work out flexible schedules, he suggested, me with my construction jobs and he with a blend of yoga and consulting for the law firm. He promised me things could be different between us, and I was beginning to actually believe him.

CHAPTER *sixteen*

He'd come up with the surprise he'd promised me, Declan said. He didn't want to tell me what it was. "Just come in," he said. "I want to cook you dinner."

I hesitated, thinking of Frank, who was right that moment upstairs putting Amanda to bed. "I have something to tell you, too," I said.

"Tell me when you see me," he said. "We'll swap surprises."

"I don't really like surprises," I said.

"Ah, now, darlin'. I told you I would do something to surprise you and I'm damn well going to go through with it. Please. Don't ruin the fun."

So against my better judgment I said I would go into New York and see him the next night, looking forward, just a little bit, to slipping away to see another man, an ex-lover at that, without telling Frank about it. I wasn't lying exactly, I thought, remembering Declan's words: I was omitting. It was payback time for all the omitting Frank had done to me.

And Declan, too, for that matter, making myself feel better for the information I'd omitted on the phone, even at his insistence. He'd hidden some pretty large facts from me, first that he was seeing another woman, and then that he had a child. In that context it wasn't so wrong for me to drop a bombshell of my own.

Even so, I was nervous the next evening standing on the corner across from Declan's bar, feeling queasy about the situation despite my best rationalizations. The place was transformed, with the scaffolding gone, the trim painted a fresh white, and the letters that spelled out McGlynn's sporting a shiny new coat of gold. I looked up at the dark glass of Declan's windows and suddenly his face appeared. He broke into a grin and waved at me. I smiled weakly and waved back. No more agonizing: I crossed the street and the buzzer was already sounding to let me in when I reached the door. And when I got to the top of the stairs he was standing in the hallway, smiling down at me.

"Kennedy," he said.

"Hello." I felt at that moment as traitorous, as low as I thought it was possible to feel.

And then, as I reached his door, he spread his arms wide and standing behind him grinning up at me was a little girl about Amanda's size.

"Here she is," he said. "My daughter, Katherine. Isn't she a beauty?"

And she was a beauty, with her strawberry hair pinned back with a Minnie Mouse barrette and her enormous beaming smile and her dimple in one cheek and her little glasses, so thick her eyes looked as big as quarters. She was wearing a lime green sundress printed with strawberries and trimmed with bright pink rickrack.

"Wow," I said. "I am surprised. That's great, that you have her here."

And then I had a terrible thought, one that made me feel much worse than lying to Frank, or than hiding Frank's return from Declan.

"You're not . . ." I tried to look beyond them into the apartment. ". . . going to introduce me to her mother, are you?"

He burst out laughing. "No, don't worry, not a chance," he said, letting me into the apartment and locking the door behind us.

I felt a tug on the hem of my dress. Katherine was gazing up at me.

"Do you like my dress?" she said.

I squatted down so that we were eye-to-eye. "That's a gorgeous dress," I said. She smiled all the wider but threw her arms around her father's waist and snuggled shyly into his side.

"I'm Kennedy," I said. "I bet your Dad told you that."

She nodded, gazing at me.

I straightened up, looked at Declan.

"Okay," I said. "I'm surprised."

"And that's not all," he said. "Come in, come in. Katherine and I have a special dinner planned for you."

It had been over two months since I'd been in Declan's apartment and all the work that had been in progress the past spring had been completed. Now the walls were cool and beige, the woodwork a shimmery white, the floors pale and shiny, no plastic or drop cloths anywhere. On an elegant beige silk ottoman sprawled one of the most common decorating accessories from my own house: a naked Barbie.

"Wow," I said.

Declan had disappeared into the kitchen, Katherine trotting behind him as unfailingly as if she were leashed.

"Wow?" He popped his head out from the kitchen.

"Your place. It looks beautiful."

"Yeah," he said. "Well, I've had a lot of time to work on it."

What if I went in there and just told him now? Just said, "I'm sorry you and Katherine have made me this wonderful dinner, but I can't stay, you see Frank came back, and we're trying to see if we can work things out, and so there's really no point in having dinner with you."

Declan emerged from the kitchen holding a silver tray with a cocktail glass on it. The glass was frosty and in it was a pale pink drink. He was walking slowly because Katherine was bouncing along beside him, with one hand clutching the tail of his shirt and with the other gripping a little crystal bowl full of nuts, her fingers submerged in the salty cashews. Nuts fell in a steady stream, leaving a trail behind her.

"Here," said Declan. "Your aperitif."

"Ah."

"Okay? Are you okay?"

"Sure."

"I have to finish up something in the kitchen. Katherine, sit here with Kennedy and keep her company while I get the you-know-whats ready. The—" He bent down and whispered in her ear.

She giggled.

"Sit right here and talk to Katherine until I tell you guys—I'm sorry, I mean ladies—dinner is served, okay?"

"Okay."

I settled onto the dark blue sofa and Katherine perched on the edge of a black footstool across from me, gazing solemnly at me as I sipped my drink. After just a few seconds I realized I had sucked down almost the entire thing.

"You're pretty," Katherine said.

"Thank you. So are you."

That made her smile and visibly relax. "My daddy took me on a boat and we saw the Statue of Liberty," she said.

"My little girl went to the Statue of Liberty with her dad."

"Where is your little girl?"

I knocked back the last of the drink. "She's home," I said. "In my home." Home being baby-sat by her father, whom I lied to.

"I have a Mommy," Katherine informed me.

"I know that," I said, thinking of how Amanda must have felt meeting Sunny for the first time, wanting to like her and be liked, but to remind both Sunny and herself that her mother still existed.

"How did you know?"

"Your dad told me."

"Oh," Katherine said. She crossed her legs, then uncrossed them, then crossed them the other way.

"My mommy's pretty, too," she said.

"I'm sure she is," I said truthfully, though for jealousy reasons I hadn't ever let myself speculate in too much detail on Lucy's indubitably good looks.

"How did you know?"

"I guessed, because you're so pretty."

This inspired her to drop to the floor, now entirely undone by laughter, and hide her face in her hands. Then she parted her fingers and looked up at me, only to dissolve into another round of giggles.

"Come on, girls," said Declan. "Dinner."

The table was set beautifully, with a cream tablecloth and candles in silver candleholders and cream china and damask napkins. The place cards, hearts cut

from construction paper, had been decorated by
Katherine.

"Wow," I said. "This looks beautiful."

"Katherine and I did it together."

We started with a salad made from romaine, feta
cheese, and avocados, followed by a cold tomato soup,
and then steamed seafood with homemade aioli.
There was white wine, which I drank copiously, and
caffeine-free Coke, apparently Katherine's favorite.
Dessert was raspberries and lemon sorbet. Then Declan made us cappuccinos and we went to sit in the
living room, he on the sofa with Katherine leaning
heavily against him, her eyes beginning to close after
the big dinner, and me perched on the beige ottoman
formerly occupied by Barbie.

"That was delicious," I said.

"I'm glad you liked it."

"No after-dinner cigarette?" I asked.

"I gave up," he said, brushing the hair back from
Katherine's brow. "For her."

"You're a good dad, Declan," I said. "A wonderful
dad."

"Do you think so?" he said earnestly. "You inspired
me, you know, hearing you talk about how crazy you
were about your girls."

I was watching Katherine, whose eyes had dropped
closed and who was beginning to leave a thin trail of
spittle on Declan's shirt.

"I think she's asleep," I said softly.

He looked down at her and then, shifting, took off her glasses, folded them carefully, and then laid her head gently on his lap. "If I try to move her too soon," he said, "she wakes right back up." His voice was filled with awe and newfound authority, as if he'd made an unprecedented discovery in a land no one else had ever explored.

"How long has she been here?"

"Actually that's the rest of my surprise, Kennedy," he said. "Lucy and I have broken up. I realized it wasn't Lucy I wanted to be with—it was Katherine. Katherine's here for the summer, maybe longer. And she's in my life forever now."

What I felt was beyond surprise: I was shocked. "Oh, no."

"What's wrong?" he said, frowning. "Do you have some problem with Katherine being here?"

"It's not Katherine, Declan. It's Frank. Frank came back."

His hand, the one that had been brushing back Katherine's hair, stopped moving.

"It happened after I saw you that last time. He just showed up one morning, with Amanda. He'd broken up with his girlfriend. He wanted to get back together, and at first I thought it was absurd. But I don't know, we've been talking."

"You've been talking about getting back together?"

"Yes."

"This is what you want, Kennedy?"

"I don't know what I want. But I feel I owe him a hearing, you know? That I owe Amanda that. That I should at least give it a chance. Like you gave it a chance with Lucy."

Declan's hand was resting now on Katherine's head.

"You and I, we're not together now," Declan said stiffly. "You don't need to consider me in this decision."

"I know," I said. "But I feel, I don't know, responsible. You left Lucy, and now you have Katherine here, based on thinking I was still available."

He stared at me as if I'd started speaking a different language, one he didn't like the sound of.

"Do you really think," he finally said, "that you're at the center of this, of me and Katherine, even of what happened with Lucy?"

"I just meant—" I began.

"What do you think of me," he said, "to suggest that my being with Katherine and being a good father to her has anything at all to do with whether you're going to be in my life?"

"I don't know," I said, ashamed. "I'm not sure what I think."

He was looking at me with something close to contempt.

"You know," he said, "maybe the reason things never worked out between us is that you basically think I'm a loathsome person."

I was thoroughly aghast. "Oh, no, Declan," I said. "Quite the opposite."

"Really?" he said. "You said it yourself, that I was the kind of man who couldn't be counted on, who couldn't be true. If you didn't have that basic faith in me, no wonder you never wanted to stay with me. To love me."

"I did want to love you," I said. "You wouldn't let me."

And with that I broke into tears, shielding my face from him, not wanting to cry in front of him but equally unable to stop. He didn't move to comfort me, and I didn't want him to.

"Oh God, I've made such a mess of everything," I said finally. "I'm sorry if I've been wrong about you, but now I feel that I've gotten tangled up with Frank again and I have to see it through."

He eased himself out from under Katherine then, setting her head down gently on the sofa and crossing the room and opening the door. He stood there holding it open until I got up and gathered my purse.

"I don't know the right thing to do," I said.

"You know, darlin'," said Declan, "do what you like. Just do it in fucking New Jersey, all right, because I really can't stand to hear about it any longer here in my own living room."

CHAPTER *seventeen*

Faith. Frank would have to use that word, Declan's word, in accusing me of not making a serious enough commitment to us getting back together.

"I don't think you have enough faith in me, in the fact that I've changed," he said.

"No, Frank, I can see that you've changed."

"Perhaps you don't have faith things can be different for us and our family."

"I don't know," I said. "It's been such a short time you've been here again. Such an unusual time."

"But during that time," said Frank, "have things been different from how they were before?"

"Very," I admitted.

"Then I believe I've proven to you that I can be different and that our relationship can be different."

Why did I feel as if I was on *Court TV*?

The issue that prompted this argument was whether I

would allow Frank to go with me when I picked up Maya. I said that I should go alone, break the news of his presence to her in the car so we'd have time to talk about it before she actually had to deal with him.

He said no, that if we were going to be more of a team on the domestic front than we'd been before, we should start here. He wanted to be close to Maya again, and if he hid out at home she'd be even more pissed off at him. It was important that I allow him to come along as a statement to Maya—okay, to Marco even— that we were a couple again now, united in everything.

"We're not really a couple again, yet," I pointed out.

"Are you saying you want me to leave?"

"No."

"Then the message you're sending is that you've lost faith in our family."

What I really seemed to have lost faith in was myself. Since that night at Declan's, I felt as if I were second-guessing every decision, every emotion, feeling as if no matter which way I turned it was wrong.

So since Frank seemed so sure his way was right, I went along with him, but then knew I'd made a mistake even on the drive to Marco's. If there had been enough time, I would have turned around and dumped Frank off at home. But Maya was waiting, had sounded anxious to see me again. The best thing to do seemed to be to forge ahead and hope everything would work out okay.

When we pulled up in front of the long stairway leading up to Marco's big white house, Frank started to get out of the car.

"No," I said. "I'll go up alone."

"I think I should go with you."

"Frank," I said. "Stay in the car."

Maya answered the door herself, throwing her arms around me and practically leaping into my arms. It had been hard for me, on the phone, to get a clear reading on how her month with Marco and his family had gone. Every time I asked her, she said "fine," which for Maya was not a particularly positive word. But she didn't sound unhappy, either, and never complained. Now, though, her lime green duffel was packed and waiting near the door, and she gave Marco and Tina only the most perfunctory of kisses before stepping out into the night.

"I'll carry your bag to the car," Marco said.

"No, that's all right," I said, not wanting Marco to see Frank. "I can get it."

But it was so heavy I had trouble, even with my new beefed-up muscles, lifting it.

"I said I'll get it," Marco insisted.

Tina and the little boys retreated inside as I led the way slowly down the steps. You couldn't see Frank or Amanda from here and I was trying to plan ahead: If I could get Marco to give me the duffel bag by the last landing before the bottom flight of steps, if he would only kiss Maya good-bye there, if Frank and Amanda stayed inside the car until I actually put Maya's bag in the trunk, if Maya didn't freak out the second she saw Frank, if she got in the car and drove home with us while I talked to her, if she would only agree to give it a little time, then everything would be okay.

And just as I thought that, Amanda popped out of the car and screamed up, "Maya, Maya! Guess what? Daddy came back!"

Maya stopped in her tracks. I turned to look at her. Marco was glowering down at the car. And Frank stepped out from the driver's seat and waved up at her.

"What's he doing here?" Maya said. Her voice was calm; that was a good sign.

"Maya, honey, we have a lot to talk about. Frank brought Amanda back from the beach and he's been staying at the house."

"Then I'm not going back," Maya said, whirling around and trying to push past Marco up the stairs.

"Stop!" Frank called. "Kennedy, stop her!"

I tried to grab Maya's arm but she yanked it away from me. She still couldn't get around Marco, though, whose face was contorted in fury and who was stabbing his finger toward Frank, yelling, "You asshole! You stay away from my kid, you hear me?"

"You have no legal jurisdiction here!" Frank shouted. "Kennedy is the custodial parent and if you keep Maya here we will have you arrested for kidnapping!"

"Oh, yeah?" Marco said, beginning to advance down the stairs, brushing right past me. "You're gonna have *me* arrested for kidnapping? What about you, fuckface?"

Down below, I saw Amanda wander out onto the sidewalk, looking in puzzlement up to where Marco was screaming.

"Amanda, get back in the car!" I cried, torn between rushing down to protect her and running after Maya, who was halfway up to the house now but no longer retreating, instead standing rooted on the steps.

Amanda disappeared inside the car just as Marco reached Frank. "Maybe I should have you arrested for coming down here even trying to see my kid," Marco said, shoving Frank. "For taking her away for all those fucking years." Another shove.

"Stop it!" Maya shrieked. "Dad!"

Both Marco and Frank froze and looked up at her, as did I. She was standing above us on the stairs, her arm raised, ready to issue her queenly decree.

"Dad," she said. "Leave him alone. Come on. Let's go inside."

"Maya," I said, again starting up after her. "Please. Please come home."

"Don't even think about it," she said, pointing at me.

I stood there.

"Dad," she called. "Come on."

This time Frank didn't look her way. As Marco finally took a step backward and turned away, Frank scrambled to duck inside the car.

"Maya," I said. "Please. I love you. I want you to come home."

"I'm sorry, Mom. But I'm not going with you."

I kept standing there as she turned and began walking up the stairs with Marco, not looking back at me. I could not turn around and leave my daughter. Her father put his arm around her and led her into the house. The door slammed and then there was quiet.

How could I leave my child? But what else could I do? Camp there on the stairway? Call the police? Then she'd really hate me. Even more than she hated me now. I was furious at Frank for insisting on coming with me, for fouling up my relationship with Maya. But by letting him come with me, I had fouled up my relationship with her all by myself.

"Mommy!" Amanda was calling me from the car.

I did not want to leave. I wanted to bring Maya home with me and make Amanda forget the horror of tonight and resolve things once and for all with Frank and with Declan. Finally, I knew exactly what I wanted out of life. I knew what I wanted, but I did not know if I would get it.

CHAPTER *eighteen*

Ironically, it was seeing Marco again, or rather Marco and Maya together, that made me feel I owed Frank one last chance. I didn't want to worry, ten years from now, that I'd raised the bar too high for him to jump over, that I'd made it impossible for him to find any way back into our lives, the way I was afraid I had for Marco.

"Close your eyes," I told him.

"Why should I close my eyes?"

"Just close your eyes."

I was showing him the new house for the first time. It wouldn't be fair to let him see the ragged garden first, I thought, or the unpainted window frames, or the cracked stucco. I knew that he, never a fan of funk in any form, would not be able to see beyond the roughness to the beauty that would one day be. But if I could just get him inside the door, inside where I'd done so much and where it had come so far toward looking the way I wanted it to look, maybe he would see it the way I saw it.

"Keep them closed," I said, holding his hand, leading him up the bluestone path and onto the porch, opening the front door, propelling him into the living room just as the bells in the tower of the church on the corner started to ring for noon. "Okay. You can look now."

He opened his eyes and blinked, gazing around the living room, where the walls were smooth and painted the lavender gray I'd envisioned when I first saw the house. The woodwork and the fireplace mantel were repainted, too, and the cracked windowpanes had been repaired. I'd even hung my gold mirror on one side of the room, reflecting the green through the windows opposite. The wood floor was still rough and unfinished, and the kitchen was still a disaster, but this room had more than fulfilled its promise.

"Wow," Frank said. "Well."

"Isn't it beautiful?"

"Incredible."

"It's going to be so great, Frank. You wouldn't have believed it if you'd seen it before. Come here, look in the dining room. Can you believe this wainscoting? And this mural—I had to do this really intricate restoration of the plaster around the edges here."

"God, I didn't realize. I mean, there's still so much to be done."

"Not that much. Compared to where I started. But

that's what I was thinking. I mean, what I was hoping. That maybe you could work on it with me. Mom says she'll watch Amanda, and there's less than a month until we have to move in."

"I have to go back to work, Kennedy. I thought you realized that."

"Work? You mean the yoga thing?"

"God, no—I mean at the firm. My leave is up and they're pressuring me to make a commitment, and it seems the best thing for now is for me to go back full-time."

"But we talked about you consulting part-time," I said, puzzled. "Me finishing up the work on this house, and then maybe starting the contracting business."

"That was talk," Frank snapped. "Somebody's got to earn a living around here."

"But in this house," I said, "expenses will be a lot lower."

"The truth is, Kennedy, I think we should stay in our old place. Less upheaval for Amanda and everything."

I couldn't believe what I was hearing. "The house is sold, Frank. We have to be out September first."

"I'll get us out of that."

Just like that? He could undo all of my work with a wave of his pen?

"I don't want to get out of it! I want to move here!"

"Come on, Kennedy, face facts. This place is a

wreck and you're not even close to being ready. If you really want to move, I'll go along with it. But then let's get rid of the old house *and* this place and shop for a new house that's right for both of us. For all of us."

I felt my temper about to explode and I struggled to keep myself in control. "You know, Frank, I haven't even decided for sure that I want us to get back together. You just started assuming and then I guess I started assuming but I never really decided."

"Kennedy, come on. You know it's the right thing to do. It's what Amanda wants and it's what I want and deep down I know it's what you want, too."

"I'm not so sure about that."

"What are you going to do, choose this old dump of a house over your family's happiness?"

"You're twisting things, Frank." I'd had this same feeling when he talked me into letting him go with me to pick up Maya. It was a feeling that went way back, I realized, a sense of confusion that tended to come over me when we disagreed, and I found myself doing things and agreeing to things I didn't really believe in. Staring at him there in the house over which I'd labored so hard for the past months, I noticed for the first time that his hair wasn't blond anymore—except for a few bleached-out tips, it had reverted to its old mousy brown. "And what about Maya? What about Maya's happiness?"

"You can't let Maya emotionally blackmail us into

splitting up," he said. "Even your mother told you that."

She had told me that. She'd also told me that if I got back together with Frank it would be the biggest mistake of my life, far bigger than dropping out of college or getting pregnant with Maya or even marrying Frank in the first place, given that I'd had a very nice little girl with him and had also come out of the deal with a house worth several hundred thousand dollars. Though I hadn't passed those opinions on to Frank.

"Frank," I said, trying to stay focused, to keep my voice calm. "I would like to think that you and I could get our marriage back on track. But I am not willing to sacrifice Maya for you. And I am not going to give up all the work I've invested in this house. I am not interested in being your satellite out here doing exactly what you want me to do while you work at the firm every day. No matter what you think or what you want, I am going to have both my daughters with me and I am going to live in this house."

"You couldn't even get a mortgage on your own!" Frank said, spittle bubbling up in the corners of his mouth. "I could put in a call to the mortgage company and say I'm not going to cosign and that would be the end of your deal, right there!"

"Are you threatening me?" I said, incredulous. "Are you really trying to threaten me into giving up this house and giving up Maya and staying with you?"

"Kennedy," Frank said, downshifting his voice to neutral with stunning ease. "No. You misunderstand. I'm just pointing out the problems inherent in going ahead with your plan alone. You're not thinking clearly because the situation is too pressured. All I'm saying is that the sensible thing is for us to stay in our house and work things out without the stress of deadlines and rush construction jobs."

He sounded so reasonable, so seductive, that for one minute I thought, Yes, of course, he's right, this is too tense, I should step back, think more clearly about what I really want.

And then I happened to look up and see the light spilling down the staircase, the staircase I'd fallen in love with the first time I walked into the house, the sunlight that had illuminated my vision of how I could make a life on my own for myself and my daughters, reminding me of the choice I'd made after Frank had left me without any choices.

"No," I said.

"What do you mean, no?"

"No. No us. No going back. It's over, Frank. You were right that day in April about how it was time for me to make my own life. This is what's right for me, for me and Amanda and Maya. Having a little house like this, a place that's all my own, is what I should have done way back then instead of looking to you to rescue me."

He stood there, blinking. "All right, then," he said.

"If this is so important to you. I didn't realize you were nonnegotiable on the house. I'm sure I could learn to love this place. And if you want, I could probably extend my leave from the firm until after Labor Day so I could help you get the place into shape."

I laughed then. I actually laughed. I felt giddy because I knew I was free of him, free in a way I hadn't been when he'd walked out with his suitcase or when I discovered he was engaged to Sunny or during my interlude with Declan. Our marriage was really over for me now, because I was the one who was ending it.

CHAPTER *nineteen*

Frank's departure solved one problem, aside from the problem of Frank himself. Marco called me and said Maya had agreed to come home. But she had some conditions, which he would outline for me when we met. All information was funneled through Marco these days—Maya refused to take my calls or respond to my e-mails or letters—so I'd had to rely on him as my messenger, without any confidence that he was actually on my side. He suggested we meet the following evening at a Dunkin' Donuts along the highway, halfway between our two houses.

"That's ridiculous, Marco. Why don't I just come out there and pick her up? Or you can bring her here."

"She wants me to talk to you first."

"We can talk on the phone," I said, not relishing the prospect of another encounter with his paw.

He sighed. "You know how she is, Kennedy," he

said. "Very definite about what she wants. Just like you."

I laughed at that. "She's a lot tougher than I am."

"I don't know about that," he said. "Just meet us at the doughnut place. The deal is we'll talk inside and she'll wait in the car."

The next night, I left Amanda with Jeannie and drove to the designated spot, feeling like a character in a low-budget suspense movie. At least the ridiculousness of the situation helped to ease the pressure of seeing Marco as well as negotiating—if indeed that's what we were doing—Maya's return. I was missing her desperately and feeling as if I would go to any lengths to get her back, but it was hard to be too grim about it when surrounded by jelly doughnuts.

I was already waiting inside, sipping a coffee, when Marco pulled up in an enormous shiny red truck. I could see Maya's silhouette in the front seat but when I waved to her she turned her head away. Marco came inside and ordered a coffee of his own as if he didn't even know me, and then, nodding at me, led me to a table in back just out of her view.

"What's this all about?" I asked.

"She's nervous," he said. "She thinks you're going to try to trick her again, about Frank."

So I was still mopping up the fallout from Frank's misguided insistence on coming with me to pick her up.

"I'm not tricking her. Frank and I are really and finally broken up. I told you that a dozen times on the phone."

"I know. She just wants a guarantee that she's not going to get there and find him waiting."

"She has my guarantee. You have my guarantee."

"And then there's the other guy," he said. "Declan. She wants to know whether you're seeing him again."

"No," I said, taken aback. "I'm not seeing him either. But I didn't realize that was a big issue for Maya."

"I think she's concerned about the overall situation, who's going to be around the house. Any other boyfriends on the scene, any other guys you're involved with?"

"*No*, Marco!" I said. "Wow, I had no idea she was worried about this."

"Yeah, well, you never know," Marco said. "It's got to be hard for you, there all alone."

He was looking at me with what I realized with a start was tenderness, and then he reached out and brushed a stray curl back from my forehead, his fingers trailing against my skin. I gasped and, without thinking, grabbed his wrist. He was muscled, even there where normal people were just bones, but after a summer of working on my house, I was pretty strong myself.

"Marco, you have to know something," I said. "You and me, that's not going to happen."

"We had something good," he said.

"We did," I told him. "But that was a long time

ago. Too long, Marco. You've got your family now, and I've got . . ."

What did I have? I had my girls. I had myself.

"I'm glad things are going so well for you," I told him, changing direction. "I'm really happy that you and Maya have found each other again. But no matter what happens, I am not going to sleep with you, ever again."

Once Maya was home, I was able to turn my attention to my second most pressing problem: the house. I got in touch with Mrs. Glover in Maine, which involved calling the local postmistress, who sent a note to Mrs. Glover with a neighbor, who drove Mrs. Glover to a local pay phone where she called me.

"Mrs. Glover, I need an extension," I said.

"What kind of an extension?"

"I need an extra month to work things out. My ex-husband refused to cosign my loan, so I need until October 1 to put together the financing. If you could let my daughters and me move in before then, I'll pay you rent for September, whatever you think is fair. . . ."

"Nein," Mrs. Glover said.

"What?"

"Nyet. Nix. No."

"But it's only for . . ."

"If you don't have the mortgage figured out by now, why should I believe you'll have it figured out by October? You know, after I made the deal with you that developer fellow came along and offered me more money."

"But we'd already signed a contract."

"He offered me more money," she continued, as if I hadn't said anything, "and I told him if the deal fell apart with you, I'd sell it to him. He's just waiting for me to say the word."

"I thought you wanted to sell it to a single mom who'd love it as much as you did."

"Yeah? That was just a sales pitch, sister. All I really care about is the bucks."

That left only one option, the option I'd been avoiding for the past fifteen years. I put on a skirt. I put on some heels. I borrowed a Gucci bag from Jeannie and let Maya do my makeup. I made a reservation at one of the hottest restaurants in New York and invited my mother to lunch.

"Oh, how fabulous," she said. "We'll celebrate your impending divorce. But I insist on paying."

I was about to protest, but figured that would seem a tad ridiculous, once she found out why I'd asked her there.

She also insisted on having Stanislav drive us into the city in the white Mercedes wearing his chauffeur's cap.

"How kinky," I said, going for droll.

"Exactly," smiled my mother.

Heading into the city on the big day, I felt ashamed

of waiting until I had an ulterior motive to invite my mother on this outing. She was so delighted at the prospect of spending a few hours alone with me, of going with me to the kind of sophisticated place that didn't interest Stan or any of her provincial horse country friends, that I wished I'd suggested we do this long ago. Inching along the crowded noontime city streets, she exclaimed about everything from the tightness of the young women's skirts to the displays in the shop windows to all the restaurants that had set tables out on the sidewalks. By the time we pulled up in front of Epernay, my mother was clapping her hands in delight. "Ooooh," she squealed. "This is going to be so much fun!"

She turned down the first two tables the maître d' showed us, holding out for a corner banquette from which she could view the whole room.

"We look important sitting here," she whispered to me.

The waiter appeared. "I'll have a sidecar, please," Mom said, in the cultured voice she'd adopted for special occasions since the days of Hal the nightclub singer.

"A sidecar? Not a cosmo?"

"Sidecars are the new cosmos," Mom said, with the authority of someone who spent her days reading *InStyle*.

The waiter turned to me.

"I think I'll have an iced tea."

"She'll have a Long Island iced tea," my mother said.

"Plain, unsweetened iced tea," I corrected her, telling myself I hadn't said anything yet about the loan; I could still just forget the whole thing.

When the waiter was out of earshot, I turned to my mother and said, "You've got to stop doing that."

"Doing what?"

"Ordering my drinks! Trying to direct my every move!"

"Oh, pooh," Mom said. "I just want us to have fun."

"I want us to have fun, too," I said. "But I can't have a drink because after we get back to New Jersey this afternoon I've got to go to work on the house and I'll probably be there until midnight."

"I thought we'd go shopping after lunch," Mom said. "We have Stan and the car right outside and I'd love to see all the new fall clothes. Maybe I could even buy you something tight and chic, now that you're back on the sex market."

"Mom, I do not have time to go shopping and I am not back on the sex market!" I said this loudly enough for every nearby table to look toward us in curiosity.

"You don't have to get mad," my mother said.

"Apparently I do! This has been going on my entire adult life, Mom! I appreciate your offer to take me shopping, I'm delighted that you want to have fun with me at lunch, but you have to respect me as an equal or we're never going to work this out."

My mother blinked. "Maybe you need to start acting like an equal."

"What in hell does that mean?"

"Be more sure about what you want!" my mother cried. "Have a solid plan for making things happen! State your needs in a clear and confident voice!"

I sat there with my mouth half-open. I hadn't been doing that? Wait, even that thought sounded somewhat uncertain. All right, then! I hadn't been doing that! I was going to start being more direct and clear and confident about my wants and needs.

"I need $50,000," I told my mother.

Now she was the one who was speechless, holding her sugar-rimmed sidecar glass just below her open lips.

"I need you to cosign a mortgage for me," I continued.

Still, she was frozen.

"And I need it now."

She took a gulp of the sidecar. Sticking out her tongue, she licked the sugar from all the way around the rim. Then she burst out laughing.

"Good job," she said. "That's exactly what I was talking about."

"So will you do it?"

"Hmmmm," she said, looking toward the frescoed ceiling. "What kind of interest were you thinking about on the loan?"

I'd been thinking about none. But I said, "Three

percent?" And then, remembering that I was supposed to act more adult, I ramped up the confidence in my voice. "Three percent."

"Let's say five," she said, whipping a tiny calculator from her bag and punching in some numbers. "Yes, I could live with five."

I was about to agree, but then something moved me to say, "Four."

Mom looked surprised but then laughed again. "Okay, four. And if you default on the mortgage, I get to tear down the house and build a modern one."

A few months ago, that might have sent me running in tears for the door. But now I said, "I'm not concerned about that. Within a year I'm going to have enough of my own income to refinance."

"How are you going to do that?" Mom asked.

This part of the plan was still a little shaky, though I wasn't going to admit that. "I'm going to help one of my new neighbors design her kitchen. I've learned a lot working on the house and I'm considering becoming a professional."

Mom drained her sidecar. "A professional what?"

"A—someone who manages renovations. Sort of a designer but also someone who can hire the workmen and supervise the construction. The women I know in Homewood are always complaining about how contractors never call them back and don't treat them with respect even though they're usually the ones who are managing the whole job."

"You're going to become a contractor?" my mother said.

"Yes, Mom! What's wrong with being a contractor?"

"Well, what man wants to marry a contractor, for land's sake? A male nurse?" She chuckled and signaled for another drink, just as the waiter arrived with our salads. "Kennedy, you have to get serious now, thinking about your future."

"I am thinking about my future. That's exactly what I'm doing."

"No, I mean what are you going to do about a husband. You're still young, girl. You look fantastic, better than ever since you dropped that little marriage weight you were carrying around. It's time to be planning out the next step."

"Mom, I learned my lesson with Declan. I rushed into that relationship and made a mess of it. You told me yourself I shouldn't get involved."

"What kind of a mess?"

"I took it too seriously. I was too vulnerable. Instead of becoming lovers right away, we should have just stayed friends."

"Friends," my mother said scornfully. "Men make terrible friends. You don't want to marry the kind of man who would be capable of being a good friend."

"Yeah," I said, thinking of how unlikely it was that I'd ever want to be friends with Frank or with Marco, my quasi-ex-husband. Or rather my ex-quasi-husband. "But you don't want to marry the other kind of man either."

"Sometimes I don't think you're even related to me," Mom said, sighing from somewhere down near the Fendi bag nestled in her lap.

Given our history, I was reluctant to ask the next question but I couldn't stop myself. "What would you do, Mom?"

Mom considered that for a moment. It didn't take her long to formulate a plan of action. "I'd see if I could break up Bill Gates's marriage."

"If you were me, Mom."

"Okay, if I was really impractical and romantic and fixated on the past?" Mom said. "Was this Declan person good in bed?"

"Mom!"

"Was he?"

I'd been trying to avoid dwelling on that. "The best," I admitted.

"Well, then I'd do whatever I needed to do to get back into bed with him," she said, laughing her gurgling smoker's laugh, "and trust that everything else would fall into place."

The waiter brought Mom's new sidecar, and looked questioningly at my untouched iced tea.

"You know, on second thought," I told him, "I'll have what she's having."

CHAPTER *twenty*

It was September 1, moving day, the Saturday of Labor Day weekend, and the hottest day of the entire summer. The closings had taken place the night before.

I felt, finally, as if I was marching steadfastly into my future, utterly alone. Frank had left a message saying he'd be away until after Labor Day, when he was due to return to work at the firm, promising to see Amanda then. Declan hadn't called me since dinner at his place, not surprisingly, and I was afraid to call him, to confront his anger. And the truth was I hadn't had the time or energy to think about much besides getting Maya back home and making sure we had a home. Sometimes, right when I opened my eyes in the morning, I thought of Declan. And then immediately life charged into high gear and I was off.

Now, we were barely an hour into our move and already Amanda was in deep meltdown, watching in horror as I started to strip the sheets off her old bed so I could wash them before carrying them over to the new place.

"Don't do that!" she screamed.

"Amanda, we don't have a washer and dryer yet in the new house. I have to wash these here so I can put them on your bed clean in your new room."

"No!"

"Amanda, don't you want to have nice fresh sheets on your bed tonight after we move?"

"No!" she squealed. "I want everything to stay just like it is!"

I let go of the sheets and, even though Stanislav and Maya and Jeremy and three of Jeremy's friends were rushing all around us, carrying everything down to the rented truck, I knelt beside Amanda and put my arms gently around her.

"You don't want to move to the new house?" I asked.

"I want my bed the same! I want everything the same!"

"But I have to pack your sheets and blankets and pillows into one of the big boxes," I said. "Then we're going to put the boxes and the bed onto the truck and drive it over there."

"Mom?"

It was Maya, standing in the doorway.

"I think what Amanda wants is for you to fold up everything on her bed and move it just the way it is."

"Really?" I grimaced so that only Maya could see me. Amanda's sheets probably had not been washed for six weeks—and at this rate would not be washed for another six. But the sheets' griminess was less important than making Amanda feel better, which Maya seemed to have become particularly adept at doing. "Is that what you want, Amanda?"

Amanda nodded tearfully.

"All right, honey," I said. "Don't worry. We'll do it just the way you want it."

Hours later, at the new house, I gave thanks for Amanda's tantrum. Her unsorted stack of dirty bed linen made at least one job of settling in easier. All those essential items I had carefully placed in the boxes marked IMPORTANT were nowhere to be found. So while my nightgown and pillow and the coffeemaker and the silverware and the Advil were all missing, Amanda's sheets were in place on her bed, every stray hair and grain of sand undisturbed.

"What do you think?" I asked her.

Amanda didn't answer me. She was busy sticking the pictures of Barbie and Pokémon that had adorned her old room up on her new wall with packing tape. I bit my lip to keep from saying anything to her. I'd painted this room so carefully, wanting it to be perfect for her, following Declan's advice to the letter. Thinking of him here made my heart seize up. Get him out of your head, I commanded myself. Just think about your house, your kids, your life alone. All Amanda cared about was unpacking her books and toys and making everything look as much as possible like we hadn't moved at all.

Maya, meanwhile, was ignoring the mountain of boxes that were piled every which way on her floor. Her dresser was wedged into one corner behind her upended bed and her curtains lay in a puddle on the floor. She was sitting, back to the wall, on her unfurled sleeping bag, Jeremy stretched out beside her.

"So," I said. "What do you think?"

"About what?"

"The house."

I knew what I thought. I thought it looked wonderful. Asters were blooming in the beds around the front porch, the black velvet couch looked perfect in the living room, and I couldn't wait to shut the door on all the helpers and sink into a hot bath in my new pink bathtub.

But Maya scrunched up her face. "I wish we'd had more time to get it in shape," she said. She'd done a lot these past few weeks, alternating between taking care of Amanda and pitching in with me and Jeremy to paint and hammer and clean. "What's with these floors?"

"Now that I have the money from Grandma, I can hire someone to refinish them. But nobody was available to do it before we moved."

"Well, they're gross," said Maya. "I even got a splinter."

"Maybe I could do it, Mrs., I mean, Kennedy."

He was trying to get out of the habit of calling me Mrs. B. now that I'd told him that I was dropping Frank's last name, Burns, and becoming just Kennedy McAndrew again. Maya, Amanda, and I were about to become a family with three last names.

"That's okay, Jeremy. You've got to go back to school this week. But thank you for offering."

"God, you two have gotten pretty chummy," said Maya.

"I thought you wanted us to be friendlier."

"I didn't want him to become, like, your favorite child," Maya said.

Jeremy and I exchanged a look.

"I'm sure the house will look fine when you're finished," Maya snapped. "Could you leave us alone for a while now?"

"I thought I'd take one more trip up to the old house," I said. "Make sure I didn't forget anything. Want to come?"

"No, I do not want to come. Could you please get out of my room and shut the door behind you?"

She was back and I was delighted to have her, teenage attitude and all.

Amanda was lying in her bed, nestled under her blankets despite the still-hot weather, gazing at the ceiling, her thumb in her mouth.

"Since when did you start sucking your thumb?"

"Since now," she said, speaking without unplugging the thumb.

"Your room looks beautiful."

She looked around, as if seeing it for the first time. "I know." I wished I had that five-year-old confidence.

"So," I said. "Do you want to go over to the old house? Say good-bye?"

"I don't like to say good-bye."

"It's up to you, sweetie. If you'd rather stay here with Maya, you can, but this is our last chance to go back."

She thought for a minute. "Okay," she said, popping her thumb out of her mouth and hopping down from her bed.

Back inside the old house, she seemed surprised that the rooms were empty.

"We moved all our stuff to the new house," I said. "Remember?"

She nodded slowly, her eyes wide. "It looks different."

She walked slowly from one room to the next as if she were in a museum, somewhere where she wasn't really supposed to run through the halls or speak loudly. I followed her, holding my breath. She'd been so fragile lately, since Frank left for the last time, so prone to bursting into tears when I had no clue why. I wanted to protect her, to make everything all right, but I couldn't stop the forward motion of our lives. All I could do was keep being her mom.

She tiptoed upstairs and I trailed her. "Do you want to go into your room?" I asked.

Amanda peeked in but didn't step inside. "That's not my room anymore," she said.

She went in the other direction, into the room that had been Frank's and mine. She stood in the spot where our bed had been, and then suddenly sank to the floor and started sobbing.

"Oh, honey!" I cried, dropping down beside her, taking her in my arms. "What is it?"

"I had a memory," she said. "I remembered laying in bed with you right here, nursing."

"You remember nursing?"

She nodded, her eyes staring straight ahead. I passed my cool dry hand over her damp face, smoothing the hair back from her forehead.

"I miss it," she said, the tears starting again. "I miss everything."

"Oh, sweetheart," I said. "Your room will be just as pretty as your old room and next week you'll start first grade and now we have Maya back. And pretty soon I'm sure we're going to see Daddy. I think everything's going to be great."

We sat there for what felt like a long time on the hard floor, staring into the darkening light of the empty room. Amanda was slumped across my lap and my legs were beginning to cramp.

"Mom," she said finally. "Can people tell the future?"

"I don't know," I said. "Sometimes I think so." I thought for a moment. I wanted to make her feel better, to make everything better for her, but it also seemed important, right now, to tell her the truth. "But usually," I said, "I don't believe they can."

"Well," she said, "then I don't know if everything's going to be great."

I didn't want to admit that I didn't know either.

CHAPTER *twenty-one*

It seemed throughout September, though, that everything *was* great. Being in the new house, finally believing it was mine, gave me the feeling that I could make anything happen. With the money from my mother, I hired a plumber to install a shower in the bathroom, an electrician to put in a new circuit breaker, someone to come in and sand the floors. That freed me up to spend more time with Jeannie in the shop, where I was inspired to start selling our stock on eBay. I could manage that side of the business at night on the computer, leaving my days free to tackle my kitchen renovation job.

After some initial rockiness, the girls were doing fine. Frank seemed to be punishing me for filing for divorce by remaining incommunicado, refusing to return my calls even after he was back in the city and at work. Amanda was so upset about not seeing him that

I threatened to report him to the state as a deadbeat dad. That brought him back in line, and he finally scheduled a weekend visit with Amanda. Maya, sympathetic to her little sister's father issues, offered to go too, which astonished me.

"Frank's so desperate to get me back on his side he said Jeremy could sleep over," Maya said.

When I started to protest, she just laughed at me. "Don't worry," she said. "Jeremy's too big a wuss to actually do it."

Speaking of wusses, Frank neglected to tell me, until he had the girls in his car and was about to drive away, that he and Sunny had gotten back together. If he expected that this news would make me angry or distraught, he was disappointed. All it made me feel was free, and I broke into a grin and waved cheerily at him.

"Congratulations!" I called, as they pulled away from the curb. "Have a great time!"

Then I was alone, facing the one issue in my life I could not forget, and could not resolve.

Greenwich Village, on that beautiful early autumn afternoon, was swarming with people. At first, I almost didn't recognize Declan's place. The brass letters of the McGlynn's sign were polished to a high sheen and tables stood on the sidewalk outside the newly painted front door. Young couples and families and groups of friends sat in the sun, drinking beer and eating burgers. A waitress darted in and out of the kitchen door, and I couldn't get close enough to the dark windows to look inside.

My only choice was to go into the place itself. I could tell right away that Declan wasn't behind the bar, but once my eyes adjusted I spotted him, sitting on a stool drinking a bottle of water, Katherine on his lap. He was talking to the bartender, smiling and laughing. He looked relaxed, happy, which made me feel more bold. I hadn't dressed up for this occasion, didn't want to expect anything special to happen or give him the impression that I was trying to seduce him. I was wearing the same jeans and brown sweater I'd thrown on three hours before to rake the yard, and when I reached up to smooth my hair my fingers hit the crusty edge of a leaf.

"Hi," I said, but my voice didn't come out loud enough. Oh God, what was I thinking of? I'd failed with Frank and I was going to fail here, too. And then, just as I was considering turning around and walking away, Katherine looked in my direction and, giggling, waved. Declan looked up. I smiled. But he didn't smile back.

Katherine slid off his lap and came over to me, throwing her arms around my thighs in a huge hug.

"I knew you'd come back," she said. "Daddy said you wouldn't, but I said no, you were our friend and you'd come back."

"And here I am," I said.

"Here you are. Look, Daddy! Look who's here!"

I remembered him once when I'd worked there acting this cold, when an old friend from Australia showed up and Declan refused to return his smiles or stand near him at the bar and talk. When the man finally left, defeated, Declan said, "The shit owes me money and then he shows his face here expecting me to put him up. Arsehole."

And now he was ignoring me in the same way.

"Declan," I said, getting close to him. "I don't blame you for being mad at me."

"Good," he said, not meeting my eye.

"The last time we met . . ." I shook my head. "I handled that really badly. I'm sorry."

"You should be."

"I am. God, Declan," I said. "I see Katherine's with you."

Declan ran his hand over her head. "I talked her mother into letting her spend the school year with me. It turns out Katherine has some learning problems—it's connected to her vision—and there's a great school for her here in the Village. Better than anything in California. So her mother's been staying down at the Jersey Shore with her sister, and Katherine's with me during the week and with Lucy every other weekend."

"Wow," I said. "That's . . ."

"It's great," Declan said. "Great. I mean, it's difficult, trying to work out the hours and such, but that's not your worry. What was it you wanted?"

I hadn't expected that he would ask me that question so directly. And now that I was here, with him before me, I realized I wanted much more than to say I was sorry. I wanted to see his face break into a grin at the sight of me. I wanted him to kiss me, I wanted him to hold me, I wanted us to make love. I wanted him to say he'd been waiting for me, he wanted to be with me only, and again.

"I wanted to see you," I said.

"Well, there," he said. "You've seen me." He nodded his chin at the bartender. "Brian, I've got to take Katherine down to her mother's place. I should be back by five but if I hit traffic it could be a bit later." He hopped off his bar stool and brought his empty water bottle behind the bar, tossing it in the bin and then busying himself at the cash register, his back to me. I stood there, waiting for him to turn around, but he didn't.

Finally I cleared my throat and said, "Declan?" He punched some keys on the cash register, waited while it churned through its calculations, and then examined the length of paper with numbers on it. More loudly: "Declan?"

He turned around, the paper still in his hand, looking annoyed.

"Declan, please," I said. "I'd really like to talk with you. I don't want to leave it like this."

"What's the problem?" he said. "Looking for a shoulder to cry on after another spat with your husband?"

Tears sprang to my eyes but I blinked them back. "Frank and I have been apart for almost two months now," I said. "The divorce is in progress."

That at least got some reaction. He hesitated for a moment, seemed about to say something, then shook his head as if he'd changed his mind.

"So what do you need?" he asked. "Help painting your house?"

"Declan," I said, noticing Katherine watching us, wide-eyed, over the rim of her Coke glass. "That's not fair."

"No," he said, "what's not fair is you coming back into my life after all these years and making me fall in love with you and then pulling it all out from under me."

I stood there stunned. All I could think of was the "fall in love with you" part.

"It wasn't just something I did to you," I said. "You were seeing Lucy, hiding that from me."

"Your life was complicated, too, Kennedy. We're grown-up people with all kinds of messiness involved. But I was willing to deal with the fact that you were still legally married and you had two kids of your own and you were determined to move into a crumbling little fairy tale castle when you didn't even know how to drive a nail into a wall."

"But you're not willing to deal with me now," I said.

"What?"

"Now I'm here, and I'm free, and my marriage is truly over, and I know how to use a hammer, and you've got your little girl and I've got mine, and we have a chance to see whether anything real could happen between us, and you won't take that step."

He shook his head and folded his cash register receipt carefully in half, in quarters, in eighths. "We gave it a chance, Kennedy. It wasn't right."

"But we didn't give it a real chance. We tumbled into it, and we weren't really honest with each other, and we didn't really know what we wanted. And now we do. At least I do. This is our moment, Declan." I hadn't realized it, when I'd decided to come into the city to see him, but saying it now it seemed as true as the blueness of the sky.

I noticed that the look on Katherine's face was like the one Amanda wore when she was watching the end of Cinderella, when the Prince was about to fit the glass slipper onto Cinderella's dainty foot. But Declan folded his paper again and shook his head. "We had our moment. Twice. And it's passed." He came around the bar and lifted Katherine off her stool. "Come on, sweetheart. I need to check on something in the kitchen and then we'll leave for Mommy's."

And, still carrying Katherine, he walked away from me into the kitchen, just like that. Brian looked at me with a sympathetic face and shrugged; I remembered whichever of us was on duty giving that same look to half a dozen women Declan broke up with during a slow afternoon at the bar. I remembered the women crying, or screaming after Declan. Once or twice, the bartender had to put his arms around one of them and lead her firmly outside, nodding in sympathy but really just trying to get rid of her. I wasn't going to let that happen to me.

I turned, wiping off my cheeks with the back of my hand, and went out blinking into the bright early October afternoon. I had to stand there on the corner for a moment until I could see clearly, and then I started walking away, not really caring which direction I was taking or where I was going. Declan was still the only thing on my mind and I felt less hurt by the way he'd treated me, I realized, than furious. And I didn't have a right to feel furious, I knew that: However badly he'd treated me, I'd treated him three times worse. Ten times worse. But I was angry nonetheless, because while everything I'd just said to him was unplanned and unrehearsed, I knew it was true and he wouldn't listen to me.

You can't force someone to be with you, I told myself as I trudged along, people whirling around me though I stared straight ahead.

But he loves me, I thought. He loved me in the spring and he loves me now.

I couldn't be sure of that. If he really loved me, wouldn't he want to be with me, at least give it a try? And I couldn't bully him into being with me. Look how I felt when Marco tried that, or Frank.

But I told myself I couldn't just give up, walk away, when I knew it was right. I did that when I left him for Frank, all those years ago, and then spent all that time living a life that was wrong for everyone.

I had Amanda. That wasn't wrong. He had Katherine.

Don't push it today, I cautioned myself. It was a mistake rushing into this relationship before. Maybe I was rushing into it again. Be patient. Sit back. Maybe it would be better if I waited six months, a year, ten years. Almost ten years went by last time and I came back, I was able to come back. Life is long.

Ten more years. And what would happen during that time? I'd marry someone else, he'd marry someone else? And those relationships wouldn't be quite right, and would break up, and we'd find each other again, or maybe the timing would once again be off and when I was alone he'd be with someone or vice versa, or we'd both feel too battered, or get too used to being on our own to ever be together again. Or one of us would get sick. Or one of us would die.

I turned around and without thinking ran back in the direction of the restaurant. It seemed as if everyone in New York was walking the opposite way and I had to dodge people and push past them and maneuver around them, fighting to dive into the ocean through the breaking waves.

I love him, I thought. I had to tell him, straight out, letting him know I meant it. I pictured myself walking in, him back behind the bar, the cash register tape in his hand, Katherine on the barstool drinking her soda, and me, breathless, saying, "I love you." Just that, "I love you." And him, after a moment's hesitation, coming around the bar and taking me in his arms and breathing, "I love you, too. Oh, darlin', I love you, too."

When I finally got to the bar and pushed through the heavy door, I had to wait again for my eyes to adjust. Then, in the darkness, I looked around blinking for a few minutes before I could believe that he really wasn't there. Brian was still behind the bar, rinsing glasses, turning them upside down onto a snowy towel. He had noticed me but was trying, I could tell, not to have to deal with me.

"Where's Declan?" I asked him.

"He's gone."

"Gone? Is he upstairs getting ready to take Katherine to her mother's?"

"No, they've left."

"But I've only been gone a few minutes. He said they had to get ready. They must still be upstairs."

Brian shrugged. "Ring the bell if you don't believe me," he said, "but they went up and got Katherine's bag and drove away about three minutes ago."

"Oh, shit," I said. "Maybe I can still catch them. The traffic's pretty bad out there."

Brian shrugged. "He tore out of here pretty fast. All I know is they're gone."

CHAPTER *twenty-two*

The time had come for me to pay a special visit to Jeannie. I didn't warn her I was coming, wanting to give myself a chance to back out if I got too nervous. I just walked down there—I could walk, from my new place—stopping at Starbucks for two lattes on the way and planning my arrival for a little before opening time so I wouldn't be interrupted by a customer.

"Hey," Jeannie said, breaking into a grin when she saw me. "Check out these pumpkins."

Lined up along the pine table were a quartet of enormous pumpkins, two reddish-orange and two ghostly white, ripe for a Fairy Godmother.

"Aren't these amazing? We took a drive in the country on Sunday and I found this weird farmer who grows them in his backyard. Think we could sell some on eBay?"

Jeannie, strictly a low-tech girl, didn't grasp the fundamentals of electronic commerce and, frankly, didn't want to.

"I think the shipping charges would be pretty prohibitive," I said, setting down the coffee and trying to lift one of the pumpkins, which definitely weighed more than Amanda. "God, what are they, filled with lead?"

"Gold," Jeannie smiled.

"Listen," I said, taking a deep breath. "I have a favor to ask you."

"What?" Jeannie said. "Did Mother Dear reneg on your loan?"

"No, nothing like that. In fact, you're going to like this one."

"Okay," she said. "Shoot."

"I want you to read my cards."

"Whoo-hoo!" Jeannie cried, rushing to the cabinet and extracting the silk-wrapped bundle. "I've been waiting for this for months. Hey, listen, this reminds me, I have a money-making idea for you. What if I taught you how to do this and when you were working here, you could do readings for twenty bucks?"

"Just do the cards, Jeannie."

"What changed your mind?"

"I'm desperate."

"Desperate? That sounds . . . desperate. What's the problem?"

"You know," I said, sighing. "It's Declan."

"I thought that was definitely over."

"For him," I said. "But I can't stop thinking about him. I'm just trying to figure out what I can do, if there's anything I can do that will bring us together again."

"You came to the right place." She'd finished shuffling, and then pushed the cards across the table for me to cut.

"It's my last resort," I told her.

Jeannie began laying out the cards in the cross pattern I remembered from long ago, with four cards rising on the right. My last card was the Ace of Wands. I thought I remembered an ace was good.

"What do they say?" I asked.

"Hmmmm," Jeannie said. "Hmmmmm."

"Jeannie, come on," I said, my heart skipping a beat. "Is it that bad?"

"No," she said. "Not exactly bad."

"Well, what do they say, for Christ's sake?"

"Okay," she said, looking up at me. "They say you should have a party."

"What?"

"That's what they say, that you should have a party."

"What kind of advice is that? I want to know about me and Declan."

"This is about you and Declan. See, there you are, The Lovers."

"I wish."

"You're surrounded by turmoil—look at this weeping woman with the swords—"

"That's me?" I said.

"She just represents unhappiness. But there are lots of good things, too—friends, family. I see romantic fulfillment resulting from a large gathering. So tarot's advice is: Throw a party."

"Maybe the large gathering means the bar," I said hopefully. "Maybe it's just trying to tell me to go back and see him at McGlynn's."

Jeannie shook her head firmly. "I'll help you," she said, trying to ease my party phobia. "But there's no way out of it. A party is what you have to do."

The girls were over the moon with excitement. Sure, they'd had birthday parties, of course, we'd hosted small dinner parties, but this was our first all-family pull-out-every-stop mondo bash.

The first idea was a simple housewarming party. Then, given the season, Amanda began mounting a campaign to give it a Halloween theme. Maya liked that idea because everybody could wear costumes and she and her friends could treat it as a campy, kitschy thing, much cooler than hanging out at some lame-ass party with a bunch of grown-ups and little kids.

I mailed an invitation to Declan and Katherine. I tried calling him to tell him how important it was to me that he come, but he wouldn't take my calls. So I just sent him the same invitation—a black construction paper bat with spidery silver writing on it—we'd sent to everyone else, and enclosed a note saying I'd love it if he could be there. Emphasis on the love.

Without warning me first, the girls also invited Frank, who asked if he could bring Sunny. Figuring this might be some weird part of my destiny as foretold by tarot, I agreed. Amanda, who was dressed as Barbie, natch, wanted Frank to come as Ken, but Sunny apparently had alternate costume plans for him. So I had been drafted to play Ken.

The night of the party, I came downstairs dressed in my baggy thrift store suit and white oxford shirt, accessorized with an old tie of Frank's that hadn't sold, with my hair up in a bun and a black mustache drawn across my upper lip. Maya groaned.

"Nobody's going to know what you're supposed to be, Mom," said Maya. "They're just going to think you're some old dyke."

"No," I said. "Look." To the lapel of my suit jacket, I'd pinned a nametag that said HI, MY NAME IS KEN.

"Oh, like that makes it real obvious," said Maya. "Come here. At least take off the tie."

"Noooooo!" cried Amanda.

"Amanda, don't you want Mommy to look pretty for the party, too, even if she is Ken?"

There was an argument Amanda could understand. She nodded in agreement.

"Okay—here, Mom." Deftly, Maya untied my tie and whipped it off. Then she unbuttoned the top three buttons of my shirt and, after considering, also undid the fourth.

"Yikes!" I said, pulling it closed. "You can see my bra."

"So? At least they'll know you're a woman. And take your hair out of that bun."

"Ken can't have long curly hair. I was going to wear a fedora."

"Okay, well, do you have to wear oxfords, Mom? Can't you at least wear high heels?"

"I'll never be able to dance in high heels. I'll never be able to even walk."

Maya sighed again. "I give up."

"It's not like you look so glamorous," I pointed out.

"Hey, I'm not the one who's trying to trap a guy," Maya said, grinning to reveal where she'd blacked out her two front teeth. Her costume was one of her own invention, a look she called "Bride Risen from the Dead." She'd shredded a white satin thrift store wedding gown and splattered it with fake blood, and she had the handle of the rubber knife plunging into the chest of the dress, with the blade coming out her back. Her hair was ratted so it stood straight out and was decorated with dead leaves. She'd smeared mascara under her eyes and bright red lipstick across her mouth.

Amanda, meanwhile was resplendent in a floor-length hot-pink sequinned gown and a blond wig that reached her waist.

"Do I look pretty?" she asked.

"Gorgeous, Barbie."

Amanda giggled. "Thanks, Ken."

"Look what I found!" It was Jeannie, in full witch regalia, in from the darkening garden with arms full of dried-out flowers and weeds: blackened rose hips, papery silver dollars, branches with a few shriveled leaves still hanging from them. She had several tin flower buckets, the kind florists use, lined up on the dining room table and she began filling them with her dead bouquets. On each vase she tied a black organdy bow, the effect appropriately macabre.

The night before, she'd taken me to the discount warehouse to buy supplies, and we'd spent the whole day preparing the food, decorating the house, and even embedding plastic spiders in the ice cubes. It was a full-scale extravaganza à la Jeannie, and I had my fingers crossed it would prove more than an evening of torture for me. The doorbell rang. Show time.

I couldn't move. I could barely breathe. My hair had come out of the bun of its own accord and my shirt sleeves were rolled up. If I had been wearing an undershirt I would have taken the shirt off altogether. My fedora was lost in the crowd, my suspenders kept slipping off my shoulders, and my oxfords had, I think, been thrown out the window. All the windows were wide open. The music was blasting. It was a good thing I'd invited all the neighbors, because otherwise they would have called the police.

I moved through the crowd, stopping to shout hello in someone's ear or smile and nod to a comment I couldn't really hear. In the yard, the trees twinkled with little white lights; golden lanterns swung from the branches. I could see the shadows of the children dashing through the dark, free and wild in the suddenly warm night, my own little Barbie among them. There were dozens of children out there, dozens of teenagers, too, sitting on the front porch and on the fringes of the garden, bending in close together, trading secrets beneath the overgrown rhododendrons.

"Wonderful party, darling!" It was my mother, arrayed as the fairy godmother, wafting by, unflaggingly waving her magic wand, which was actually a long cigarette holder with one of her gold-tipped cigarettes jammed into its end. She looked like Glinda the Good Witch. Stanislav followed, her obedient footman.

A short bald man in glasses and a frog's costume stopped me. "Hey!" he yelled in my ear. "Do you know who Kennedy is?"

This was the third time this had happened to me tonight.

"That's me," I yelled back.

"No, the guy Kennedy."

"I don't know any guy Kennedy."

"He's a contractor."

I laughed. "That's me. The girl and the contractor."

He looked taken aback but then he recovered. No suburbanite would risk insulting a contractor, not even a female one. "I wanted to talk to you about my kitchen," he said. "I live around the corner on Oak, and we're doing an expansion."

I promised to stop by the next week, and pushed on. Earlier in the evening, I'd been too busy and too distracted to eat or drink anything, but now I popped a carrot stick in my mouth and poured myself a glass of chardonnay from one of the innumerable bottles of wine that seemed to be sprouting up everywhere. Even though there was no sign of Declan, I was actually enjoying myself. Before this night, the house had been finished, but the party had made it home.

Some of the people had shown up in their regular clothes and some had come in costume, but none were as elaborate as the head-to-toe Cruella De Vil get-up on the woman who'd just come through the front door. She was wearing a full black-and-white wig, with a tailored suit, dalmatian-fur muff, and long cigarette-holder. From the looks of it, she'd brought her own dog with her: a shortish, thinnish man in an absurd dalmatian suit. When he turned around and faced me, I gasped and spilled the entire glass of wine in my hand. It was Frank.

Thank God there were enough layers of people between me, Frank, and Cruella that I didn't have to say hello right away. And that the bottle of wine was still within reach: I poured myself another glass, and drank it in one gulp. And Maya came to my rescue by choosing that moment to put on her dance mix and crank up the volume.

"Come on, Mom," she shouted in my ear. "It's time to kick this party into high gear."

She pulled me into the center of the floor, yelling, "This song is for you!"

It was Destiny's Child, "Independent Woman." I knew it because Amanda owned the *Charlie's Angels* video and we'd watched it at least fifty times. If the lyrics hadn't already been engraved upon my brain, I wouldn't have been able to understand them from the CD blaring at my noisy party, but I moved with Maya and closed my eyes and silently sang along.

Some of the older neighbors and the parents of small kids began to edge toward the door. Jeannie's husband Chip, who was dressed as a horse, trotted into the night carrying the equestrian Phoebe on his back. Still dancing, I stood on my toes and craned my neck, hoping that somehow Declan and Katherine had arrived without my seeing him. But they were not there. In the archway leading to the dining room, I saw Stansilav smiling down at Cruella, until Mom shot in and yanked him unceremoniously away.

I felt a rhythmic thump on my shoulder—less someone tapping me with their finger and more someone pummeling me with a small pillow. Swiveling around, I found myself eye-to-eye with my former husband, the dog.

"Hey," I said. "You look really ridiculous."

"What?" Frank shouted.

The next song had started, some rap number I didn't know but that inspired all Maya's friends to scream and start dancing. Maya was dancing with Jeremy, who had a green face and a large bolt sticking out of his forehead, Frankenstein-style.

"Never mind," I said.

Laying his paw on my arm, Frank pulled me gently away from the dancers and the stereo speakers.

"I can't hear," he shouted. "Can we go outside?"

The kids were still out there, racing around the moonlit garden with Amanda in the lead, though it was not as warm as you'd guess from inside. I shivered in my shirt sleeves and Frank tried to put a plush-clad arm around me. Though I believed he meant it kindly, I moved away.

"What is it, Frank?"

"I wanted to thank you for inviting us to the party," he said. "For including Sunny."

I shrugged. "I did it for Amanda."

"I know. But I think it's a good idea, for us to be friends. Well, maybe not friends, but friendly, you know, for Amanda."

I had my arms folded across my chest and I was watching the kids run like phantoms through the night. I remembered how much, as a child, I'd loved racing through the dark like that at parties, while the grown-ups drank and talked, oblivious.

"Don't you agree?" Frank said.

"Oh." I struggled to remember what we'd been talking about. Inside, Maya turned up the music yet again and a shout went up; everyone was dancing now. I saw her take the hands of her tow-headed Frankenstein and smile up at him. "Yes. I suppose."

"So instead of just barging ahead and doing this," he said, "I wanted to talk to you first, about the divorce."

I turned slowly, eyes narrowed, to look at him, ridiculous spotted ears sticking up from his head. "What about the divorce?"

"I don't think we should go through with it."

"Frank," I said, my heart suspended in my chest, "we've been through all this, we tried this summer . . ."

"No," he said. "That's not what I mean. I don't want to go through with the New Jersey divorce because the waiting time is twelve months, and I don't have that long. I want to go to the Dominican Republic, Kennedy. You don't have to go; you just need to give me a sworn statement that you agree with the divorce and the terms. Don't worry, I'll give you all the money that you need, for the girls and for you, too. And it will be over in a couple of days."

I was staggered. I was sure I wanted to be divorced from Frank, but I'd always seen it as a long process stretching out ahead, moving through several stages until finally we both would be legally free.

"When do you want to do this?"

"Next week," he said. "I'd like to leave Monday night, if you can get to your lawyer in time to sign the agreement."

"I'll have to see," I said, "and talk to him."

"Is there some problem?" the dalmatian asked.

"No, not really. I mean, I agree in principle. But I'm curious: What's the rush?"

"I don't want to tell Amanda this yet," he said, "but Sunny's pregnant."

It was just on that beat, when Frank said the word pregnant, that I saw Declan materialize through the gate, holding Katherine in his arms and pointing toward the lights and the people dancing inside. Katherine was dressed in the most beautiful and elaborate costume I had ever seen on a little girl, a dress of silver net and glitter that glowed in the moonlight, with a white fuzzy stole around her shoulders and a jeweled crown on her head, a miniature of the matching one Declan was wearing.

"It's okay, Frank," I said, laying my hand on his arm but staring at Declan. "The Dominican Republic, whatever, that's fine about the divorce."

"So you'll sign the papers on Monday?"

"Yes, sure, first thing, no problem." I patted him, much like I would pat a dog. "Tell Cruella I said congratulations. Just—excuse me now."

I left him then and walked as if in a dream around the dark side of the house to where Declan and Katherine were still standing near the hedges. I could see, as I drew close to them, that Katherine was wearing a perfect tiny pair of glass—or rather plastic—slippers.

"You came."

Declan smiled down at me, and for the first time in so long he looked relaxed, and gentle, and happy to see me.

"We came. Katherine wanted a chance to show off her costume. And I thought she might like meeting Amanda. We don't know many kids, down where we live."

"Katherine," I said, touching her gently. "You look so beautiful. Are you a fairy princess?"

She buried her face in the collar of Declan's gold brocade cape—from the looks of it, a remnant of upholstery fabric, and then looked up at me again.

"Cinderella," she said.

"And is your daddy Prince Charming?"

She nodded shyly.

"I'm so glad you're both here," I said, touching Declan's back and guiding him toward the house, a perfectly gallant Ken, feeling, now that my fingers were against his skin, that I would never be able to bear to let him go.

Katherine and Amanda were both stretched out on the sofa, lying on their backs with their heads touching, fast asleep despite the bright lights overhead. The neighbors had all gone home and Maya and a few of her friends, including Frankenstein, whose bolt had fallen off, exposing a disk of non-green flesh in the center of his forehead, were helping clean up. Jeannie was there, too, her witch hat still firmly on her head, Chip and Phoebe having left hours before. She was gathering orange and black paper plates while Declan held open a plastic bag for her. Beyond where he stood, through the window, I could barely make out a knot of teenagers, the tips of their illicit cigarettes glowing like tiny lanterns.

"Maya," I said. "You can go now if you want."

She cast a look at Declan, who was knotting the top of his bag while Jeannie moved on to wineglasses, then back at me. "Are you sure?"

"Sure I'm sure. Thanks for all your help. Have a good time. And don't smoke."

She kissed my cheek and gave Declan a friendly little wave, then took Frankenstein's hand and vanished outside with the rest of her friends.

"Jeannie," I said. "You don't have to do that. Really. You should go home, too."

"It's all right," Jeannie said, holding four glasses in each hand. "I don't want to leave you alone with this mess."

"I'm not alone," I pointed out. "Jeannie, thank you. But go home."

She stopped, looked at me, looked at Declan, and set down the glasses.

"Good night." She kissed me on the cheek.

And then she went over to Declan, stood on her toes, and kissed his cheek, too. "I never would have believed it," she said, "but you've turned into a really nice man."

And then she was gone, and outside the teenagers were gone, and except for the girls' soft snores, it was absolutely silent.

"Let's turn out these lights," I said to him, "and sit on the porch."

A wind had blown up, sending the mounds of dried leaves in the corners of the property skittering across the garden, crackling through the night. Just as Declan and I sat on the green-painted bench I'd set on the porch, the wind changed direction hitting us head on, blowing out the only jack-o-lantern candle that was still burning. I shivered and inched closer to him and the bench wobbled beneath us. He sat stiffly beside me and I was afraid for an instant that he was going to move away, or stand up, but suddenly he lifted his arm and wrapped his golden cape around me. I felt his hand through the thin cotton of my shirt and leaned against him.

"I love a man in a cape," I said.

"I love a woman in suspenders."

"I love a man who cleans up after a party."

"I love a woman who throws a party."

I love you, I thought. "I missed you," I said.

He sat there, looking straight ahead, waiting, it seemed. Then he said, "I saw Frank here tonight."

"Yeah," I said. "Could you believe that costume?"

"So what's happening between the two of you?"

"Nothing," I said. "He was here with his girlfriend. Did you see her? Cruella De Vil? Amanda asked me to invite them."

He fell back into waiting mode.

I touched his chest and said, lightly, trying to make it sound like a joke, really just wanting to get him to talk, "Are you jealous?"

"I'm wary, Kennedy. If I opened myself up to you again, and you left me again for him, three times . . ." He shook his head. "I think it would do me in, darlin'."

"But that's not going to happen. The divorce, we talked about it tonight. He wants to go down to the Dominican Republic for a quickie divorce. It seems Cruella's knocked up."

I was watching closely; he didn't even crack a smile.

"But even if she wasn't," I told him, wanting to make sure I was perfectly clear, "even if Frank weren't pushing it at this moment, we'd still be getting divorced."

"When it happens," he said, "I'll believe it."

I leaned closer, and kissed the corner of his mouth. "It's going to happen."

"Mmmmm." I could feel him wanting to resist. But he still kissed me back.

"Declan. It's going to happen."

I kissed him again, so hard I knocked the crown

right off his head. He wrapped his arms around me and pulled me to him. The bench swayed dangerously, creaking more loudly than the wind, but I climbed onto his lap. Inside, over his shoulder, I could see our daughters, still sleeping soundly, a pair of bare feet on each arm of the sofa.

I love you, I thought, and kissed him again.

Suddenly the church bells started ringing from the next block, the second quickly followed by a teenager's howl.

"What's that?" Declan murmured.

"Probably one of Maya's friends."

"No," he said, more alert now. "The bells."

"They ring them at midnight. You get used to it."

"Holy shit," he said, inelegantly pushing me aside and stumbling to his feet. "I promised Brian I'd take over for him. I was supposed to be back before now."

"Wait," I said. "Can't you call him? Try to get him to stay?"

"It was hard enough to convince him to come in for a few hours tonight." He was already moving through the door, crossing the dim living room, lifting Katherine from her sleeping place. "I'm sorry, Kennedy, I really am, but I've got to go."

I was still rooted in the front hall, trying to take it all in, but he swept through the door as the bells sounded for the eleventh time, then the twelfth. I hurried after him but he had already disappeared through the gate, and by the time I made it to the street all I saw were his taillights flash on and then vanish at the corner.

Slowly, I walked back to my house. There, beside the porch bench, lying on its side, was his crown. And in the living room, next to the sofa, was a tiny—a really, really tiny—glass slipper.

CHAPTER *twenty-three*

Frank and I stepped out of my lawyer's office in Montclair into a cold November rain. Frank patted the place above his heart to make sure, for probably the fifth time in the minute and a half since he'd put it in his breast pocket, that the document attesting to my agreement to the divorce was still there. Then he squinted up at the sky—the water falling down on his face apparently not evidence enough that it was raining—and opened his big black umbrella, sending a shiver of déjà vu down my spine. But it wasn't an illusion: We had in fact been in almost exactly this situation before, the day we met outside McGlynn's a dozen years ago. It had been November, and it had been raining. He'd been wearing a tan trench coat over a white shirt and a red tie and a gray suit, exactly like the ones he wore now. His hair and his face had gotten wet before he put up his umbrella, his oversized black umbrella. And then he'd said just what he was saying now: "Do you want to get a cup of coffee or a bite or something?"

I couldn't help myself; I smiled. I'd been planning to meet Jeannie at the shop—it was Monday, the day we were closed—to start setting up Thanksgiving displays. But that could wait.

"I could use some coffee," I said, the same thing I'd said back then. I wondered if he'd notice.

"I'm starving," he said. Also, the same thing he'd said back then.

"What's the matter?" I said. "Didn't you want to eat the food at McGlynn's?"

He looked at me quizzically. "What are you talking about?"

"The day we met," I prompted. "The conversation we just had."

"What do you mean?"

"Oh," I said. "Never mind. Sure, let's find a coffee shop."

The only coffee shop left in downtown Montclair was one that seemed to be frozen in 1974—neither old enough to be hiply retro nor modern enough to have sushi or organic mesclun on the menu. Instead, this one had brown leatherette booths, their seats held together with silver or bright blue duct tape, and tan marbled formica tables. The smell of onions on the fry permeated the air, although there didn't seem to be any actual onions on the grill, and the waitress had a

Marge Simpson hairdo recolored in bright orange. They served, of course, no cappuccino.

"Only regular coffee, hon."

With non-dairy creamer.

Frank ordered what he'd ordered that first day we'd gone out together and in fact the same thing he always ordered in coffee shops: a turkey club on two slices of whole wheat with mustard instead of mayonnaise and ketchup on the side. I should have known that first day, I thought, as I sat there watching him dip the most minimal edge of the sandwich into the ketchup—wouldn't want to get too liberal with a condiment—that Frank was all wrong for me. I should have paid for my coffee and stood up and shook his hand and gone back to my little girl in the East Village and the next day gone to work again at McGlynn's and told Declan we were obviously perfect for each other so we should just get on with it.

"I'm glad you're taking care of the divorce," I said. "It's better, getting it over with, now that we're both sure."

Frank nodded, exerting great effort to keep his lips tightly sealed while he struggled to chew the enormous bite he'd just taken. "The law imposes the standard waiting period for some very good reasons," he said, "but in essence we've been living separately for nearly a year now so I don't feel that I'm circumventing the state's divorce law or its underlying intent."

"There was that period this summer," I said. "Don't you have to restart the clock if you reconcile for a time?"

I was really only trying to annoy him, but he turned bright red and furiously swiped at his lips with the flimsy paper napkin. "We weren't living as man and wife, sharing a bed or, you know. So technically it doesn't count."

Frank always took very seriously the dictum that lawyers operate, personally and professionally, above the reproach of the law. He had receipts to document every dollar he deducted on his taxes, and claimed that he had never in his entire life gone through a red light, even at 3 A.M. with no one on the road for miles around. The closest he'd come to breaking up with me before we got married was when I told him I'd smoked at least my fair share of pot. But then he rationalized by saying that he hadn't personally done it, and I hadn't done it during the time we'd been together. So it was all right.

"I'm sorry, Frank," I said, touching his arm. "I was only teasing you."

"Oh," he said. "Oh. Okay."

"So how is it," I said, "being back at the firm?"

"Oh, it's fine, I suppose. Now I realize the whole yoga thing was just a fantasy. I mean, it would have been great if it had worked out, but law is really what I do."

"You're a good lawyer, Frank."

"Yes," he said. "Life isn't perfect, but I made my choices and I intend to make the best of them."

The old Frank, the brown-haired gray-suited straight-laced responsible Frank, had fully returned. It seemed he had finally left his old teenaged Ramones-loving self back on the beach forever. But I was surprised to find, sitting there across from the Frank I knew so well, that I was almost sad to see that rebellious surfer boy go.

"So how is it with you and Sunny?"

"Good," he said. "I mean, not ideal, but that's what relationships are like, right?" He gave a little laugh. "You and I have certainly lived through this. You meet, you fall in love, you think the other person is the moon and the sun, you think you're going to be happy and madly in love from then on. And then one day you find it's just . . ." His voice trailed off and he stared out the window, wiping his hands on his now-balled-up napkin. ". . . normal."

"Normal?"

"Yeah, you know. You come home, you have dinner, you talk about your day, you go to bed, you don't necessarily make love." He laughed again. "Well, Sunny, she's feeling really sick with the pregnancy. I mean, the morning sickness is terrible. And her breasts—well, you don't need to hear about that."

No, I didn't.

"I'm surprised," I said, "about the baby. After how she felt about Amanda."

"Oh, she likes Amanda. I may have, I don't know, exaggerated that a little bit. And the baby will be, you know, her own and everything."

He turned red again then and I thought of reassuring him, saying it was okay, I understood, that of course Sunny would love her own baby more than she could ever love Amanda, but instead I said, "But both children, I mean Amanda and the new baby, will be yours. I don't want you ever to abandon Amanda, Frank, and I mean abandon her in any way."

"I know that," he said. "Don't you believe I will always be a good father to Amanda?"

"You weren't a good father to her when you disappeared in September."

"I'm sorry," he said. "It was just so complicated. Wanting to come back, then you kicking me out, starting to see Sunny again, going back to the firm . . ."

"I know," I said. "But I have to watch out for my daughter."

He looked at me across the table, then suddenly he leaned toward me and reached for my hands. "Kennedy," he said. "After all this, I just have to say, I mean, I think." He shook his head and took a deep breath. "What I'm trying to say is, I'm happy with Sunny and all, but when I look back, I think, I wish she had never walked into the Oyster Bar that day. I wish I'd had lunch somewhere else, and come home to you like always, and that we were still together."

And I knew, his eyes shining with tears, what he expected me to say at that moment. He expected me to say that I wished it, too, that it was too bad, that we'd had a good marriage, and I would always remember it fondly.

But sitting there with him, being with him in so much the same way that I'd been with him at the very beginning, I knew that I was happy he'd met Sunny, that he'd needed her because he wasn't really getting the kind of love he wanted—deserved, really—from me. That I'd never loved him the way I now believed a woman should love her husband: without reservation, and totally, his body, his mind, his soul, him. I'd told myself that my resistance to the security and stability he was offering me was really immaturity, that I should grow up and be a good mother and love Frank, this man with a regular job, with a real dining room table, with an opening in his life for me and Maya. So I said yes, when all the time, deep in the core of me, from the very first day we met and throughout our marriage and even now, I was saying no. My unspoken and unheard no was what really propelled him to Sunny. I'd made him feel that the breakup of our marriage was all his fault when really it was all mine.

I took his hand and looked straight into his eyes and realized that if I had never loved him enough before, I loved him now, loved him as the father of my child and the companion of so many central years of my life and even as the agent of my freedom.

"Frank," I said. "Listen to me. I think Sunny is the right person for you. I know that Amanda is going to be okay and that she loves you, even that Maya loves you. I believe we're both going to be happier apart than we were together. You shouldn't feel guilty or sorry or any of that anymore. I wish you nothing but the best. And that is the truth."

CHAPTER *twenty-four*

Katherine's tiny glass slipper spent the entire week sitting on the hall table next to the silver bowl that held my car keys, waiting. A hundred times I wanted to call Declan and a hundred times I resisted. The next time I saw him, I wanted to have that piece of paper in my hand, proving I was a free woman. I imagined Frank running into problems with the Dominican authorities and not being able to get the divorce, I envisioned him losing some vital document, even losing his determination to go through with the whole thing.

But Thursday night Frank called me, back safe and sound with papers in hand, and I arranged to go into the city on Friday morning and meet him in the lobby of his office building to get my copies of the documents.

"Why are you so dressed up?" Amanda asked me in the morning before school.

"I'm going into the city today."

"What are you going to do there?"

"Oh, lots of things. I'm probably going to see De-clan."

"He's handsome," Amanda said. "Do you think next year on Halloween he'd be Ken?"

"Maybe," I said. "We'll have to ask him."

Frank was waiting when I got to his building. He handed me a manila envelope, which I hugged close to my chest, my bag being fully occupied by Katherine's glass slipper. Then he kept standing there, looking as nervous as he had on Monday and much paler than anyone should after three days in the Caribbean.

"Didn't you even get to the beach while you were down there?" I asked.

"No," he said. "Sunny didn't want to chance the trip, so I just stayed in the hotel in Santo Domingo, took some work along."

"Well," I said. "I guess this is it."

"Um, Kennedy?"

"Yes?"

"I have something I have to tell you."

I noticed tiny beads of sweat along his hairline. He'd left me, his girlfriend was pregnant, we'd officially gotten divorced—what more could he have to tell?

"Sunny and I are getting married."

"I figured that was the idea."

"No," he said. "I mean this weekend. I mean to-morrow. We're getting married tomorrow."

"Wow," I said. "That's—wow, congratulations, Frank."

"Really?"

"Yes," I said. "Really." And I did mean it, completely and thoroughly. "You should tell the girls."

"I will. But what I'm really trying to say is, I'd like the girls to be there. Originally we were talking about having a bigger wedding, but now with the baby and everything, by the time we plan it, it's just going to take too long. So we decided we'd get a judge I know to marry us in the apartment, and have a few friends there and Amanda and Maya. I mean if that's okay with you. And with them."

"Sure, Frank. Of course that's okay with me. And I'm sure they'll want to be there. But you should be the one to talk to them. They'll both be home by 3:30 today."

"Thanks, Kennedy. Thanks for being so nice about this."

"Not at all," I said. "I hope someday you'll do the same for me."

I stood on the sidewalk in the Village, staring unbelievingly at Declan's place. There, where the brass letters spelling out McGlynn's had shone just a month ago, a new sign was going up. The M, c, G, l, y, and one of the n's were down, and in their place were a B, an r, and an i. A man stood on a tall ladder, affixing an a. My mouth open, all I could do was stand there, shaking my head.

Finally, I was able to pull myself together enough to cross the street and go into the place, which except for the sign still smelled and looked and felt the same. A man moved behind the bar and, my eyes not yet adjusted to the dark, I said, "Declan?"

"No," he said. "It's Brian. We're closed yet."

"It's me, Kennedy," I said. "Is he here?"

Brian hesitated a moment and then said, "No. No, he's not."

"Well, where is he? Is he up in the apartment?"

"I said he isn't here. Now I'm sorry, but we're closed yet, so you'll have to go."

Brian then steered me, none too subtly, to the door, holding it open for me and locking it behind me. I stood there for a second, considering whether to press the buzzer to Declan's apartment, and then decided to cross the street and look up at his windows to see if I could discern any signs of life inside.

I was nervous, feeling as if the divorce papers I carried were my heart, which I was here to offer to Declan, now and forever. I'd been so focused on getting the papers, on getting ready to present myself to him, free and available, that I hadn't really worried about what was going on with him. I'd assumed, I realized now, that he was simply waiting for me to show up. But now, in the time since I'd seen him at the Halloween party, McGlynn's was no longer even McGlynn's and I realized I had no idea what else might have happened.

A siren sounded and I looked toward the traffic at the corner, and when I turned my attention back to the window I saw Katherine's small round pale face appear like a ghost's in the thick glass. She gazed down at me, and then she lifted her little hand and waved. I put up my own hand to wave back, when I saw another face appear behind Katherine's. A woman's face, pretty, with flame-colored hair and the mouth set in an angry line.

Another woman. The way paint behaves. I lurched away and started running then, and kept running, the sound of my heart and my pounding feet drumming in my ears. I should never have come here. God, I was such a fool, to think Declan could really be mine, to imagine he could be forever. He'd always been like this; he always would be. What idiocy, to think a suburban mom with plaster dust under her fingernails could inspire him to settle down.

I thought I heard him calling my name. You've got to learn to tell the difference, I chided myself, between what's really happening and what you want to happen. You did that with Frank, wanting him to be the perfect husband when he was actually smothering you to death, and now you're doing it with Declan, wishing he would be your one true love when he's never been able to be true to anybody, least of all you.

When I felt the hand grab my shoulder, I screamed and wrenched away, moving instantly from a trot to a sprint. In all my years in New York, I'd never been mugged and I wasn't going to let it happen to me now. I'd gotten fit over my months of working on the house and, as afraid as I was, it felt good to be able to run this fast, to feel the air searing my lungs and know I could keep going as far as I needed to.

"Kennedy!"

I couldn't believe it was real.

"Kennedy, for fuck's sake!"

Finally, I slowed down, and stopped, and turned around.

Declan was twenty paces behind me, doubled over, his hands on his knees, his back heaving with his breath.

Slowly, I walked back to him. He held up a finger, signaling me to wait. "Jesus," he finally managed to gasp out. "I. Thought. You. Going to. Kill me."

I laughed, I couldn't help it, partly from relief that he hadn't actually keeled over, and mostly because I was so thrilled he was there.

"Oh yeah," he said, standing upright, beginning to breathe normally again. "It's hilarious."

"I'm sorry," I said. "I thought you were a mugger."

"Is that why you were running?"

"No," I said. "I was running because of what I saw."

"What did you see?"

"That woman," I said, wondering how he could be so dense. "That redheaded woman in your apartment."

He looked puzzled for a moment, then burst out laughing. Now it was my turn to be confused.

"That's Lucy," he said. And, when I still looked confused, "Katherine's mother!"

"Katherine's mother. Oh! Oh. Katherine's mother."

"What did you think?"

"I thought she was your girlfriend."

Declan turned serious. "Kennedy, there's no other woman in my life."

"Am I in your life?"

He gazed down at me. "I don't know," he said. "Are you?"

I thrust the envelope toward him. "Here."

"What's this?"

"What I told you I was going to get this week. My divorce papers."

"Really?"

"Yes, really. This is it, Declan. The thing you said you needed."

"God," he said. "I don't know what to say."

"Say you want me. Say you want to be with me."

He opened his mouth, about to speak, and then he stepped to the side. "Let's walk," he said. "Do you want to walk?"

It was sunny but cold. He took my arm and I walked close to him, past the low brick houses that made this part of Greenwich Village so charming, my favorite corner of New York.

"I have to tell you something," he said finally. "I'm going on a trip."

"A trip?"

"Katherine and I. We're going to visit my mother in Ireland, and we're planning to stay at least through the holidays, probably longer. I've sublet my place for six months."

Six months. Two whole seasons. It had been nearly that long since I'd last slept with him, since that day after the flea market. I didn't know how I could wait for him that long again. But many of the things that had seemed puzzling now made sense.

"So this explains the sign on the bar."

"Brian and I have been talking about this for a while. When Katherine came to stay full-time, we got more serious."

"I thought you said you'd found a great school for her. I thought you said she was happy here."

"At school, yes. But the city isn't good for her. You know that, you tried to raise a child in the city. It's hard enough when your child doesn't have any problems. But for Katherine, it's all too overwhelming, too frightening. And with the bar, I just didn't have the time for her she needed."

"But Ireland. I can understand that you want to see your mother. And that she'd want to meet Katherine. But why do you have to stay so long? And what are you going to do after you return?"

He shook his head. "I don't know, Kennedy. I want to do what's right for Katherine. Sometimes I think the best life for her might be over there, where my family is, where things are gentler. My mother hasn't been well. I've been gone from home for so long, and I don't know how much time there's left to spend with her."

I was stunned. "But Katherine's mother . . ."

"Lucy's moving back to California. That's part of what precipitated all this."

I stared at him, fear beginning to simmer up from deep down inside me. Don't blow it, I told myself. Don't drive him away again. But if you don't tell him how you really feel, then you're starting out with him the way you did with Frank, not being honest, not saying the difficult thing and thinking that's going to make everything go more smoothly. And in ten years, the two of you will be trying to deal with the wreckage.

"Why didn't you tell me any of this?"

"You were a married woman, Kennedy. No matter what you said, no matter what you felt, you were still married to another man. I cared about you too much to let myself get hurt again if you were just going to end up going back to him."

"So why did you come to my party?"

"I was going to tell you then. I thought it would make it easier."

"And so why didn't you?"

"I couldn't," he said. "There were so many people, then Jeannie and Maya were there, and then when we were alone . . ."

"What? When we were alone what?"

"You were so beautiful. And I couldn't help it, I wanted just a few more minutes to be with you without your being so angry at me, the way you are now."

I was breathing deeply through my nose, gathering courage. "Don't go," I said suddenly. "Come live with me, you and Katherine. Please, Declan. Everything's right."

"I've got the tickets," he said. "We leave tomorrow. My mum is expecting us. Katherine's her only grandchild and I'm sure she'll have the whole fucking village out to greet us when we arrive."

"So the whole fucking village will be there next month. Or next summer. But if you leave now, Declan, it's just one more opening for things to go wrong between us."

He shook his head. "Maybe you need some time to let all this settle, Kennedy. The divorce, Katherine, the new house."

"No, maybe you're the one who needs time! All fall, you've been putting this on me, that I'm the one who needs to be sure, who needs to be free, that you're afraid I'm going to change my mind and hurt you again. But I think what you're really afraid of is making a commitment to me."

He opened his mouth, then clamped it shut and shook his head. "That's not true. I want to be with you. But I need to go to Ireland to see my family. And when I get back, if you still want me then, you'll be all the more ready and we'll take it from there."

"You're running away."

"I'm not going to Ireland to leave you."

"Yes, but funny how it takes care of that."

Fumbling in my purse again, I pulled out Katherine's little glass slipper and thrust it into his hands, and then I wheeled around and started walking away. He didn't come after me, and I didn't want him to. But before I crossed the street and disappeared around the corner, I turned to face him again, and said the only thing left for me to say.

"I love you, you know. I loved you the first time I met you and I've loved you all along. And anything you do without me from now on is just a big fucking waste of time."

"You really said that?" Jeannie asked, incredulous.

"I did." I was still reeling. I'd come straight to Jeannie's from my encounter on the street corner with Declan, and I'd been so unsteady on my feet that she'd run next door to buy me a bottle of beer, returning with Barb in tow.

"Anything you do without me is a big fucking waste of time." Barb chuckled and shook her head. "I've got to remember that one. I'll use it on my clients."

"So then what happened?" Jeannie asked, biting into a meatball hero.

"Then I just walked away."

Thinking about it, how hard it had been not to

turn around and look at him, how torn I felt getting into my car and driving out of the city, as if I was the one leaving him, I thought I was going to burst into tears.

"What now?" said Jeannie.

"I don't know," I said. "He's going to be gone until after New Year's, probably longer. He's sublet his place for six months."

"Well, you can't just sit around waiting for him to come back," said Barb. "You've got to find something to do that makes you happy, really happy."

"I've been thinking," Jeannie said, "that with the holidays coming and the house finally finished, maybe now's the time to expand the shop."

I looked around the shop. Branches, their dried leaves dangling, reached from a pair of stone urns I'd found in my new neighborhood in someone's garbage. Jeannie had found a great source in Wisconsin for fake wooden fruit, so real-looking it even had worm holes, and we'd filled the shop's vast collection of wooden and pottery bowls with golden apples and dark purple plums, gorgeous and inedible.

"It looks great in here," I said. "And I love doing the eBay thing. But I realize I can't be tied to the hours of a shop. I've got to be out and about, like I am with the renovation stuff, and also have flexible hours so I can deal with the kids."

"I remember when Patricia dumped me," Barb said.

Jeannie and I froze. We'd always suspected Barb was gay, but until now she'd remained resolutely in the closet.

"Same thing," Barb said, "whether the person you love is a prince or a princess. Anyway, my one true love was named Patricia, and when she left me I was so devastated I needed something hugely good in my life to balance out the pain."

"So what did you do?" I asked, expecting her to say she'd gone on a trip around the world, or blown thousands on an antique-buying orgy.

"Silky!" Barb crowed. "My ferret! I started with one, then I began breeding them and I've never looked back."

I shook my head, stifling a smile—at least she'd made me smile—and ignoring the meatball sandwich Jeannie was offering me. "I don't see my fulfillment coming from the animal kingdom."

"Okay," said Barb. "When were you happy? I mean really happy, as happy as you are when you're with Declan."

I thought. "Does it have to be with another person?"

"No! You just need to go after your passion, the thing that makes you so excited you plunge into it and forget all about the person you love, and then so tired at night that you don't wake up at 3 A.M. obsessing about them. Is there anything that makes you feel like that?"

I considered. With each of my babies, I'd fallen in love so thoroughly my feelings for everyone and everything else had paled for months and months. But I wasn't about to go off and have another baby to make me forget about Declan. I loved buying things for the store at auctions and flea markets, but that was temporary, a few hours of intense pleasure and then it was over.

"I loved working on my house," I said.

"So now you have the design and contracting," Jeannie said.

"And I like that," I said, "but I don't think that's what Barb's talking about. That's more like a job. But when I was fixing up the whole house—I mean doing the work myself, literally up to my elbows in it—I loved it. I'd wake up at six in the morning and I couldn't wait to get started, and the day would fly by and still I wouldn't want to stop at night." I shook my head. "I would never believe that I would say this, but I'm sorry that it's finished."

"But it *is* finished," said Jeannie. "You're not going to keep working on it just because you like to."

"I don't know," said Barb. "Maybe there's something here. You know there are people in town who fix up old houses and resell them. A lot of them are realtors, or work in partnership with realtors so they can get the really great deals. If you hadn't gotten in there your house would have been snapped up by one of those people."

"I hate those people!" I cried.

"But that's because you hate what they do to old houses—take out all the beautiful old windows and replace them with those horrible snap-in frame jobs, rip out every kitchen and bathroom and put in cheapo cookie-cutter cabinets and fixtures. I'd pick you to be my partner above any of these guys with ten times the experience but not a tenth of your taste."

For the first time since I'd walked away from Declan on the street, I stopped thinking about him, I stopped feeling as if I was on the verge of tears, and my heart began beating more quickly.

"But are there really good houses out there?" I asked Barb. "I mean, places that would be worth all the investment of time and energy? Plus, where would I get the money to buy the houses in the first place?"

"I've got the money and you've got the talent," Barb said. "And if you agree we'll split the profits, I'll find us the places."

"And then I'll move in lots of cool furniture when it's time to put them on the market," said Jeannie.

"That's the idea," said Barb. "Come on, girls. We're gonna look at some houses."

CHAPTER *twenty-five*

Silence. The girls had gone into the city, to Frank and Sunny's wedding, and were planning to spend the night in a room adjoining the honeymooning couple's at The Plaza hotel. I'd offered to pick up Maya and Amanda after the reception, but Frank had reassured me it was fine for them to stay over. "We don't have sex anymore these days anyway," he'd explained with a grimace—way more than I needed to know.

I built an enormous fire in the fireplace and spread photos of the house Barb had shown me, along with the disclosure forms and surveys and listing information and drawing paper, all over the living room floor. Yes, I was sad about Declan. But compared with last summer or last spring or even last year, when Frank and I were still together, I now was able to relish time alone and to feel happy and settled exactly where I was.

Several developers had already been scared away from the property that Barb was considering buying for me to fix up. It was originally the guesthouse for a large estate, now derelict, and was tucked behind the larger property on a little square of land that didn't have its own access to the street. The reason I thought I might be able to make this work was that the house on the other side of the guesthouse was owned by none other than Mrs. Trevino, Amanda's teacher. She had a strip of unusable land on the far side of her driveway—maybe she'd sell that to us to create a right of way.

I stood up and gazed out the window. New Year's wasn't that far away. Maybe Declan would come back after New Year's. Where would he live then, if he couldn't move back into his place? Here, I thought. He and Katherine could live here with us. Stop thinking this way, I told myself. He probably won't be back until the spring, and who knows whether he was even going to want to see me then, never mind move in with me.

I could imagine the guesthouse as lovely as it had once been, but with more practical features such as a proper kitchen and a bathroom with a shower rather than merely a sink-sized tub. The stage left over from its incarnation as a playhouse would have to be sacrificed to make a master bedroom. But that would still leave an enormous main room, filled with light from windows on three sides. And the place was incredibly private, surrounded by tall hedges on the parklike property of the estate.

Where was Declan now? On his way to the airport, already on the plane, already there, across the ocean? I imagined him packing his suitcase and Katherine's and locking the door to his apartment, maneuvering with her in his arms through a crush of people at the airport, sitting on the airplane helping Katherine buckle her seat belt, the plane lifting into the air leaving only clouds and ocean beneath them.

Wind rattled my windows and I shivered, setting down my pencil. So much for this project distracting me from thoughts of Declan. The fire was dying down and I went out onto the porch to gather more wood. The temperature had dropped and the trees, now leafless, were swaying against the nearly white sky. It was the kind of day, when I was still married, when I would cook the first pot roast of the season, and maybe a chocolate cake to boot, and end up eating most of both by myself. I shivered again and hurried back inside.

I had to call him now, try one more time. But no, I couldn't. I'd given him a chance, a dozen chances, and he'd made it clear, he didn't want me.

I felt tears spring to my eyes and bent over my drawing paper, blinking them back and taking a big breath to calm myself. I'd see him in a few months, I told myself. Maybe he was right, maybe I did need more time. I could spend Thanksgiving at my mother's, I'd have a wonderful time decorating the house for Christmas with the girls, maybe get away for a few days around New Year's. The time would pass before I knew it.

I tried to make a detailed list of everything that needed to be done to the guesthouse, but I'd write three words and my mind would be back on Declan. Was he still in New York? Was he thinking of me, too?

I imagined myself jumping in my car, racing into the Village, ringing his doorbell, another dramatic confrontation in his apartment, or at the airport, at the gate where his plane was leaving for Shannon—or was it Dublin?—begging him not to go, him saying I was right, he would stay, us falling into each other's arms.

But that only happened in movies. Didn't it? I could go. I could do it. But where was I going to go? There were three international airports within an hour of his apartment; he could be at any one of them. Or none of them. I should start by calling him at home.

His phone rang. And rang. And rang. He always had a machine but now there was not even a way to leave an electronic message. The phone wasn't disconnected, which was, I guessed, a good sign, but no one was picking up either. What did that mean? That he'd just run downstairs for something and hadn't turned on the machine? Or that he'd left and the phone was about to be turned off?

I rushed to the hooks by the front door and grabbed my gray velvet jacket. I'd just go into the city. But maybe I should go to the airport. But which airport?

I knew. I'd call the bar. He might be there. Or someone there might know if he'd left yet, or what airport he was leaving from. Though Brian had not seemed very willing to help so far. Hands shaking, I dialed the number, and was relieved, maybe against all reason, when Brian answered.

"Brian, it's Kennedy. I have to find Declan. It's really important."

"He's not here."

"Has he left for Ireland yet?"

"I couldn't say."

"Brian, come on, give me a fucking break. Is he still in the city? Has he gotten on the plane? Do you know which airport he's gone to?"

"Why do you want to know which airport he's gone to?" he asked suspiciously.

"Listen, Brian, I've got to find Declan, I've got to talk to him. Please just tell me where he is."

"You listen to me," said Brian. "If you really want to do Declan a favor, stay in your fucking house. Do not go looking for him at any airports. Do not come into the city. Just stay out there in Jersey where you belong, all right?"

And he slammed down the phone.

I stood there, swearing under my breath, wanting to

call him back and somehow threaten or cajole or bribe him into telling me where Declan was, but then I decided that would be an utter waste of time and emotion. The only thing to do was go there, somewhere, anywhere. Newark Airport was just twenty minutes away. I'd go to the international terminal, check on any flights to Ireland, start there. I just knew I couldn't stay sitting in my living room.

I snatched up my purse and yanked open the front door, my mind already racing ahead to map out the fastest route to the airport, to figure out where I was going to park, thinking of which airlines flew to Ireland, whether there was any chance they'd tell me on the phone what flight Declan was on. I was focused on the ground but not really seeing anything, so I nearly collided with Declan before I actually saw him.

"Oh my God."

"Kennedy."

We didn't even need to step closer to one another for him to wrap his arms around me and hold me tight.

And that's when I started crying, realizing as the tears came how much I'd been holding in all day, and yesterday, and for months and probably years before that. I cried until my face was drenched with tears, my voice thick and choked.

"You came to say good-bye," I finally managed to say.

"No," he said. "No. I've come to stay, Kennedy."

"You're going to stay in America?"

"No, darlin', I'm going to stay here with you."

"You want to stay here in my house?"

"That's what I had in mind," he said, hesitating. "Is that all right?"

"Yes!" I cried. "Yes, yes! I was going . . . I don't know where I was going. I was just going to find you. To try and find you. To tell you again not to go."

Declan was smiling. "Where were you going to look for me?"

"I don't know, the airports, starting with Newark. I talked to Brian and tried to get him to tell me where you were, but he told me I should stay home and leave you alone. I know he's your friend, but that guy is such an asshole."

Declan burst out laughing. "He knew I was coming out here to see you. He was trying to keep you from leaving the house!"

"Not very elegantly."

"No," Declan said. He backed me across the threshold and into the house, kicking the door shut behind him. "But I'm not all that elegant either. Are you prepared for that?"

"I think so."

"You've got a nice tidy little female household going here. Are you ready for a big not-very-tidy male to arrive and mess everything up?"

"How much?"

"Hmmm?"

"How much are you going to mess things up?"

"Um," he said, "well, I do have a tendency to leave clothes lying around."

"Really? What do you mean?"

"Well, say, if I helped you off with your jacket, like this—" he took off my velvet jacket "—I might just throw it here." He tossed it onto the staircase.

"That's shocking."

"Oh, I know. And I'm incorrigible, too. For instance, you express your shock at what became of your jacket, but if I took off your sweater—" and here he tugged at my black turtleneck "—I'd toss it right onto the floor."

He stopped then, a look of alarm spreading across his face.

"What's wrong?" I said.

"Where are the girls?"

"With their father on his honeymoon. Where's Katherine?"

"With Lucy."

"Okay, then," I said, pulling off his jacket. "I guess we're really alone."

We kissed, a long, slow, this-really-counts kiss, and undressed each other at our leisure, and lay down on the living room floor, stopping only to pile more wood on the fire, and stayed there all afternoon and into the night. The next day we would pick up our clothes and drive into the city and collect Katherine from where she was staying with her mother and pick up Maya and Amanda from The Plaza and begin creating our family and our life together. But for that one tiny moment, we pretended it was just the two of us, and there was no other world.

CHAPTER *twenty-six*

Stanislav insisted that our Thanksgiving dinner always include a Polish ham, smoked by him on the homemade wood-burning barbeque that was the only thing he brought with him when he moved in with Mom. Mom, however, would not be pushed aside and always made a turkey, too, the one major meal she produced herself in the entire year. She had a secret technique which she wouldn't even share with me, mostly, I suspected, because her secret seemed to consist of shoving the turkey in the oven and not doing anything to it. Maya had been in charge of setting the table since she was old enough to reach it, and Amanda devoted the entire week before the holiday to constructing place cards. My job was everything else, a job that Declan had insisted on taking off my hands.

He'd been busy for days, constructing elaborate

hors d'oeuvres that he stored in the freezer, rolling out pie crusts and peeling apples, pureeing sweet potatoes and butternut squash and real pumpkins, collecting exotic varieties of potatoes and lettuces, baking bread.

"You're going to spoil my mother," I told him.

"I want her to like me."

"She's going to like you."

"I don't know," he said. "She sounds tough to please."

When I thought about it, she hadn't liked Marco or Frank, the only two other men I'd ever brought home, and she wasn't disposed to like Declan either, though I hadn't told him that. Now, the two of them were alone in the kitchen, Declan peeling potatoes while Mom pretended to do something to the turkey. I was sitting in the living room, where I had been ordered by both of them to stay, while Maya folded napkins and Katherine and Amanda played with my childhood dolls. I was wondering what Mom and Declan were talking about in there and growing more anxious by the second.

Finally I hopped up and opened the swinging door that led from the dining room to the space-age kitchen in time to hear Mom say, "Look at the size of your hands. You must be hung like a horse."

Yikes. "Mom!" I said, barging into the room. "Why don't you come for a walk with me and the girls?"

"Oh, no. I'd much rather stay here with your handsome friend. I was just telling him how much he reminds me of my dear husband Stan."

"Yes," I murmured. "I heard that. Need any help, Declan?"

"I'm fine, darlin'," he said, winking at me. "Enjoyin' myself."

"Run along now," my mother said, as if I were Amanda and Katherine's age. "We'll be just fine."

It was a bright day, warmer than usual for the end of November, but the grass was muddy from an overnight rainstorm and so we stuck to the road that led down to the grove of birches and the little wooden bridge. Stanislav, who was standing by his smoking rusted barbeque puffing on a cigar, smiled and waved to us. Once we passed beyond his smoke field, the air smelled newly washed, nearly fertile. If you closed your eyes, you could almost believe it was spring.

"This is my favorite holiday," Maya said, as the two little girls scampered ahead.

"Really?" I said, thinking that this was an unmistakable sign that she was growing up. "Better than Christmas?"

"Frank wrecked Christmas for me."

"Oh, Maya. I'm so sorry to hear that you feel that way." I hesitated. "So this is okay, all of us having Thanksgiving together?"

"Yeah, why wouldn't it be okay?" Maya stopped in her tracks and I stopped with her. Only a few weeks had passed with us all squeezed into the house together, and everyone had been forced to make adjustments. Declan had gone very quickly from no kids to one to three, my girls were alternately wary and giddy around him, and he and I were still working to balance the demands of work and kids with our near-constant desire to be alone in the bedroom, tearing each other's clothes off. And then there was the house renovation business, which, with Declan on board, had suddenly taken off, with three houses under construction.

"Maybe if I ruled the world," Maya said, "it would still be just be us, alone together. Or maybe it would be you and me, back in New York with my real dad, with Marco. But I like Declan and I'm okay with this. Really, Mom."

"And with Katherine, too?"

Maya broke into a grin at the mention of Katherine's name. If they were still somewhat uneasy around Declan, both girls had taken quickly to Katherine, who seemed dazzled to find herself suddenly with two sisters.

"I was thinking," she said, "that maybe I could help you do the Santa Claus thing for Amanda and Katherine this year. Try to get into Christmas again that way."

"That's a great idea. I'd love that. Declan would love that. He's totally inexperienced."

"So what was the deal with him and Katherine?" Maya asked. "Did Katherine's mom, like, not let him see Katherine until now?"

"No," I said, afraid the truth might turn her against Declan but not wanting to tell her anything less. "It was really Declan's fault. He didn't want to have kids, and Lucy left him before Katherine was born. It was only after we started going out that he decided he wanted to see her."

We walked along quietly, nearing the grove of birches. Up ahead, Amanda had taken Katherine's hand and had led her into the grass, where she was pointing out a woodchuck that was stripping the leaves from a plant at the edge of the woods. Even though Katherine was actually a few months older and a few inches taller, Amanda had begun behaving like the big sister, showing Katherine the world. I thought of calling them out of the grass so their matching red patent leather mary janes—which Amanda had chosen for both of them—wouldn't get muddy, but decided to let it go.

"Listen, Mom, I want you to tell me the truth," Maya said. "You and Declan aren't having a baby, are you?"

I burst out laughing. "Four kids!" I said. "No, I don't think so. Not anytime soon, anyway."

"Because I know you kept those baby clothes," she said. "From the yard sale. I saw them when we moved."

I'd forgotten about that. But now I wondered whether this was really her concern.

"Are you worried that I'm going to marry Declan?" I said gently.

Maya looked at me as if I'd pulled a booger out of my nose and eaten it. "No," she said. "I'd assumed you would marry him. Why would I be worried about that?"

"I just thought with Frank getting married to Sunny," I said, "and your dad married to Tina, maybe it would make you nervous to think of me getting married, too."

"What makes me nervous," she said, "is the idea of you guys *not* getting married. Don't you want to get married?"

I called to Amanda and Katherine, who had begun to wander into the woods, and we all began heading back uphill.

"*I* do," I admitted, the first time I'd said this out loud, "but I don't think he's ready. I don't think he really believes in marriage. I mean, I know he loves me, I know he wants to be with me, to stay with us, forever, I don't know, as much as I have any confidence in forever. But marriage." I shook my head. "He's never going to ask me."

"You should ask him," Maya said.

Amanda and Katherine were racing ahead of us, playing tag, giggling as they passed Stanislav, who still had his cigar in his mouth and was hoisting his ham from the grill with two enormous forks.

"I don't think so."

"Oh come on, Mom. Move into the twenty-first century."

"Maybe next year. Or the year after. Not now."

We stopped in the driveway. The girls banged open the door and clattered inside. I heard my mother yelling out to them to slow down, heard Louis Armstrong warbling from the stereo and caught the scent of the turkey and what I guessed was sweet potato pie.

"And to think," Maya said, "that I had almost decided that I wanted to be like you instead of like Gram."

My mouth dropped open. "Really?" I said. "You wanted to be like me?"

"Not anymore," Maya said. "Let's go inside. It's time to eat."

Pie time. The eight of us—Jeremy had shown up after eating dinner with his family, in time for dessert—sat sprawled around the table, barely able to pick at the slices of apple, pumpkin, and cherry pie piled on our plates, but unable to resist, either. Amanda lowered her head to her plate and sucked up the hillock of whipped cream mounded on top of her pie; Katherine, giggling and wide-eyed, took it all in and then followed suit.

"I don't remember you ever doing such a thing as a child," Mom said to me.

"That's because you never ate with me as a child," I said.

"Oh, poo. Poor, poor Kennedy. I ate with you *constantly* throughout your childhood. The endless cut.

ting of those vile little grilled cheese sandwiches, the orange stuff oozing out." Mom shuddered delicately.

"It's okay, Mom," I said. "You were busy."

"Did Kennedy tell you that my second husband was quite a famous singer?" Mom said brightly to Declan. "Well, semi-famous, anyway, back when singers actually sang. Hal McAndrew. Kennedy has his last name, though I think she would agree that she was more fond of my fourth husband, Murray, who left me this property and treated her the way a real father should."

"And Murray came right before Stanislav?"

"That's right. And of course Stan here is by *far* the most studly of the bunch."

I felt myself turn bright red and even Maya covered her face with her hand, but Jeremy laughed loudly and said, "Far out, man."

"But still," my mother said, "I think second marriages have real potential. Who knows what great things might have happened if Hal hadn't died?"

I stood up. "Mom, you divorced Hal long before he died. Is everyone finished with their pie? Are you going to eat that, Mom?"

"Put down that plate," my mother snapped. "Sit down. I'm not finished lingering at the table. Tell me, Kennedy, what about you and Declan? He's a very nice man, fabulous cook, huge hands . . ."

I hurried to cut her off. "Mom, you're embarrassing me."

"Okay, I'll ask Declan then. What about it? Let's face it—neither of you are spring chickens. You've got three children under your roof. You're living together, for land's sake. When are you going to make it official?"

Declan's face was bright red. He was leaning back in his chair and looked as if, at any moment, he'd fall over backward.

"Mom," I said. "Will you please stop? We only just got together. Our children are going through these huge adjustments."

"I think what Gram is trying to say is that, if you decide to get married, she'd be fine with it, and so would I," Maya said, giving me a significant look.

"Don't push me!" I cried, casting a nervous glance at Declan.

"I don't understand," said Mom, still oblivious. "I was a single mother, too, you know, and if I met someone, and they were nice, I either married them or that was it, it was over. Otherwise, what was the point? Onward, I always say. Up—"

"Upward. I know." I was on my feet again, hyper-aware of Declan sitting speechless beside me, but afraid to look at him. I was so agitated I couldn't control my voice and found I was shouting. "Mom, I'm serious, leave me alone! We're not getting married!"

With that Declan leaped to his feet, knocking over his chair. He started to bend to pick it up but then just scowled and stalked out the French door, leaving it open as he strode away down the lawn toward the nearly dark woods. We all gaped after him, long after he disappeared from sight, until I finally walked over to the door and shut it.

"Now look what you've done," I said.

"No," said Mom. "Now look what *you've* done."

Katherine and Amanda were settled in front of *The Wizard of Oz,* lying on the floor on pillows dragged down from the chairs and sofas, and Maya and Jeremy half-reclined beneath an afghan on the pillowless sofa, watching the childhood favorite through hooded eyes. My mother announced that she and Stan were going to bed early. Everyone seemed to be making a great effort to ignore the blowout, though they all seemed to be succeeding better than me. I finished the dishes and wiped the counters three times and stood in the kitchen staring out the window thinking that any second I would catch a glimpse of Declan coming back.

Finally I couldn't stand it anymore and asked Maya to watch the girls while I went out searching for him. I grabbed the big silver flashlight that Stan kept stashed under the sink and went out into the night, shivering against the chill that had settled over the countryside with the darkness. Declan had been out here at least an hour. Our car was still parked around the corner on the gravel drive—that made me breathe a sigh of relief—but he could have walked into town, even hitchhiked back to our place, or into the city.

Hugging myself, I walked tentatively down the drive toward the woods. It was so dark.

"Declan?" I called, not wanting them to hear me inside. "Dec?"

I was nearing the woods. I didn't want to go in there, even if I stayed on the road and the bridge. Something scuttered through the dry leaves, making me stop cold.

"Declan?"

I turned around then, really just for a reassuring glimpse of the house, and that's when I saw the fire. Slowly, not knowing what it was I was looking at, I walked back up the driveway until I could make out the shape of Stanislav's huge barbeque and realized the orange glow was coming from it. My heart thumping, I moved faster, thinking it was not supposed to be burning, might be about to burn out of control, when I saw something that made me stop again. There was Declan, leaning over the barbeque, poking at the fire in what I guessed was an attempt to keep warm. I hurried toward him but he didn't look up, didn't seem to see me.

"Declan," I said, when I got close enough not to shout.

He started and then smiled enough to at least let me breathe again. "It's fucking freezing out here."

"What are you doing? Why didn't you come in?"

"I just needed some time," he said. "Clear my head. Is everything okay in there? Is Katherine . . . ?"

"Katherine's fine. Listen, I'm really sorry about my mother. She loves to be outrageous and a lot of the time she crosses the line."

Declan shook his head and rubbed his hands over the fire. "That's all right," he said. "What she said didn't bother me."

"Oh come on, Declan, be honest. You jumped up and left the house. You've been standing out here in the cold for over an hour. Don't tell me that what she said didn't bother you."

"Okay, Kennedy, you want me to be honest?" He stopped rubbing his hands and looked straight at me. "What your mother said didn't bother me. What you said bothered me."

"Declan," I began. "I know you haven't lived in a big extended family for a long time, but some squabbling at the dinner table . . ."

"I'm not talking about the squabbling. I'm talking about what you said, about not wanting to marry me."

I caught my breath and peered through the darkness at him. I ventured a step closer.

"You mean you're upset because I said I *didn't* want to marry you?"

"Yes, you eejit! What do you think?"

"But I *do* want to marry you!" I cried. "I said that because I didn't want to scare you away!"

"Scare me away?" Now he was moving next to me, gathering me in his arms. "Why would that scare me away?"

"I don't know. I didn't think you were interested in marriage. I thought it was too soon."

"I thought it was too soon for you," he said.

I took a deep breath. He was all around me now, and I only had to whisper for him to hear me. "I'm ready," I said.

"Marry me," he whispered back. "Marry me, Kennedy, as soon as we can arrange it."

"Yes," I said, without a sliver of doubt in my heart. "Yes I will."

CHAPTER *twenty-seven*

I woke up at dawn on the morning after Christmas and reached for Declan, but he wasn't there. I had a moment of panic but then I remembered, of course, he'd left late last night. Today was our wedding day and he'd gone to stay with Brian, who would be his best man. We'd meet again today at the altar—or rather, at the fireplace downstairs in the living room.

I stretched, the air in the bedroom icy against my arms. With all the leaves off the trees the house was bright, even this early in the morning, and this morning seemed even brighter than usual. When I edged out from under my down comforter and pushed one corner of the filmy white curtains aside I saw why: In the night, a crust of icy snow had fallen and the branches were covered with a layer of sparkling white, glistening like diamonds. I thought of waking the girls to show them, in case the sun melted it all before they were out of bed, but then selfishly decided no, not today.

I pulled on a thick pair of socks and a huge old cashmere turtleneck over my nightgown, tiptoeing my way downstairs. I flicked up the heat but not too high: I was going to treat myself to an early morning fire. Flipping the switch on the coffeemaker and then plugging in the Christmas tree lights, I knelt by the fireplace and carefully built a teepee of wood, then set it all aflame.

A year ago I hadn't even known how to build a fire. A year ago, exactly a year ago, I'd woken up early, before anyone else in the house, and lain there beside Frank, wanting to get out of bed so I wouldn't have to deal with the possibility that he might try to make love, fantasizing about sitting alone in front of the fireplace with a hot cup of coffee, but not knowing how to build a fire or even work the bells-and-whistles coffeepot he'd bought me for Christmas, tossing my old one in the trash. Pathetic.

I didn't want to get married on the anniversary of the day Frank left me, but we couldn't do it before or on Christmas because that would steal the holiday from the kids, and we couldn't do it after New Year's because we had too many construction projects launching then. Plus we couldn't bear to wait that long. And between Christmas and New Year's, we had to squeeze in a wedding trip to Ireland, *en famille,* replacing the trip Declan didn't take in November, since his mother wasn't well enough to travel here for the ceremony. When I realized that December 26 was the perfect day, my first impulse was that I couldn't marry Declan on that cursed day. And then I thought: that day isn't cursed. That was the luckiest day of my life.

As the sun rose higher, I heard the *drip drip drip* of the ice and snow melting from the trees onto the roof. The girls were snoring softly overhead. I poured myself another cup of coffee and threw an extra log on the fire.

With Marco, I had always, from the first morning we were together until the day I changed the locks, been on edge, tense, wondering—What does he feel now? What will he do next? He was like a storm whose course and intensity I was powerless to alter. And I had loved that, for a time, had loved living in a romantic drama, ripe with sex and kisses and passion and fighting and making up from fighting. But then we had a child, and I got tired of the drama, the fighting; I couldn't do it anymore. Didn't want to, and couldn't.

Frank was a decision, an affair of the head rather than one of the heart. But it was, I realized now, a decision I was constantly revisiting, continually trying to talk myself into. I talked myself into going out with him, taking him seriously, moving in with him, marrying him, staying with him. Except after a while, certainly after Amanda, I stopped second-guessing our relationship, because I was too scared, and didn't know how I'd make my way in the world. But I never stopped wanting to leave.

With Declan, there was no storm, no decision. He just was. We just were. Being with him was like being with one of my children, in a sense, in that I loved him absolutely and without question, and knew that I would love him always. We were already in the same family. And yet, looking at him across the kitchen as he mixed twin glasses of chocolate milk for Katherine and Amanda, or working with him to refit a cupboard door in a customer's kitchen, I sometimes could hardly stand to wait the hours until we were in bed alone.

Tires crunched on the icy gravel outside and my mother's white Mercedes pulled into view. Hearing the car door slam I braced myself for the sound of one of the girls calling me from upstairs but they seemed to sleep on as I scrambled to my feet and pulled open the door so Mom wouldn't ring the bell, holding my finger to my lips to warn her to be quiet. She held out two large silver boxes to me.

"What's this?" I asked, setting them on the hall table.

"Presents. Girls still asleep?"

I nodded. "For the moment. It's still early. Sit down with me and have a cup of coffee."

"The house looks great," Mom said.

"I thought this was enough," I said, indicating the Christmas decorations—the tree, the boxwood gar-

land, the silver ornaments hanging from the chande-
liers. "But Jeannie's bringing more, if you can believe
that. She says right now the look is Christmas, and it
needs to be Christmas wedding, whatever that
means."

"Darling," Mom said, taking both of my hands in
hers. "I have to ask you this. Are you absolutely sure
about going through with this?"

"Absolutely."

"Good. I could tell. When you married Frank, I
didn't even ask you because I thought it might send
you screaming away from the altar."

"You mean you knew I was conflicted about marrying Frank?"

"Well, of course. Everybody knew, especially when
the minister said, 'You may kiss the bride,' and you
turned your head so Frank had to kiss your cheek."

"Oh God, I'd forgotten about that," I said. "You
know Frank is going to be here today."

My mother stiffened. "No, I certainly did not
know that. What a perfectly ridiculous idea."

"Amanda really wanted him here," I said, "and he
and Sunny are taking her for the night so they can celebrate Christmas before we leave on our trip."

"What about Maya?"

"Maya's going to Marco's for the evening."

"Land alive. Don't tell me he's going to be at the
wedding, too."

"No, Mother. But he'll show up during the reception and if he wants to drink a glass of champagne I'm not going to throw him out."

"I would never invite an ex-husband to any of my weddings."

"Marco and I were never married."

"Ex-boyfriend, lover, you know what I mean. A wedding is a fresh start, Kennedy. If you can't say no to all these men lurking around from your past, you should elope the next time you get married."

"I'm not getting married again, Mom."

"You've said that before."

"Jesus, Mother, I hope I never get as cynical as you."

"Don't worry, dear, for better or worse, you're nothing like me. Now listen, are you certain you want me to give you away? Stanislav is perfectly willing to do it."

"Mom, I'm very fond of Stanislav, but I'd really rather have you, if you think you can stand this break with tradition. If not, I don't mind at all walking down the stairs by myself."

"Nonsense. Of course I'm delighted to do it."

"Mommy!" It was Amanda, calling from upstairs.

By the time I coaxed Amanda and Katherine out of bed and through their bathroom routine, bundled them in warm socks and sweaters over their pajamas, and the three of us piled into Maya's bed and worked on her to wake up, my mother had made another pot of coffee and scrambled a pan full of eggs. Then, while Mom was feeding the kids in the kitchen, Jeannie arrived with yards of white moire ribbon to tie at the edges of the garland, and buckets full of white roses and holly and a trove of silver containers to put them in. Then the caterers showed up, and someone put on some music, although the radio was already spewing news from the kitchen. The little girls were squealing as they chased each other through the house while Jeannie barked orders from atop a ladder and my mother gave Stan instructions via cell phone. The doorbell rang; the wedding cake was here. And then the cases of champagne arrived. Someone was setting up folding chairs in the living room while another person put leaves in the dining room table then laid it with a starched white cloth. I stood on the stairs watching it all, unnoticed by everyone, feeling first as if I should be helping or at least offering advice and then thinking, No, this is perfect. My part comes in when my hand finally touches Declan's.

I tiptoed upstairs and hopped into the shower, feeling as if I'd pulled off a coup more remarkable than buying the house by making it in here before Maya. I took my time, too, washing my hair twice and shaving even the backs of my thighs. Once my shower was over, I rubbed lotion carefully all over my body, and moisturizer into my face, and massaged styling cream into my hair. I clipped my fingernails and toenails. Downstairs, I heard Amanda shriek—nothing serious, I could tell—and then heard Mom tell the caterers to be careful of something, I didn't know what. The bathroom window rattled against the icy wind, but I kept moving slowly, luxuriating in having both a reason to get ready and plenty of time in which to do it.

No one had seen my wedding dress, not Jeannie, not Mom, not Maya although she'd begged relentlessly. I'd hidden it from her by hanging it in the basement, where she was afraid of encountering spiders, and had smuggled it upstairs with the Christmas presents, concealed beneath an oversized linen dress. Now, hearing Maya slam the bathroom door and then turn on the shower, I took it out from beneath its linen shroud and admired it: a slim strapless satin Valentino, vintage mid-sixties, that fit as if it were made for me. In red. Very bright red.

I'd bought black and red lace hooker-worthy underwear to go beneath it, and pale shimmery stockings that hooked to a garter belt, and silver shoes with curvy heels and pointy toes. Now, I put all these things on and then I slipped on my red dress and stepped back, looking at myself in the mirror. I'd tried on the dress in the store and not since then, obeying some vague feeling that to wear it before the proper time might bring me bad luck.

There came a sharp knock at my bedroom door and I heard Mom's voice: "Kennedy? Do you need anything right now or can I get Katherine and Amanda ready?"

"That'd be great, Mom," I called.

I'd already decided that the only jewelry I wanted to wear was the silver and onyx pendant that Declan had bought me that day at the flea market. I had just managed to fasten the clasp behind my neck when another knock sounded at my bedroom door.

"Yeah, Mom?" I said.

"No," said Maya. "It's me. Can I come in?"

I opened the door for her, hiding behind it so no one else would accidentally see my dress. Then I closed the door slowly and stepped back and spread my arms. Her eyes widened as she took it in.

"Wow," she said. "Awesome."

"You really like it?"

"Are you kidding? Totally. You know Chinese brides wear red. I'd wear that for my own wedding."

"You mean if you were Chinese and already had two kids with two different men, neither of them the groom?"

Maya giggled. "That's right. If I was a slut like you, Mom. Hey, can I do your hair?"

"I thought I'd just wear it down."

"Long curly hair with that dress? No no no. Sit down. I've got an idea."

I closed my eyes as she worked more styling gel through my hair, pulling it straight with a comb, her fingers smoothing and twisting. I didn't know what she was doing, but it felt wonderful.

"So," she said. "Are you ready for this wedding?"

"I am."

"How do you tell?" she said. "I mean, when he's the one."

"It's hard," I said, opening my eyes. "You make a lot of mistakes."

She laughed. "You and grandma do. I'm not going to. I'm going to get married just once and it's going to be forever."

"I said I'd never get married," I told her.

"Really? Why not?"

"I didn't want to be like Grandma."

In the mirror, I saw Maya nod.

"That's why I didn't marry your dad, you know," I told her. "It wasn't because I didn't love him. I did love him, before things went bad. He would have married me in a shot. But I wouldn't get married because I thought if you got married that wrecked your relationship."

"So what changed your mind now?"

"Declan," I said. "Declan changed my mind."

Maya kept brushing, beginning to twist and pin up pieces of hair. Finally, when I'd almost forgotten what we'd been talking about, she said, "I want to get married by the time I'm twenty-five. I'm going to have five children."

"Five children? Are you planning to be a full-time mom?"

Maya shuddered in what I assumed was horror. "Absolutely not. I'm going to be a foreign correspondent."

I thought of when she was four, and said she was going to grow up to be a ballerina fireguy. Maybe she'll be able to pull it off, I thought. Maybe after watching all that Mom and I went through, she'd choose her husband more wisely from the start. If Jeremy was any indication of the kind of man she'd eventually end up with, she was on the right track.

The advantage, I thought, in holding your wedding at a church was that you got to leave your house and go somewhere else, where all the guests would be waiting for you rather than camping out in your living room, unwittingly holding you hostage upstairs.

At least if we were going to get married in a church, I would have had the opportunity to tromp through the cold streets, working off some of my nervous energy.

I wasn't nervous until Declan was late. The ceremony was supposed to start at two, and even when it was ten past, I still felt okay. He and Brian were coming all the way from Long Island, through two tunnels and across the busiest street in the busiest city in the country, and they hadn't planned on arriving until right about wedding time, not wanting to lurk around the house for too long before the event. But when it got to be twenty after, and when I couldn't reach Declan on his cell phone, I began to grow anxious. And by the time it reached two thirty, which it was now, I was flying out of my skin.

"I'm leaving," I announced to my mother and

Maya and Jeannie, who were all huddled with me in the bedroom.

"Leaving!" my mother cried, for everyone downstairs to hear.

"You're not taking off for the Caribbean or something, are you?" Maya said worriedly.

"Wait," said Jeannie. "I'll come with you."

I was already pulling on the enormous black cashmere coat I kept in my closet for truly frigid occasions, plunking a raccoon fur hunting hat, circa 1959, on top of the careful French twist Maya had fashioned in my hair.

"I'll be back," I said to Mom and Maya. "Keep the little girls distracted."

Jeannie was already hurrying after me. I ran down the stairs, keeping my eyes trained at my feet and my chin tucked into my upturned collar. Most of the guests didn't even notice me, but out of the corner of my eye I saw a few heads turn in our direction.

"It's okay, folks," Jeannie said. "We're just going outside to, um, refreeze the windshield."

Halfway to the corner and the main road, Jeannie caught up to me.

"Refreeze the windshield?" I said.

"Yeah," she said. "I had to say something."

I started laughing. "It's defrost. Defrost the windshield, not refreeze it. And why would we have to do either?"

"Oh, fuck you," Jeannie said.

I remembered, in a flash, that this was how we first became friends, back at Miss Forster's: me correcting a word Jeannie used—she'd called some boy a cock-head, and I'd pointed out the term was "dickhead"—and she lobbing back a "fuck you." I scooped up some snow in my bare fingers and flung it at her.

"Oh ho," she said. "You're going to be that way, are you?" She reached down and grabbed a few icy chunks of snow to throw at me.

"Stop!" I cried. "You can't hit the bride."

She dropped the snow. "That's true," she said. "It would be very bad for your wedding dress."

My wedding dress. That brought me back to why I'd come out here in the first place.

"He's not coming," I said, "is he?"

Jeannie looked at me, confused. "Do you really believe that?"

"What am I supposed to believe?"

"If you're marrying this man," she said, "you're supposed to believe that his car broke down, that he got stuck in traffic, that he'll be here any minute. Or he'll be here at four or at six, and you'll get married then."

I thought about that. "You're right," I said. And then I thought about it some more. "I do believe that. But I'm afraid it's not true. I'm afraid that things can't possibly go right for me."

"You're wearing red," she said. "Red is good luck."

"I wish you had your tarot cards with you," I said. "They were so right that day, about having the party.

That's what started everything with Declan in motion."

Jeannie bit her lip. "I have to tell you something," she said. "The cards didn't really say you should have a party."

I was incredulous. "So why did you tell me they did?"

"I just thought you should throw a party in your new house and I knew you wouldn't want to do it," Jeannie said. "Plus I thought it would give you a good excuse to get back in touch with Declan."

It was then we heard the sound, not like a car, more like a train, or a bulldozer, or a Volkswagen-sized airplane. It was coming closer, from the direction of the school, and then there was a squeal and the thing that was emitting the sound—a tow truck the size of a small house, it turned out, and seemingly made entirely of chrome—came squealing around our corner on two wheels. Jeannie and I jumped to the side of the road and the tow truck sped past us, then stopped with a theatrical whine of its brakes and backed up as fast as it had been going forward. Someone—Brian, I saw—jumped down from the cab, nearly as tall as a high-dive platform, and then Declan leaped after him.

"Cheers, mate," Brian called up to the truck driver, saluting him, while Declan strode over to me and lifted me in the air, swinging me around and around the way he swung Katherine and Amanda.

"I'm so sorry," he said.

"My fault," said Brian.

"Fucking right," said Declan. "Car breaks down in the fucking Lincoln Tunnel. Cell phone is dead, took forever for the cops to get to us, fucking horrible feeling stuck down there, and all I could think about was you here wondering where I was." Declan kissed me, his lips warm against my face.

"Your boy here was going to walk," Brian said.

"I wasn't going to just sit down there like I was buried alive." He began walking toward the house, with me still in his arms. "And then when the fucking tow truck came and got us out of there, it turned out my so-called best man had left the cell phone and the charger in the car."

"Declan," I said. "You can put me down."

"I don't want to put you down."

I laughed. We were nearing the house, walking up the front path, Jeannie and Brian trailing us.

"How many people are there?" he asked me.

"All of them," I said. We were standing on the porch. I pointed my chin toward the living room windows; Declan ducked so he could see inside.

"Holy shit," he said. "They're all waiting?"

"Yup."

"Okay."

He set me down, opened the door, took my hand, and led me inside. Everyone looked up and when they saw it was us, burst into applause. Declan began laughing and held up his left hand like an emcee thanking the crowd. Still holding my hand, he started heading toward the fireplace at the end of the living room, where the minister from the church around the corner was now standing.

I yanked him to a standstill. "Where are you going?" I whispered.

He looked baffled. "To get married."

"No," I said. "Mom and the girls are waiting upstairs. We've got to do the whole processional thing."

"Oh," Declan said. "Right."

It was then that I spotted Jeremy with his band, up in the front corner of the room near the fireplace, where the St. Mark's string quartet was supposed to be. He waved one of his drumsticks at me, a huge grin on his face, and I waved back, delighted to see him, if baffled as to what was going on.

"What happened to the string quartet?" I asked Maya when I got upstairs.

She blushed, a rare occurrence. "Oh," she said. "I told them they didn't have to come."

"What do you mean?"

"Jeremy wanted to give you a present," she said. "The music."

Sweet. But alarming. "What's he going to play?"

"He wouldn't tell me. That's part of the surprise." And then, perhaps responding to the look of panic on my face, she said, "He swore to me that you would like it."

"What happened to Declan?" my mother asked, helping me off with my coat and hat. "Your hair needs a little work, sweetheart."

"Here, let me do that," said Maya.

Jeannie popped her head into the room. "I almost forgot," she said. "Here are your bouquets. Katherine and Amanda, here's a basket for each of you. When you come down the stairs and walk up the aisle, just scatter the rose petals gently to each side, like this." Jeannie mimicked a rose-petal-scattering motion.

"Jeannie," I said. "I haven't even thanked you. Everything looks beautiful."

Jeannie kissed me on the cheek. "Okay, now, I'm going to wait at the bottom of the stairs, and when I see Katherine and Amanda about to start down, I'll give Jeremy the signal to begin playing, all right?"

"What's he going to play?" I asked Jeannie.

She shrugged. "He wouldn't tell me. I'll be waiting down there. You look great."

Once she was gone, Maya said to me, "Does Jeannie feel bad because you didn't ask her to be your maid of honor again this time?"

"Nah," I said. "She understood when I told her I wanted to have you. Plus she's worried that maybe she put a hex on my marriage to Frank so she thought it was a good idea for me to change attendants."

"Mommy," Amanda said. "Will you fix my headband?"

I knelt down before Amanda, who smiled at me.

"You look lovely," I said, adjusting the green velvet band and kissing her forehead. She and Katherine were both dressed in white taffeta dresses—at least someone was wearing white—with green velvet sashes. Maya's dress, tight and strapless, was dark green satin.

"Mommy," said Katherine. "Will you fix my head-band?"

She looked so sweet, the dark green beautiful against her pale red hair. I kissed her forehead, too. "Katherine," I said. "Do you want to call me Mommy?"

"You're my other Mommy," she said. "I have two mommys."

"I don't have two mommys," said Amanda. "I have a mommy and a Sunny."

"I have a mommy and a Sunny, too," said Katherine.

"No you don't. You have a mommy and a Kennedy."

My mother clapped her hands. "Girls, girls," she said. "Stop fussing now. It's time to begin our march."

The girls rushed to get in place, Amanda leading the way, a position on which they'd both easily agreed.

"I'm nervous," Maya said. "Do I have to do anything special? Do I need to say anything?"

"Just take care of your mother," Mom snapped. And then, taking my arm and fanning herself. "I'm nervous, too."

"Come on, mother. You've been through this a hundred times."

"Not a hundred. Five."

"Ready, everybody?" I said.

"Ready!"

"Okay: one, two, march!"

The band started playing, as promised, when Amanda and Katherine were starting down the stairs and my mother and I were still in the upstairs hallway. I didn't recognize the tune at first—though I gave silent thanks that it wasn't "Sexual Healing" or "Let's Get It On," two of the least appropriate possibilities that had occurred to me—and then I had to keep myself from laughing out loud when I realized what the band was playing. It was "I Can't Get Started," the ancient tune I'd always loved on the jukebox in Declan's bar.

Amanda and Katherine, instead of strewing their red rose petals artfully in my path, had taken to flinging them at the crowd, Amanda giggling wildly and Katherine, as always, following suit. From where he stood by the fireplace, Declan tried to give them a stern look, but they were as oblivious to him as they were to Jeannie and after a moment he looked over their heads and straight at me, his face breaking into a smile.

As we reached him, Declan touched Amanda's head and then Katherine's, helping each of them to a seat in the front row, and kissed Maya on the cheek. My mother gave my arm one last squeeze and then flung her arms around me and kissed me full on the lips, saying out loud, "I love you!" which got a laugh from the crowd. Then she went and sat next to the girls and Declan took my hand, gripping it tightly in both of his. He was trembling, I could feel, and there were tears in his eyes.

God help me, when I said those words at the altar to Frank—in sickness and in health, till death do us part—I was qualifying them, even to myself, as I stood there: Maybe, I think so, I'd like that to be true. But saying them with Declan, they felt as vivid and as heartfelt as if they had sprung directly from my brain to my lips. We didn't need to write our own vows because the standard promises said it all, and we'd warned the minister not to clutter up the service with too much talk. We were rushing toward the kiss, and when it came I thought it would never end, Declan's arms were wrapped so tightly and so completely around me, our lips moving over each other's, until we felt the not-so-gentle shove of Amanda and Katherine pushing their way between us, giggling and squealing.

Then the crowd broke into a roar of applause and Jeremy's band started playing again—and this time it *was* "Sexual Healing." But what could I do but laugh? What could I do about anything, in that most wonderful of moments, but laugh and touch Declan and assure myself that all this happiness was indeed real, and my own.

*   *   *

At some point the wedding ceased to feel like our own private affair and started to feel like a mob scene. At least, for us, that took longer than for many couples, pushed by their parents or the photographer or the catering hall to go through someone else's paces even before the ceremony took place. We were in our own home on our own schedule. We had our kiss and then instead of getting stuck on a receiving line we moved through the crowd together shaking hands. The food was a conglomeration of our favorites, from salt bagels to walnut brownies, from goat cheese to mashed potatoes, laid out for anyone to eat when they wanted, in whatever combination they wanted. Forget about a sit-down dinner: no room. Forget about sitting down, unless you wanted to perch on a kitchen counter or on the stairs, which many of the guests did. Otherwise, once the folding chairs that had been set up for the ceremony were cleared away, the entire downstairs of the house was turned into a dance floor.

Declan and I managed the first few dances together, and then my mother cut in and twirled Declan away while I did a courtly waltz—to James Brown's "It's Your Thing"— with Stanislav. I saw Declan dancing with Jeannie, while I danced with Brian. Maya danced with me, Amanda danced with her dad, and Declan took a twirl with Mrs. Glover, who made a point to tell me how beautiful she thought the house looked: "almost as lovely as when I lived here myself." I almost panicked—it seemed like hours later—when I saw Declan dancing with Sunny. But then he winked at me over her shoulder and I suddenly felt almost a sisterly fondness for her, with her swollen ankles and her burgeoning waistline and her not-very-helpful and almost-totally-insensitive new husband.

I was standing by the dining room table, sipping champagne, when Sunny approached me.

"I just want to say," she shouted in my ear, as Jeremy and the band were doing a passable and rousing rendition of Aretha Franklin's "R-E-S-P-E-C-T," "that I'm sorry."

I looked at her in surprise. "What for?"

She looked just as surprised back. "Well, for stealing Frank, I guess."

I laughed, loudly and merrily. "That's okay," I assured her. "Really. So when's the baby due?"

"May."

I'd done enough calculating of due dates to recognize instantly that that meant the child had been conceived in August. Late August, when Frank had already left? Or early August, when he was still trying to win me back? Oh, who cared.

"Perfect time to have a baby," I said.

"Let me ask you this," she said. "When you were pregnant with Amanda, was Frank a little, I don't know, uninterested? Or is it only with the second baby that they don't show up to hear the heartbeat

for the first time or look for very long at the sono-
gram pictures?"

I flashed on Frank, rushing into the delivery room
just as Amanda shot out of the womb, too tied up in a
very important deposition to get there earlier.

"Don't worry. I'm sure it will be fine," I said, patting her hand. From across the room, I caught sight of
Declan signaling to me, pointing downward, presum-
ably at Katherine. I patted Sunny again. "Excuse me."

"Lucy's here to take Katherine," Declan told me
when I made it over to him, "but Katherine doesn't
want to leave."

Katherine was sitting on the polished wooden floor
in her shiny new dress, convulsed with laughter as
Amanda spun her around. Judging from the plate-
sized circle of dust on Amanda's bottom, they'd been
taking turns.

"That's okay," I said. "Tell Lucy to stay for a while."

"Are you sure?"

"Of course. Make the gang complete."

I was talking to Lucy, who was charm itself, about
San Francisco, when I saw Marco arrive and stand in
the doorway, looking around but making no move to
take off his black leather jacket. I peered beyond him,
expecting to see Tina, but he seemed to be alone. He
looked supremely uncomfortable, shifting from one
foot to the other and craning his neck to look all
around the house. I felt that old feeling whenever he
walked into a room and didn't seem happy—I wonder

what's wrong, I better go fix it before he gets mad at me—and even though I chided myself for giving in to this old compulsion on this most happy and secure of days, I couldn't help it: I went over to him.

"Wow," he said, taking in my dress. "Red."

"Chinese brides wear red," I informed him.

"Sexy," he said.

"The red dress? Or Chinese brides?"

"You," he said.

Despite myself, I blushed.

"Congratulations," he said, leaning over and kissing my cheek.

"Want some champagne? Some food?"

"Nah. I don't want to crash your party. I just came to get Maya."

"Remember, she's got to be back by noon tomorrow. Our plane leaves at seven and she isn't even packed yet."

"I'll remember." He looked at me fondly. "Kennedy, listen, I know I wasn't always the most responsible guy. But I gotta say thank you."

"Thank you?" I said lightly, caught off guard. "For what?"

"For raising our kid so nice. For not making her hate me."

"Her feelings about you—you're in charge of that."

"Yeah," he said. "And there's something else, too. That thing I blamed you for, taking Maya, making me hit bottom. I needed that, back then. If you hadn't have done that, I don't know, maybe I never would have gotten better. So thank you for that, too."

Declan appeared at my elbow, and Marco tensed. He'd always been jealous of Declan, I knew that, and my first impulse was not to touch Declan or focus on him, but then I thought: I'm nuts! It's my wedding day! I grabbed Declan's arm and clung to him, feeling certain as I stood there that Marco could never hurt me again. He shook Declan's hand and wandered away to find Maya.

Declan put his arms around me.

"How do we get rid of all these people?" he said in my ear.

"I know. I didn't think about this when we decided to have the wedding here. Maybe we should leave?"

Declan considered for a moment. "Nah," he said finally. "I want to be with you here. Maybe I should just tell them all it's time to go home?"

Together, we looked out at the crowd, which seemed to have swelled throughout the evening. Or maybe they had just grown more boisterous. No one showed the least inclination to go, the band had just struck up another set, and the crowd was whooping and dancing. Even the caterers were dancing.

So we danced. We danced together and with, it seemed, everyone else in the place. When it got toward midnight, my mother seized control. Marching up to where Jeremy's indefatigable band was still playing, she grabbed the microphone.

"Okay, all you people," she said. "You all know what weddings are for, right?"

"Getting drunk!" someone, I think it was Brian, shouted.

"No, making love!" my mother cried. "Now it's time for everyone to leave so the honeymoon can begin!"

A cheer went up from the crowd, the band began packing up their equipment, the caterers started lifting bowls from the dining room table, and suddenly the departure was in motion. I made a move to begin picking up glasses but my mother held up her hand in a kind of traffic cop, "Stop in the Name of Love" motion.

"You two go upstairs," she said. "I'll get all these people out of here in no time and I'll help the caterers finish clearing up."

So instead of rushing out of a church or climbing into a waiting convertible, we walked up our own staircase, where instead of rice we were pelted with balled up cocktail napkins. We locked the door to our room and then huddled there giggling as we listened to our loved ones making their way out into the night. Declan reached up under the skirt of my red dress, his big hand warm against my skin.

"I love you," he said.

"I love you."

"My wife."

"My husband."

People were still downstairs, but we'd waited long enough. He pulled my dress over my head and I unbuttoned his shirt. He unhooked my bra and I unzipped his trousers. And then we made love, no longer hearing anyone anywhere, except when we were finished—the first time, I mean—and we realized that there was still a gang of stragglers beneath our bedroom window, beating on pots and pans. We lay back on top of the covers, hot now, and laughed, until they got tired and went away. Then we made love again.

Early in the morning, I woke up to find Declan lying beside me already awake, staring at me, a smile playing at the edges of his lips.

"What are you thinking about?" I asked him.

"How much I love you."

"I wish we'd gotten married long ago," I told him, thinking of what had gone through my mind as I started down the aisle. "You're the man I should have married in the very beginning."

"Oh, no, darlin'," he said, looking shocked. "That wouldn't have been any good."

"Why not?" I asked, shocked, too.

"I wasn't any good back then. You knew it. You knew everything that was wrong with me, with how I behaved with women."

"And so what made you change?"

"You," he said, as if he couldn't believe I didn't already know the answer. "It was all you."

Up Close and Personal with the Author

DOES EVERY WOMAN HAVE A MAN SHE SHOULD HAVE MARRIED?

Absolutely. I think for every woman there's a man—or sometimes several men—who live on as real possibilities. If things had been different, if you'd been smarter, if he'd been available, he would have been THE ONE. He might be someone you had an actual relationship with or maybe just a friend, someone you were attracted to but the timing was wrong, which was the case for Kennedy and Declan. I think who that man is changes depending on where you are in your life. For Kennedy, at one point, Frank actually *was* the man she should have married because of his dependability, his steadiness. But when Frank changes and leaves the family, that forces Kennedy to change too, and the man she needs—what she needs out of life—becomes very different.

WHY *IS* DECLAN THE MAN KENNEDY SHOULD HAVE MARRIED?

As Declan says at the end of the book, he wasn't always the right man for her. But he's grown up, he's ready to be devoted to one woman, which is something Kennedy needs despite her best efforts to be free and independent. Declan's efforts to work things out with the mother of his child ironically prove his interest in having a serious, exclusive relationship. Declan's and Kennedy's sexual chemistry is one reason they're right for each other: I'm a big believer in the importance of attraction and good sex to making a relationship last. But Kennedy and Declan also managed to have a good non-sexual friendship for a long time, and that's important too. They have the capacity, as Kennedy says in the book, to both talk and be quiet together. And then there's their willingness to confront each other about the difficult issues, another vital component of a successful partnership. They're equals, which is another thing I believe in—and something Kennedy never had with Marco or Frank, something she wasn't ready for herself before now.

DO YOU BELIEVE PEOPLE CAN CHANGE AND REINVENT THEMSELVES?

A novelist has to believe in the human capacity for change: Change is at the heart of every novel. Yet so is character, the immutability of character and all of our resistance to making the smallest kind of change. We've all had the experience of meeting up with an old friend or lover and being amazed at how little they've changed over the years. They may look different, they may have traveled far in the world, yet after a short time with them it all comes back, what you liked and hated, all those little ticks that drive you crazy or make you fall in love all over again. For myself, I always feel as if I've changed so much, yet I can see someone who knew me as a teenager, say, and they'll claim I'm exactly the same, which I find shocking.

DO YOU THINK PEOPLE SHOULD TRY TO MAKE THEIR MARRIAGES WORK FOR THE SAKE OF THE CHILDREN?

Of course, and sometimes going that extra distance to understand your partner, to be kind to your partner, to rediscover the spark between you by taking a vacation away from the kids, can make a foundering marriage start working again. But I don't think Kennedy was wrong to leave Marco—his personal problems with drugs were too immense for her to solve and too dangerous for their child—and neither do I believe she should have stayed with Frank. In fact, I believe that ultimately Frank did the right thing to leave the marriage, which was ultimately more a marriage of convenience for both of them than a real meeting of minds and hearts. He really did Kennedy a favor by leaving. She would have stayed in that marriage forever, out of fear and dependence. His leaving forced her to rediscover her own strength and also to own up to the ways she shortchanged Frank and herself by staying in a marriage that was wrong.

WHAT ABOUT THE TUG BETWEEN CITY LIFE AND SUBURBAN LIFE, BETWEEN KENNEDY'S OLD WILD SELF AND HER NEW TAMER ONE?

I think this is a tug that a lot of women feel. Most suburban moms today did live independent city lives before marriage and motherhood, did have careers and their own apartments and lots of lovers before the men they married. They have former lives that are very different from their current ones, and often that can leave you wondering: What happened to that free spirit I was before? How did that life impact the life I have now? Especially when you're in the thick of raising kids, you wonder: Where's the individual I used to be? How much attention can I pay to her—what she wants and needs—without shortchanging my husband and children?

WHAT DOES THE THEME OF MOTHERS AND DAUGHTERS MEAN TO YOU?

This has been a huge issue in my own life, as I think it is for many women, especially when they're adolescents themselves or when their daughters are teenagers. Kennedy's confronting her own sexuality again at the same time her daughter is starting her first romantic relationship, and that's confusing for both of them. How much can they reveal to one another, how will the men in their lives affect their relationship with one another, how do you balance your sexuality with your role in the family? Kennedy's mother always put her husbands above her daughter, and Kennedy suffered for that as a child and does not want to impose the same burden on her daughters. But can she be totally in love with a man without leaving her daughters out in the cold? Does putting your children first mean you inevitably end up with a second-class relationship? In some ways, Kennedy is just beginning to wrestle with these questions at the end of the book.

WHERE DO YOU SEE THESE CHARACTERS IN FIVE YEARS?

I don't think Kennedy's and Declan's marriage is going to be infinitely blissful—I think that's beyond the power of any marriage. But I believe these two have the strength and depth to work out whatever problems they encounter, to figure out a way to have an intense love affair and also a rich family life. Maya is going to go off to college and become either a physicist or a movie star, continuing her relationship with Jeremy for many years, though I think ultimately they'll end up as friends and she'll marry someone less nice but more powerful. Mom and Stan, I'm afraid, are going to have to break up, but Mom, through Kennedy's good example, may end up with someone more her equal in intellect, age, and bank account. Declan's and Kennedy's business will prosper, Katherine will end up living with them full-time, and I think they will have a baby together—I see them with an all-girl family, with Declan happily supplying the household's full quota of testosterone.

WHO IS THE CHARACTER IN THE BOOK YOU IDENTIFY WITH THE MOST?

It would have to be Kennedy, because she's wrestling with the kinds of issues that concern me, that I find fascinating. How do you be a good mother, daughter, partner, while also pursuing your individual dreams and desires? When do you listen to your friends and family and when do you follow your own heart? How do you overcome your fears and try something new?

HOW MUCH DOES YOUR LIFE INFLUENCE YOUR FICTION?

I feel I really became a novelist when I learned to let go of reality—hard to do for someone like me who'd written magazine articles and nonfiction books for years—and created fictional characters and invented their unique story. So I'd say that women's issues, family dilemmas that I find interesting in real life and that I personally have lived through, get explored in this novel. Some of the settings are based on places I've known: Kennedy's apartment in the East Village is one where I lived, and I worked as a waitress in an Irish bar. But the bar was owned by a woman, sadly, not a sex god like Declan, and there was no Marco in my life, and I did not become a single mom at nineteen. I do not have a rich much-married mother and my husband did not leave me for a surfer. But I have worn a strange outfit while throwing a yard sale and I have tossed a potholder that was crawling with roaches out an apartment window.

WHAT ADVICE DO YOU HAVE FOR FLEDGLING NOVELISTS?

You can use elements from your real life—places you love, people you've met, stories you've heard—but as a novelist your job is to reshape them into a work of fiction, to create a story that's compelling for the reader. Before you start writing, create your characters and sketch out your settings, know your title and your ending. Write in scenes: The scene is the building block of any novel. And write every day. It's much more productive to spend an hour a day on your novel than to spend seven hours once a week. The last piece of advice is to get comfortable with criticism and rejection, a major factor in every writer's career. The difference between successful people and non-successful people isn't that the successful people get rejected less, it's that they keep going after they do.

DOWNTOWN PRESS

PROUDLY PRESENTS

YOUNGER

Pamela Redmond Satran

Coming soon from Downtown Press

Published by Pocket Books

Turn the page for an excerpt of *Younger.* . . .

CHAPTER ONE

I almost didn't get on the ferry.

I was scared. And nervous. And overwhelmed by how out of place I felt, in the crowd of young people surging toward the boat bound for New York.

Not just New York, but New York City on New Year's Eve. The mere thought of it made my hands sweat and my feet tingle, the way they did the one time I rode to the top of the Empire State Building and tried to look down. In the immortal words of my daughter Diana, it made my weenie hurt.

I would have turned around and driven right back home to my safe suburban house—*I can see the ball drop better on TV anyway!*—except I couldn't leave Maggie waiting for me on the freezing pier in downtown Manhattan. Maggie, my oldest and still closest friend, didn't believe in cell phones. She also didn't believe in computers, or cars, or staying in New Jersey on New Year's Eve, or for that matter, staying in New Jersey ever. Maggie, who came out as a lesbian to her ultra-Catholic parents at sixteen and made her living as an artist, didn't believe in doing anything the easy way. And so I couldn't cancel our night out, and there was nothing for me to do but keep marching forward to my potential doom.

At least I was first in line for the next boat. It was frigid out that night, but I staked my claim to the prime spot, hanging on to the barricade to keep anybody from cutting in front of me. These kind of suburban yos who were milling around on the dock with me, I knew, majored in line-cutting in kindergarten.

Then a weird thing happened. The longer I stood there, guarding my turf, the more I began to want to go into the city—not just for Maggie, but for myself. Looking out across the dark water at the lights of Manhattan sparkling beyond, I began to think that Maggie had been right, and going into New York on New Year's Eve was exactly what I needed. Shake things up, she said. Do something you've never done before. Hadn't doing everything the way I'd always done it—the cautious way, the theoretically secure way—landed me precisely in the middle of my current mess? It had, and no one wanted that to change more than me.

And so when they opened the gate to the ferry, I sprinted ahead. I was determined to be the first one up the stairs, to beat everybody else to the front of the outside deck, where I could watch New York glide into view. I could hear them all on my heels as I ran, but I was first out the door and to the front of the boat, grabbing the metal rail and hanging on tight as I labored to catch my breath. The ferry's engine roared to life, its diesel smell rising above the saltiness of the harbor, but still I sucked the air deep into my lungs as we chugged away from the dock. Here I am, I thought: alive and moving forward, on a night when anything can happen.

It wasn't until then that I noticed I was the only one standing out there. Everybody else was packed into the glassed-in cabin, their collective breath fogging its windows. Apparently I was the only one who wasn't afraid of a little cold, of a little wind, of a little icy spray—okay, make that a *lot* of icy spray—as the boat bucked like a mechanical bull across the waves. It was worth it, assuming I wasn't hurled into the inky waters, for the incredible view of the glowing green Statue of Liberty and the twinkling skyscrapers up ahead.

As I gripped the rail even tighter, congratulating myself on my amazing bravery, the boat slowed and seemed to stall there in the middle of the harbor, its motor idling loudly. Just as I began to wonder whether we were about to sink, or make a break for the open seas at the hands of a renegade captain running from the law, the boat began to back up. Back up and turn around. Were we returning to New Jersey? Maybe the captain had the same misgivings about Manhattan on New Year's Eve that I did.

But no. Once the boat swung around, it began moving toward the city again. Leaving me facing not the spectacular vista of Manhattan but the big clock and broken-down dock of Hoboken, and darkest New Jersey beyond. Frantically, I looked over my shoulder at the bright, snug cabin, which now had the prime view of New York, but it was so crowded, it would have been impossible to squeeze inside. I was stuck out in the cold facing New Jersey, all alone. The story of my life.

Half an hour later, I was hobbling through the streets of Soho arm in arm with Maggie, cursing the vanity that had led me to wear high heels and fantasizing about grabbing the comfy-looking green lace-up boots off Maggie's feet. Maggie was very sensibly striding along beside me in boot-cut jeans, a down-filled coat as enormous as a sleeping bag, and a leopard-print hunter's cap, with the earflaps down and a velvet bow tied under her chin.

"Are we almost there yet?" I asked, the shoes nipping at my toes.

"Come on," she said, tugging me away from the crowded sidewalk of West Broadway toward a dark, unpopulated side street. "This'll be faster."

I stopped, looking with alarm down the deserted street. "We'll get raped."

"Don't be such a scaredy-cat." Maggie laughed, pulling me forward.

Easy for her to say: Maggie had moved to the Lower East Side at eighteen, back when Ratner's was still serving blintzes and crackheads camped under her stairwell. Now she owned her building, the entire top floor turned into a studio where she lived and worked on her sculptures, larger-than-life leaping, twirling women fashioned from wire and tulle. All those years in New York on her own had made Maggie tough, while I was still the soft suburban mom, protected by my husband's money, or should I say, my soon-to-be-ex-husband's ex-money.

My heart hammered in my ears as Maggie dragged me down the black street, slowing only slightly when I focused on the sole beam of light on the entire block, which seemed, for some strange reason, to be pink. When we reached the storefront from which the light was emanating, we saw why: in the window was a bright pink neon sign that read "Madame Aurora." The glow was further enhanced by a curtain of pink and orange glass beads covering the window, filtering the light from inside the shop. Beyond the beads, we could just make out a woman who could only be Madame Aurora herself, a gold turban askew on her gray hair, smoke curling from the cigarette that teetered from her lips. Suddenly, she looked straight at us and beckoned us inside. Taped to the window was a hand-lettered sign: "New Year's Wishes, $25."

"Let's go in," I said to Maggie. I'd always been a sucker for any kind of wish and any kind of fortune-telling, so the combination of the two was irresistible. Besides, I wanted to get out of the cold and off my feet, however briefly.

Maggie made a face, her "You have got to be out of your fucking mind" face.

"Come on," I said. "It will be fun."

"Eating a fabulous meal is fun," Maggie said. "Kissing someone you have a crush on is fun. Dropping good money on some phony fortune-teller is *not* fun."

"Come on," I wheedled, the way I did when I called to read her a particularly good horoscope, or suggested she join me in wishing on a star. "You're the one who told me I should start taking more risks."

Maggie hesitated just long enough to give me the confidence to step in front of her and push open Madame Aurora's door, giving Maggie no choice but to follow.

It was hot inside the room, and smoky. I waved my hands in front of my face in an attempt to signal my discomfort to Madame Aurora, but this only seemed to provoke her to take a deeper drag on her cigarette and then to emit a plume of smoke aimed directly at my face.

I looked doubtfully at Maggie, who only shrugged and refused to meet my eye. I was the one who'd dragged us in here; she wasn't about to get us out.

"So, darling," said the Madame, finally removing the cigarette from her mouth. "What is your wish?"

What was my *wish*? I wasn't expecting her to pop the big question right out of the gate like that. I figured there'd be some preamble, a few moments examining my palm, shuffling the tarot cards, that kind of thing.

"Well," I stalled. "Do I get only one?"

Madame Aurora shrugged. "You can have as many as you want, for twenty-five dollars a pop."

And no fair, as everybody knows, wishing for more wishes.

Again, I tried to catch Maggie's eye. Again, she looked stubbornly away from me. I closed my eyes and tried to concentrate.

What was the one thing I wanted, above all others?

For my daughter Diana to return from Africa? Definitely, I wanted that, but she was scheduled to come home this month anyway, so that seemed like a waste of a wish.

To get a job? Of course. I'd been so determined to support myself when my husband left that I'd negotiated sole title to our house in lieu of long-term alimony. Then I'd spent half the year humiliating myself at interviews at publishing houses. No one, it seemed, wanted to hire a forty-four-year-old woman who'd spent precisely four months in the workforce before becoming a full-time mom. I tried to tell them I'd spent the past twenty years reading everything I could get my hands on, and I knew better than anybody what middle-class suburban women in book groups—women exactly like me, who made up the prime novel-buying market—wanted to read.

But nobody cared about my experience in the reading trenches. All they seemed to see was a middle-aged housewife with an ancient English degree and a résumé padded with such "jobs" as co-chair of the book fair at my kid's elementary school. I was unqualified for an editor's position, and though I always told them I would be happy to start as an assistant, I wasn't considered for entry-level jobs. No one put it this way, but they thought I was too old.

"I wish I were younger," I said.

By the looks on Madame Aurora's and Maggie's faces, I must have said that out loud.

The Madame burst out laughing.

"Whaddaya wanna be younger for?" she said. "All that worryin', who am I gonna marry, what am I gonna do with my life. It's for the birds!"

Maggie chimed in. "What are you saying, that you want to go back to all that uncertainty? Now that you finally have a chance to get your life together?"

I couldn't believe they were ganging up on me. "It's just that if I were younger, I could do some things a little differently," I tried to explain. "Think about what I want more, take my career more seriously . . ."

But Maggie was already shaking her head. "You are who you are, Alice," she said. "I knew you when you were six, and even back then you always put everybody else first. Before you went out to play, you had to make sure your stuffed animals were comfortable. When we were freshmen in high school, and everybody else was consumed with trying to look cool, you were the one who volunteered to push that crippled girl around in her wheelchair. And once you had Diana, she was always what you cared about above everything else."

I had to admit, she was right. I may have left my job at Gentility Press because I had to, when I started bleeding and almost lost the baby. But once Diana was born, I stayed home because I wanted to. And then, as she got older, I kept telling myself I couldn't go back to work because maybe this was the year I'd finally get pregnant again, but the truth was that Diana herself was all the focus I needed in my life.

So now I wanted to undo that? Now I wished I

could go back and put Diana in day care, become a working mom, or even not have Diana at all?

The very idea was enough to send an enormous shiver up my spine, as if even the shadow of the idea could jinx my daughter, my motherhood, the most important thing in my life. I could never wish her out of existence, never dream of wishing away even one of the moments I'd spent with her.

But still, what about me? Had devoting all those years to my child disqualified me from ever claiming a life for myself? The real reason I wished I'd been different back then was so that I could be different now: ballsier, bolder, capable of grabbing the world by the throat and bending it to my will.

"What's it going to be?" said Madame Aurora.

"I want to be braver," I said. "Plus maybe, if you could do something about my cellulite . . ."

Maggie rolled her eyes and jumped to her feet.

"This is ridiculous," she said, taking hold of my arm. "Come on, Alice. We're leaving."

"But I didn't get my wish," I said.

"I didn't get my money," said Madame Aurora.

"Too bad," said Maggie. "We're out of here."

Now Maggie was walking really fast. I tried asking her to slow down, but instead of listening, she kept forging ahead, expecting me to keep up. Finally, I stopped dead in my tracks so she had to double back and talk to me.

"Give me your boots," I said.

She looked puzzled.

"If you expect me to walk this far and this fast, you're going to have to trade shoes with me."

Maggie looked down at my feet and burst out laughing.

"You need more help than I thought," she said.

"What are you talking about?"

"You'll see." She was already untying her green boots.

"Where are we going?" I always trusted Maggie to be my guide to New York, following unquestioningly, like a little girl, wherever she wanted to take me. Tonight, for instance, I thought she said we were going to a cool new restaurant. But now that I took a moment to look around at the low brick buildings and decidedly uncool neighborhood as I stepped into Maggie's boots, I was starting to wonder.

"We're going to my place," she said.

"Why?"

"You'll see."

Even wearing the heels, she walked faster than me, but at least my feet didn't hurt anymore. And once we passed out of the no-man's-land that still separated Little Italy from Maggie's neighborhood, I began to relax. The blocks around her building used to be terrifying, but had improved considerably in the past few years. Tonight, the streets were full of people and all the hip restaurants and bars were packed. Every place looked good to me—I was starving, I realized—but Maggie was not to be deterred.

"We'll go out after," she said.

"After *what*?"

She smiled mysteriously and repeated the phrase that was becoming her mantra: "You'll see."

It was a five-flight climb to Maggie's loft, which I used to find daunting but now took with ease, thanks to all the hours I'd logged on the elliptical trainer in the past year. After a lifetime as a dedicated couch potato, I'd started exercising because it was the only thing I could think of, in my past year of horrible events, that would reliably make me feel good. And after a lifetime of dieting, I'd found the pounds disappearing without doing anything at all—anything, that is, except working out for an hour or two every day. I'd even, maybe twice, had a flash of that high you're supposed to get from working out, though I still preferred a Cosmo.

To someone coming from the suburbs, where Pottery Barn was considered the height of living room fashion, Maggie's loft was always a shock. It was basically one gigantic room that occupied the entire top floor of the building, with windows on all four sides and a bright red silk tent sitting smack in the middle of the three thousand feet of open space—the closet. The only furniture was an enormous iron-framed bed, also bright red, and an ornate purple velvet chaise that provided the place's sole seating, unless you counted the paint-spattered wooden floor. Which I didn't.

"Okay," Maggie said, as soon as she'd triple-bolted the door behind us. "Let me have a look at you."

But I was too distracted by what was different

about Maggie's loft to stand still. All her sculptures, all her nine-foot-tall chicken-wire women, with their size 62 ZZZ breasts and their ballet skirts as full and frothy as flowering cherry trees, had been shoved into one corner, where they mingled like inmates in some prison for works of art. Now occupying the prime spot in Maggie's work area was a concrete block as big as a refrigerator.

"What on earth is that?" I said.

"Something new I'm trying with my work," said Maggie breezily. "Come on, take off your coat. I want to see what you're wearing."

Now I could finally focus. Maggie wanting to survey my clothes was never a good thing. She was always, from the time we were first able to dress ourselves, trying to make me over, and I was always resisting. Don't get me wrong, I thought Maggie had fantastic style, but fantastic for *her*, not for me. Her hair had turned white when she was still in her twenties, and every year it seemed to get a little shorter and messier, standing up in tufts all over her head. As her hair got more butch, her earrings became more feminine and ornate and numerous. The featured attraction tonight was green-jeweled chandelier earrings. Maggie, whose body was still as slim and limber-looking as a teenager's, also must have had the soul of a French woman. She had that knack for throwing on an odd assortment of clothes— tonight it was the faded jeans she'd had since high school with an antique lace-trimmed cream silk blouse and a long gray-green velvet scarf wound around her neck—that always managed to look enviably perfect.

She walked around me, rubbing her chin and shaking her head. Finally she reached out and grabbed a hank of the oversize beige sweater I was wearing.

"Where'd you get this?" she asked.

"It was Gary's," I admitted. One of the many pieces of clothing he'd left behind when he dumped me exactly a year ago for his dental hygienist. Clothing I'd kept because, for a long time, I assumed he'd come back. And continued to keep because, for the next few months at least, he was still paying the mortgage on the house where his clothes and I lived together.

"It's a rag," Maggie said. "And what about that skirt?"

The skirt choice I was actually rather pleased with. The same beige as the sweater, it was fitted through the hips and ended above the knee, considerably sexier than the khakis and sweatpants I'd favored for the past two decades.

"It was Diana's," I said proudly. "I couldn't believe it fit me."

"Of course it fits you!" Maggie exclaimed. "You're a stick! Come here."

She spun me around and tried to push me forward.

"Where are you taking me?"

"I want you to look at yourself."

She propelled me across the loft until we were

standing in front of an oval mirror with a curlicued gold frame, like the one the Wicked Stepmother communes with in "Snow White."

"Mirror, mirror on the wall," I said, laughing, trying to get Maggie to join in the joke. But she only gazed poker-faced over my shoulder, refusing to so much as crack a smile.

"This is serious," she said, pointing her chin toward the mirror. "Tell me what you see."

It had been a long time since I'd looked in a mirror with much enthusiasm. Sometimes, especially when Diana was small, I'd go for days without checking my reflection. And then through the years, as I got heavier, and my hair started to turn gray, and the lines began to appear around my eyes, I discovered I felt happier when I didn't look at all. In my mind's eye, I was forever some grown-up but neutral age—thirty-threeish—and some womanly but neutral weight—133ish—and looked acceptable if not gorgeous or sexy or notable in any way. I was always shocked when I caught sight of my reflection in a shop window or a car door and was forced to see that I was considerably older and heavier than I believed.

But now, compelled to confront my image, really take it in, for the first time in the year my life had been turned upside down and inside out, I had the opposite reaction. I lifted my chin and turned my head to the side; without thinking, I stood up taller and smiled.

"That's right," Maggie said. She gathered the back of my baggy sweater into her hands so the fabric was pulled tight against my newly buff body. "What do you see?"

"I see—," I said, trying to think how to put it. There was me, staring back from the glass, but it was some version of myself before child, before husband, before all the years had clouded my vision. "—myself," I said finally, lamely.

"Yes!" Maggie cried. "It's you! It's the Alice I've known and loved all these years, who was getting buried under a layer of fat and misery."

"I wasn't miserable." I frowned.

"Oh, pooh," Maggie said. "How could you not have been miserable? Your husband was never around, your daughter was growing up and leaving home, your mother was fading away, you had nothing to do—"

I felt stung. "I had the house to take care of," I said. "My mother to look after. And just because Diana was theoretically grown up and away at college didn't mean she didn't need me anymore."

"I know," Maggie soothed. "I don't mean to denigrate all you did. What I'm trying to get you to see is how much lighter you look now. How much younger."

"Younger?" I said, focusing again on my reflection.

"It's partly the weight," Maggie said meditatively, staring at my image in the mirror, "but it's something else too, some burden that seems to have been lifted. Besides, you always looked a lot younger than you really were. Don't you remember when we were seniors in high school, you were the only one who could still get into the movies for the kids' price? And even when you were in your thirties, long after you had Diana, you'd still get carded in bars."

"I don't think I'd get carded now."

"Maybe not, but you could look a lot younger than you are. A lot younger than you do."

"What do you mean?"

"I mean that with some color in your hair, a little makeup, some clothes that fit, for God's sake, you could still look like you were in your twenties!" Maggie exploded. "That's why I dragged you out of that fucking voodoo parlor! We're the only ones who have the power to turn our dreams into reality."

I smirked at Maggie. She was usually the first one to puncture what she called "that power-of-positive-thinking bullshit." I was the one who made wishes on stars and birthday candles, who believed, as Cinderella said in the Disney movie I'd watched at least two hundred times with Diana nestled into my side, that "if you dream a thing more than once, it's sure to come true." But now instead of smirking back, Maggie only gazed at me with a look of utter conviction.

"So you think," I said finally, "that I have the power to make myself younger just by wishing it were so?"

"Not *just* by wishing," she said. "We're going to need a little help from Lady Clairol. Let's get started."

Try these Downtown Press bestsellers on for size!

GOING TOPLESS
Megan McAndrew

DINNER FOR TWO
Mike Gayle

THE DEAD FATHER'S GUIDE TO SEX & MARRIAGE
John Scott Shepherd

BABES IN CAPTIVITY
Pamela Redmond Satran

UPGRADING
Simon Brooke

MY FAVORITE MISTAKE
Beth Kendrick

BITE
C.J. Tosh

THE HAZARDS OF SLEEPING ALONE
Elise Juska

SCOTTISH GIRLS ABOUT TOWN
Jenny Colgan, Isla Dewar, Muriel Gray, and more

CALLING ROMEO
Alexandra Potter

GAME OVER
Adele Parks

PINK SLIP PARTY
Cara Lockwood

SHOUT DOWN THE MOON
Lisa Tucker

MANEATER
Gigi Levangie Grazer

CLEARING THE AISLE
Karen Schwartz

LINER NOTES
Emily Franklin

MY LURID PAST
Lauren Henderson

DRESS YOU UP IN MY LOVE
Diane Stingley

HE'S GOT TO GO
Sheila O'Flanagan

IRISH GIRLS ABOUT TOWN
Maeve Binchy, Marian Keyes, Cathy Kelly, and more

THE MAN I SHOULD HAVE MARRIED
Pamela Redmond Satran

GETTING OVER JACK WAGNER
Elise Juska

THE SONG READER
Lisa Tucker

THE HEAT SEEKERS
Zane

I DO (BUT I DON'T)
Cara Lockwood

WHY GIRLS ARE WEIRD
Pamela Ribon

LARGER THAN LIFE
Adele Parks

ELIOT'S BANANA
Heather Swain

HOW TO PEE STANDING UP
Anna Skinner

Downtown Press | PUBLISHED BY POCKET BOOKS